Screw the chitch

"Tommaso, listen to me. You don't want to do this. You don't want to be here. You don't want to be one of them. And I know that I was supposed to be Andrus's mate—whatever the hell that means—but I don't want him. Yes, yes, I love his look—what woman can resist leather pants?—but that's not my heart speaking. My heart wants something that my brain can sign off on. It wants a best friend who's sexy and strong and who can kick ass when needed. So even though we don't know each other, I'm asking for the chance to find out if that's you." I drew a trembling breath. "Because I think it is. I mean to say—I want you." And I meant that. I really did, though it was difficult to imagine why at the moment. He really smelled.

His cold gaze narrowed on my face. "We will cut out your heart at sundown."

What? "What! How can that be your respon…" My voice trailed off as he simply disappeared. Like, as in, disappeared-disappeared. Gone. Poof. "What the…? Tommaso! Come back! You don't want to do this!"

Praise for Mimi Jean's Books

"Mimi Jean Pamfiloff is a paranormal romance (PNR) author that never disappoints. She writes the type of PNR that has readers smiling and laughing one moment, and cursing and making stabby motions the next."
—*Reviews by Ruckie,* on *Immortal Matchmakers, Inc.*

"Pamfiloff injects smart-ass humor into every scene…plot and characters are pure fun."
—*Publishers Weekly,* on *Sun God Seeks Surrogate*

"Smark, snarky storytelling and an inventive plot will keep readers turning the pages. Throw in a host of amusing, distinctive characters, and Pamfiloff's latest is hilarious, sexy and just plain fun."
—*RT Book Reviews,* on *Accidentally Married to a Vampire?*

"Every time I read one of these books in the series I think it is the best one. I get proven wrong by each one. They just keep getting better and better."
—*Romancing the Book,* on *Sun God Seeks Surrogate*

"This first book in the spin-off is everything I love about Mimi Jean Pamfiloff's paranormal. Sarcasm, snark, smartassness, and big sexy alphas in leather pants. Getting down and dirty no holds barred romance."
—*Hannah's Words,* on *Immortal Matchmakers, Inc.*

OTHER WORKS BY MIMI JEAN PAMFILOFF

COMING SOON:

TAILORED FOR TROUBLE
(Standalone/Romantic Comedy/
The Happy Pants Series)

IT'S A FUGLY LIFE (Standalone/Contemporary
Romance/Fugly Series, Book 2)

GOD OF WINE
(Standalone/Paranormal/Humor/Immortal
Matchmakers Series, Book 3)

THE TEN CLUB (Standalone/Dark Fantasy/The
King Series, Book 5)

BRUTUS (Standalone/Paranormal/Humor/Immortal
Matchmakers Series, Book 4)

AVAILABLE NOW:

FUGLY (Standalone/Contemporary Romance)
IMMORTAL MATCHMAKERS, Inc.
(Standalone/Paranormal/Humor/Book 1)

FATE BOOK
(Standalone/New Adult Suspense/Humor)

FATE BOOK TWO
(Standalone/New Adult Suspense/Humor)

THE HAPPY PANTS CAFÉ
(Standalone/Prequel/Romantic Comedy)

THE MERMEN TRILOGY (Dark Fantasy)

Mermen (Book 1)
MerMadmen (Book 2)
MerCiless (Book 3)

THE KING SERIES (Dark Fantasy)

King's (Book 1)
King for a Day (Book 2)
King of Me (Book 3)
Mack (Book 4)

THE ACCIDENTALLY YOURS SERIES
(Paranormal Romance/Humor)

Accidentally in Love with...a God? (Book 1)
Accidentally Married to...a Vampire? (Book 2)
Sun God Seeks...Surrogate? (Book 3)
Accidentally...Evil? (a Novella) (Book 3.5)
Vampires Need Not...Apply? (Book 4)
Accidentally...Cimil? (a Novella) (Book 4.5)
Accidentally...Over? (Series Finale) (Book 5)

TOMMASO

The Immortal Matchmakers, Inc. Series

Book Two

Mimi Jean Pamfiloff

a Mimi Boutique Novel

ISBN-10: 1-943983-01-1
ISBN-13: 978-1-943983-01-8

Cover Design by EarthlyCharms.com

Editing by Latoya Smith and Pauline Nolet

Interior design by WriteIntoPrint.com

Like "Free" Pirated Books?
Then Ask Yourself This Question:
WHO ARE THESE PEOPLE I'M HELPING?

What sort of person or organization would put up a website that uses stolen work (or encourages its users to share stolen work) in order to make money for themselves, either through website traffic or direct sales? **Haven't you ever wondered?**

Putting up thousands of pirated books onto a website or creating those anonymous ebook file sharing sites takes time and resources. Quite a lot, actually.

So who are these people? Do you think they're decent, ethical people with good intentions? Why do they set up camp anonymously in countries where they can't easily be touched? And the money they make from advertising every time you go to their website, or through selling stolen work, **what are they using it for? The answer is you don't know.** They could be terrorists, organized criminals, or just greedy bastards. But one thing we DO know is that **THEY ARE CRIMINALS** who don't care about you, your family, or me and mine. **And their intentions can't be good.**

And every time you illegally share or download a book, YOU ARE HELPING these people. Meanwhile, people like me, who work to support a family and children, are left wondering why anyone would condone this.

So please, please ask yourself who YOU are HELPING when you support ebook piracy and then ask yourself who you are HURTING.

And for those who legally purchased / borrowed / obtained my work from a reputable retailer (not sure, just ask me!) muchas thank yous! You rock.

DEDICATION

To Javi.

Thank you for letting me live my dream.

In D.F., Bacalar, Cali, AZ, New Jersey,
or Michigan, you've always dug in hard
when it mattered most.

I love you.

WARNING:

This book contains F-bombs, unicorns, golf clubs, random references to TV shows, disco balls, imprisoned clowns, leather pants, evil Mayan priests, large scary bugs, insane deities, hot immortal men, and, of course, references to extremely large penises.

If you do not like F-bombs, unicorns, golf clubs, random references to TV shows, disco balls, imprisoned clowns, leather pants, evil Mayan priests, large scary bugs, insane deities, hot immortal men, and extremely large penises, then this story is likely not for you...

TOMMASO

PROLOGUE

Lying in bed, I sifted through the darkness with my tired eyes, in search of the strange noise coming from...

Holy crap! It's above me!

The dark figure came into focus, and I let out a yelp that should've been a terror-filled scream. *What in the name of fuck is that?* I thought, feeling my entire body turn ice cold with fear.

In the yellow light of my alarm clock, I saw the monster's face hovering over mine, its eyes pits of glowing crimson swirling with black.

Oh shit. Oh shit. What is that? I opened my mouth to finally deliver that scream, but the beast quickly slapped its sickly hand over my lips to muffle the noise.

Oh, God. Help me. He smelled like death and evil. He smelled like desolation and despair—everything bad in this world mixed together.

Knowing I was about to die, I felt my eyes begin to tear.

"Please," I mumbled through the gaps in its sticky fingers, the unmistakable smell of dried blood filling my nostrils. "Please don't kill me."

Slowly, it dipped its head, allowing me to see its face up close.

Christ. He's human. Or something humanlike, resembling a man covered in black soot and the stench of death.

"Please, I'm begging you—just let me go," I whimpered.

The man slid his hand from my mouth, studying me. Then there was a flash of something I didn't expect in their depths: fear.

"Save. Me," he mumbled in a deep gargle. "Please...save...me..."

What the...? I was the one who needed saving!

"I think it's the oth-other way around," I stuttered and then reached for the reading lamp to my side and swung. He stopped it inches from his face, and an icy rage replaced any semblance of kinder, gentler emotions.

He roared and then grabbed me by the hair, dragging me from my bed.

"Let go!" I yelled, and he did. He tossed me to the floor as if I were completely weightless.

Oh, God. He was so strong.

I yelled for help, but no one was coming. I lived alone out in the middle of the desert.

Looking pleased by my fear, he reached into the waistband of whatever he wore as clothing and drew a buck knife or machete or something one might use to murder an innocent twenty-six-year-old golf instructor who lived ten miles outside of Palm Springs, liked to binge on crunchy food, and owned two Jeeps, a cat that hated her, and four rescue chickens. Yeah. It was that kind of knife. A really, really big fucking knife.

"Oh, God. Please no. Please…I'm sorry," I cried. "Whatever I did, I'm sorry!" Of course, I wasn't sorry. I was simply terrified and wanted to live. Unfortunately, the odds were not in my favor.

I watched in terror as the blade barreled down toward my face.

PART ONE

TOMMASO

CHAPTER ONE

9:42 a.m., Los Angeles

Covered in bright red blood, Tommaso Fierro stumbled from his sleek black Mercedes and staggered across the litter-filled 7-Eleven parking lot, clutching the front of his sticky gray dress shirt.

"Sonofabitch," he groaned. *This can't be happening.* He'd gone through far too much, survived far too much, only to end up like this.

No. No. No. You are not *turning evil again.*

But then why had his turquoise eyes—the telltale sign of his godsgiven immortality—turned black? Why did his heart feel like it was being prodded with a red-hot poker?

And where the fuck did all this blood come from? It sure as hell wasn't his.

He looked at his sticky red hands, suddenly seeing images of the dark-haired woman in his head. She was bound and gagged in his closet, screaming at him through a rope knotted between her lips.

Shit. Please don't tell me I killed her. Because she was the one. Yes, *the* one. And no, he couldn't explain why he had no clear memory of what happened, but he did remember the wave of intense desire he'd felt the moment he spotted her leaving the singles mixer last night—*Wait. Was it last night?* Everything was a blur after that, like watching a violent movie on a dark screen that sporadically flickered.

Godsdammit! Wouldn't this just be his godsdamned luck? He finally meets the woman of his dreams—his true mate—only to turn evil for no other reason than the Universe had decided to be a huge bitch and mess with everyone.

More blurry images swarmed his mind: the woman screaming and then…images of him letting her go, only to start chasing her, like a cat playing with a mouse it wanted to torment before the kill.

That is very fucked up.

Tommaso suddenly felt like his skull was splitting open. *Aaagh…* He shoved his fingers into his sticky short hair, pressing the sides of his head. Then his lungs began closing up. *I can't…breathe.* He fell to his knees on the hard asphalt. And godsdammit, he had just gotten his awesome pin-striped slacks back from the tailor. Three hundred bucks just for the hem.

A candy apple red Mustang tore into the parking lot, nearly colliding with a parked car before coming to a tire-screeching halt a few feet in front of him. The driver door popped open and out stepped a familiar face: Zac, God of Temptation.

The sound of Zac's heavy biker boots thumped toward Tommaso as he tried to keep his vision from blacking out.

"Wow," said Zac in his usual cocky tone while brushing back his mane of shaggy black hair with his usual affected gesture. "You weren't joking. You really are turning into a Maaskab—not such a great look for you, by the way."

Maaskab were an ancient sect of powerful, bloodthirsty Mayan priests who excelled in the dark arts. With their blood-caked dreads, soulless pits for eyes, and grime-covered bodies (they believed bathing robbed them of their powers), they looked like death warmed over, reheated in a microwave, and then deep fried in evil waffle batter. And though they were talented at many malevolent things, manipulating dark energy and enslaving others to do their bidding were their claims to fame, something Tommaso knew firsthand. For two loooong fucking years, he'd been pumped full of Maaskab poisons and used to spy on the gods' army. It was a miracle he'd escaped, but an even bigger miracle the gods had chosen to help him versus ending his life after he'd been discovered.

Only now, he wasn't so sure that he'd been cured (or what had happened over the last twenty-four hours or why he was in a 7-Eleven parking lot covered in blood with only a vague recollection of taking his newly found mate captive). In any case, Zac had been the first name that came to mind when he'd called for help.

Perhaps not such a wise choice. Zac wasn't known for being the most compassionate of the gods. Okay. None of the gods were compassionate.

Bat-shit crazy, the whole lot of them.

Tommaso looked up at Zac, seven feet of pure conceited asshole in leather pants. *And topless?*

"Why aren't you wearing a shirt?" Tommaso grumbled. Proper attire was essential, even when one was in the process of transforming into a monster, as in his case. Didn't see him ripping off his clothes and acting uncivilized.

"Casual Friday." Zac shrugged and then bent to help Tommaso to his feet.

Tommaso's gaze gravitated toward the hazy figure of a petite blonde standing beside the god, wearing only a pair of enormous flowery granny panties and matching brassiere. He recognized her to be Tula, the new assistant at Immortal Matchmakers, Inc., which was run by Zac and Zac's insane redheaded mess of a sister, Cimil—the Goddess of the Underworld.

"What's with Tula's outfit?" Tommaso mumbled, wondering if he wasn't dreaming.

"Casual Friday," Zac answered for Tula. "Did I not just explain that?"

"Okay, you two," said Tula, in a sugary tone, "let's get out of here before the police show and suck up another day with all their questions. I'm still trying to get them not to press charges for the singles mixer."

Tommaso hadn't stayed for more than a minute at that party, but he could only imagine the long list of reasons the police had been called. Things tended to end up decimated or lit on fire when a group of immortals got in a room and started drinking. Belch, aka the God of Wine and Intoxication, for example, held the all-time record for destroying the most hotels. Five hundred and twenty. All burnt to the ground. All by accident.

Tommaso winced, the pain of whatever searing through his veins becoming almost unbearable. "Take me home."

"Who said anything about home, compadre?" Zac said. "You're not safe to roam freely with the masses."

Zac looked at Miss Flower-Power Panties and instructed her to retrieve Tommaso's keys from his pocket.

"But Zac," Tula protested, "a man's pocket is his private space. Next to his privates."

She was standing in the middle of a public parking lot in broad daylight, wearing only her undergarments—albeit, very unsexy undergarments, but undergarments nonetheless—and she was concerned about improper behavior?

"My keys are in the ignition," Tommaso groaned, the splitting pain in his head and heart only worsening. "And I'm sorry about all the blood in the car." *Sorrier than anyone could ever know. Please don't let it be my mate's. Please.*

Zac bent his head and gave Tommaso a whiff. "Hate to break it to you, evil buddy, but if what's in your car is the same stuff that's on your shirt, that's not blood. Cherry Slurpee is my guess."

Really? Tommaso looked down at his sticky gray shirt. "I killed a woman and went to get a Slurpee? I *am* a monster."

"Do you specifically remember killing someone?" Zac asked.

"No, but—"

Sirens began wailing off in the distance.

"Time to go, big man. Let's get you to a secure location. We'll sort it all out later." Zac turned toward Tula, who was already getting into Tommaso's Mercedes. "I'll meet you back at the office."

"Yes, sir," she replied.

"And, woman?" Zac said, his deep voice filled with agitation.

"Yes?" she answered.

"The next time I see you, you'd better be wearing proper office apparel. We hold to certain standards at Immortal Matchmakers, Inc. Even on casual Friday."

"For the last time, I am *not* going to work naked, Zac!" She slammed the driver-side door shut and zoomed out of the parking lot.

"Humans," Zac grumbled. "So damned uppity! You know what I mean?" Zac looked at Tommaso, fishing for validation.

Tommaso frowned up at the deity, whose face was becoming a mishmash of swirls. *I'm losing my mind.* "Sure. Yeah. Wearing clothes is so last year."

"I know, right?" Zac grabbed Tommaso's arm to steady him as he began falling sideways. "All right, let's get you off to jail."

"You're taking me to jail?" Tommaso stumbled along toward the Mustang, without a hope or a prayer of getting free. *Not in my condition.*

"Well, I'm really taking you to Cimil's basement until we can get you moved to our real prison. But where else would I take an evil, bloodthirsty Maaskab to rot for eternity?"

Rot? Eternity? Oh hell. Maybe Zac was right; that was where he needed to go. Because if Tommaso had harmed a hair on his mate's head, he deserved to putrefy in a dark dungeon for all time.

But what if she's not dead? He had seen an image of him untying her and of her running away. *Gods be damned. I have to find out what I did...* He needed to know she was all right. Okay, and his heart demanded to see her again and beg her forgiveness.

But who was she? He'd only seen her for a moment in passing as she left the mixer—that part was clear. As for how would he go looking for her when he could barely see straight? *Not to mention you're going off to immortal jail.*

There was only one person he could turn to.

Gods help me...

CHAPTER TWO

"Where the *hell* is Tommaso?" boomed a deep, annoying voice, ricocheting off the rainbow-painted walls, through a dizzying ocean of low-hanging disco balls, and bouncing off of piles of...stuff. All making up what had to be the most frightening place on Earth: *Cimil's basement.*

"I'm here," Tommaso replied miserably, prying himself from his bale of "Cimil-certified" organic free-range hay. *So stupid.*

Tommaso bellied up to the hot pink steel bars of his cell, which was really a giant bird cage.

Like he'd said: Scariest. Place. On. Earth.

Not that *he* was afraid.

Men like him, who had been trained by the best of the best and deadliest of the deadliest in the gods' army, were lethal weapons and feared nothing. His polished exterior—manicured nails, fine Italian suits, neatly trimmed black scruff, and salon-cut "messy" short hair—were a façade. One he enjoyed maintaining, of course.

A man should always look his best. Even when kicking ass.

"Make a right turn," Tommaso yelled, "just after the guillotine urinal, and then left after the giant wooden box marked 'Danger: Randy clowns inside.'" Yes, Cimil had a wooden crate the size of an elephant filled with...well...clowns. The sounds—sadistic laughter mixed with intermittent weeping—emanating from inside were enough to make a grown warrior's gonads want to tuck and take cover.

"What?" Votan yelled. "I can't hear you over all the moaning! And what in the gods' names is that fucking smell? And why are there disco balls everywhere? It's maddening."

"She's your damned sister, Votan. Do you really need to ask?"

"Guy. My name is Guy!" he yelled, his voice getting closer. Votan, who also went by Guy Santiago (his human name), was believed to be the most lethal of the fourteen gods—the likely reason for which he was the God of Death and War. Or was it War and Death? Tommaso couldn't remember. In any case, Guy was seven feet of pompous muscle with long blue-black hair and the deity-trademark turquoise eyes—actually, the same color eyes as anyone who had been given the light of the gods and immortality. He himself had been given immortality after being infected by the Maaskab's dark powers, but only because Guy's wife, Emma, begged him to make it happen. Emma was beautiful, gracious, and forgiving and probably the closest thing he had to family aside from his best friend, Andrus. Guy was simply a jealous dip-tard.

"There you are, Tommaso." Guy scowled. "Wow. You're just as fucking ugly as the last time I saw you. No wait, you're uglier."

If I'm considered ugly, then you're considered a nice person. "Good to see you, too, asshole. Love the extra-tight T-shirt. Did you start shopping at Baby Gap, or did Emma finally leave you, so you're on your own with the washer and drier?"

Guy crossed his beefy arms over his chest, further stretching his too tight baby blue tee. His black and gray camo cargo pants looked like they might split at the seams any second now.

What's with this guy? Seriously. Tommaso was a muscular man—of normal height, thank goodness—and you didn't see him running around, trying to show off every inch. His six-two frame was always dressed in clothing that fit, that exuded confidence, not neediness. *Look at me, I'm The God of Death and War*, Tommaso whined inside his head.

"Jackass," Tommaso muttered.

"Watch your tongue, human," said Guy. "Or I will squash you like the man-whoring vermin that you are. Nice pants, by the way. But you do realize that dressing like a real man won't make you one."

Though Tommaso much preferred a finely tailored suit, at the moment he wore some ridiculous black leather pants and a plain white T-shirt that Cimil had had in her "guest prisoner" wardrobe box. Tommaso felt like he was trying to impersonate the kind of men he liked to beat the crap out of—men who had no class, no balls, and big mouths.

Basically Guy.

Tommaso shrugged. "Just because your wife, Emma, thinks I'm hot doesn't mean you have to start throwing insults, Guy."

The angular plains of Guy's face seemed to harden as his cheeks turned rage-red. "I'll fucking kill—"

"Boys!" called a female voice that was music to Tommaso's ears. "I can hear you! And will someone tell me what the hell is inside that giant box?"

"Clowns!" Guy and Tommaso replied in unison.

Just then, Emma's head of copper red curls popped through a curtain of purple streamers hanging to the side of the room. "I swear something was just following me. This place is horrifying." Wearing a flowing green dress that almost matched her eyes, and holding a small bundle to her chest, Emma weaved through several piles of fuzzy pink beanbag chairs and unopened cases of confetti cake frosting to make her way over. "Dear gods, what's with all of the disco balls? And why does anyone need so much damned frosting?"

"My love," said Guy, "have you not learned that when it comes to Cimil, it is best not to ask? And to forget anything she says? Or does? Or shows you— okay, you should really forget everything related to her. She's not right in the head."

That's what I said, thought Tommaso.

Emma nodded. "Point taken. So. What's this I'm hearing, Tommaso, about you being detained because you're a 'threat to humanity'? Because we all know that's a bunch of bull crap."

Guy turned toward her and frowned, his turquoise eyes flickering to a dark blue for a quick second. "Is that why you called me to meet you here? You said you needed to speak to me and Tommaso, that it was 'important.'" He made little air quotes with his fingers.

Tommaso's one phone call had been to Emma because she was the only one besides his best friend, Andrus, he could trust. But Andrus, like himself, was considered a bad boy of the immortal community—which said a lot because they were all highly dysfunctional beings. In any case, Tommaso had needed someone with influence to get him out of "jail."

Emma rolled her eyes. "Tommaso is locked up in Cimil's basement. That *is* important. He's our friend."

"Friend?" Votan growled. "He is *not* your friend. He is a traitor, a spy, a—"

"His mind was poisoned by the Maaskab," she snapped. "And don't forget that he was captured by them because he was working for you gods! He's nothing but kind and loyal and…"

This was why Tommaso cared so deeply for Emma. She never gave up on him, even after everything he'd done to her, including handing her over to the Scabs (aka Maaskab) for a ritual sacrifice. Of course, the Maaskab had infected him with their dark voodoo bullcrap and he had tried to fight his evil urges. In the end, however, he'd failed. Then he'd tried to help kill her. Not his best day.

Guy's facial features contorted with irritation. "Woman, I was in a summit meeting with my brethren, discussing the situation. *That* was important."

Tommaso could only assume that the "situation" was in reference to Cimil's big announcement at the immortal singles mixer party she and Zac had given a few days ago. Basically, she advised everyone that the Universe—for reasons unknown—had been thrown into some sort of moral tailspin: Any unmated immortals were about to undergo a personality change. I.e., those who were inherently evil would find themselves playing for Team Good. Those who were good, Team Evil.

Cimil's declaration sounded like a bunch of BS construed for the sole purpose of her amusement. Regrettably, however, the evidence to support her claim could not be ignored. Case in point, Cimil's new Maaskab nanny and Tommaso's inexplicable evil relapse. There were other cases of flip-flopping popping up all over the immortal community, too. And according to Cimil, the only way to avoid such a switch was to find a mate to keep one's moral compass in check. He supposed it made sense, but only hard evidence would prove this out.

If I can just get someone to help me find my woman. Tommaso glanced at Emma and Guy through his shiny pink birdcage bars. They were bickering away like a couple who'd been married for fifty years.

"I, uhhh…" Tommaso cleared his throat, trying to think of a way to get their attention back on his cause. "Is that your new baby?"

Emma immediately dropped her rant midstream. "That's right!" she said cheerfully. "You haven't met K'as Pa'achi Dzuuy Ool."

That was a mouthful. "Errr…Cazzpoochi—"

"K'as Pa'achi Dzuuy Ool," she repeated. "It means 'Badass, Tough Heart.'"

Tommaso nodded slowly, trying not to seem disrespectful. "That is…certainly…a unique name."

"We call him Kaz for short," she added and then pulled back the little blue blanket to reveal a drowsy-looking baby with long eyelashes, red hair, and pouty lips.

He's adorable. Tommaso resisted awww-ing, because that would be a very unmanly thing to do. And if Tommaso was one thing in this world, it was manly. Okay, and chivalrous. And, while he was on the subject, loyal, too. His only major flaw was being unable to let go of the past. It was at the center of his being and the reason he couldn't allow this evil change to occur. Bluntly put, he'd rather die than return to being a Maaskab minion. Those evil priests had taken everything from him—his parents, brothers, sisters, nieces, and nephews. No one had been spared that day. He never did learn what occurred exactly, but his job at the time had been tracking and killing Maaskab in the gods' army. His best guess, knowing everything he now knew, was that the priests used Uchben soldiers (aka members of the human gods' army) who were under the Maaskab's mind control to execute his family in retaliation. Then they came for him. They captured him, tortured him, and made him their mindless slave. Later, they returned him to spy on the gods' army.

In the end, he lost everything: his family, his sense of self, and his job. He wasn't about to give up his life all over again. And certainly not now, when he had a chance at a real one. *Wife, children, a family.* This woman was his chance to get that all back.

Who the fuck are you kidding, man? You're a ticking time bomb. If he overcame this current obstacle, the best he could hope for was to have a complicated relationship with this woman. One where she would always be unhappy and he would always need to keep his distance.

Tommaso looked at the beautiful baby in Emma's arms and noted the way her eyes lit up. It made him jealous. Not that he would admit it. Because he was manly. Very, very manly.

"He's beautiful, Emma," Tommaso said. "Congratulations to both of you."

"Enough with the pleasantries and ass kissing, Tommy," said Guy. "I must return to the summit meeting and—"

Hardball time. "You can't leave. Not until you've heard me out," Tommaso said firmly. "Because Emma is right. This is important."

Emma flashed Guy a warning with her eyes.

"I'll give you one minute," Guy said.

This was the part he would dread saying aloud. "I think I..." he covered his mouth, half mumbling, "found my may-mumble-mumble."

"You found a mare? Who the hell cares if you're into horses," said Guy.

"Not a mare. A mate," he said begrudgingly.

Emma squealed, and the baby cried out. "Oh. Sorry, honey. Mommy's sorry. Shushshushshush..." She began swaying. "This is so exciting," she whispered loudly.

"Once again, I ask: Who the hell cares?" Guy said.

Tommaso hated to play this card, just like he'd hated that his one phone call from Cimil's Crazy Dungeon of Pink Disco Horror and Irrational Fetishes had gone to Emma, but there'd been no other choice.

Tommaso cleared his throat. "When I was cured and given immortality by the gods, it was you, Guy, who vouched for me." Because no one, including himself, knew if being given the light of the gods would truly cure him.

"I only did it to make Emma happy," Guy said.

"Yes. And I know how much you care for her, which is why I'm sure you don't want to leave her."

"Leave her?" Guy scoffed. "Why would I do such a thing?"

"Because you vouched for me. Don't you remember? If I am convicted of any crimes, you will also have to endure the same punishment—those are *your* stupid rules, by the way, not mine."

Guy's mouth fell open just a little, and Emma's turquoise eyes went wide. Yes, she was now immortal, too. Just like Tommaso. Or, at least, he had been. Now that his eyes had darkened, he wasn't sure what he was.

"But-but," Guy stuttered.

"You wrote the laws, so don't blame me," Tommaso said.

"Guy? Is that right?" Emma asked, looking terrified.

"Well, I, uh..." Guy planted his hands on his waist and exhaled. "Yes. I suppose it is."

"What are we going to do?" she asked. "It's bad enough that we have to deal with an entire community of single immortals whose nice-switches are about to flip, but having you locked away, too?"

"That's my point," Tommaso said. "If you get me out of here and help me find this woman, I can convince her to forgive me and perhaps accept me as her mate. I won't turn evil and there'll be no reason to imprison me and Guy."

Guy crossed his arms. "I'm not going to jail. I'll change the law."

Emma shook her head. "You know how hard that's going to be. You need a majority vote, and your brothers and sisters aren't going to give it to you."

That was likely true. The gods were like children and wouldn't want to pass up the chance to see Guy in prison. Pure entertainment.

"Wait," Emma said to Tommaso. "What did you

say—that part about 'convincing her to forgive' you?"

Tommaso scratched the back of his head. "I, uhh…may have kidnapped her."

"What? *Why* would you do that?" Emma barked.

"I don't know. I woke up this morning in that parking lot. All I remember is seeing her tied up in my closet. And then I let her go and she was running away, screaming."

Guy chuckled. "Nice going there, ladies' man."

"Don't start, babies' man. Or I'll bring up the fact you were hot for Emma when she was still in diapers."

It wasn't exactly true, of course, but before Emma was born, Guy had been trapped by the Maaskab in a cenote—one of the underground springs the gods used as portals between this world and theirs. Guy couldn't go anywhere, and Emma was the only person who could hear him for some strange reason. Their long-distance telepathic connection started the day she was born, and later, once she became a woman, Guy's jealousy almost drove her mad.

Funny, how so little has changed.

"Shut your hole," Guy said, "or I'll shove something in there to shut it for you."

Tommaso bobbed his head slowly. "I am so, so not into that, but I do not judge how a god spends his free time. That being said—get me the hell out of here."

"Shut up," Guy snarled. "That's not what I meant, but you should be so lucky to have such a glorious penis in your—wait. Never mind. This conversation has gotten away from me." Guy's eyes flickered with annoyance. "You know I can't simply free you, Tommaso. Zac put you into custody for a valid reason, and to remove you without a proper review by the gods would be a violation of our laws."

"Then let's get his case reviewed," Emma said. "They're all over at your brother's beach house for the emergency summit anyway. Just get them to throw it onto the agenda."

Guy scratched his black stubbled chin, mulling it over.

"Honey," Emma said sweetly, "there's no other choice. We have to convince them to let Tommaso out to find this woman. It's either that or he's going to be declared a threat to humanity and will be sent away to prison. And so will you."

The closest prison was near Sedona, Arizona, and was where the baddest of the bad immortals were kept.

Guy bobbed his head. "We will plead our case to my brethren."

Yes!

Guy continued, "Let us go now. They'll be returning from their lunch break soon, and we want them in a good mood." Guy and Emma turned to leave.

"Before you go," Tommaso blurted, "could you please find me some earplugs? I can't listen to those groaning clowns anymore."

"Not a chance," said Guy.

CHAPTER THREE

With his shamelessly carnal gaze directed at Tula, the God of Temptation licked his lips as he sat in the corner of his brother Kinich's banquet-sized dining room, which was decorated in an ancient Egyptian palace motif complete with glyphs, those gold-plated candy-cane-looking things, and faux torches.

Dear gods, she's going to... Zac tightened his grip on the gold-painted arms of his chair, watching with bated breath as Tula, in her blue and white Hawaiian muumuu, bent over to refill another water glass on the long stone slab table in the center of the room.

Yeah, baby. So not *hot...* But watching Tula perform the most mundane of tasks, like making a pot of coffee at the office, was like porn to him. The less hot, the more painfully erotic—a God of Temptation thing. After all, he couldn't get all excited about tempting someone who was easily tempted. That would be more like fulfilling their dreams or granting wishes—not his gig.

But tempting people? Pushing them over the edge to follow their deepest, darkest desires? *Hell, yeah.* He was all over that shit.

Besides, temptation wasn't always a bad thing—it served to challenge people and sometimes got them to think about their true priorities.

But most of the time, it just makes them do shit they regret. Also fun!

Tula scratched her right boob and then continued refilling glasses.

Such a fucking turn-on. Zac crossed his legs and tugged down the hem of his "Screw World Peace, I Want a Pony" T-shirt to hide the boner pushing painfully against the zipper of his black leather pants. Thankfully, the rest of the gods were outside on the enormous patio overlooking Malibu beach, eating burgers and hot dogs prepared by his brother Kinich. Kinich was once the Sun God, but had a little issue that turned him into a vampire. Then there was that other matter regarding Zac having tried to steal Kinich's mate, thus the reason Zac was in the deity doghouse. Not that he was complaining at the moment.

Because, sweet gods, look at the titillating full coverage of her giant dress. I think I'm going to cu—

"Zac, please stop staring," Tula said, carrying on with her task of refreshing the table—water, pens, paper, and tequila for Belch, the God of Wine and Intoxication—being used for the emergency summit meeting. "It's just not going to happen between us.

Not to mention, you're my boss."

Boss? Who cares? Titles meant nothing to him, unless they were talking about his. God of Temptation. *And don't forget the Sofa King. Sofa King awesome!* He mentally fist bumped himself.

"I'm not staring," Zac said, his gaze locked on the bit of creamy ankle skin peeking out from beneath her long dress. "I'm attempting to discern what makes you so irresistible—you're the most unsexy woman I've ever met." That was a flat-out lie—he already knew what made her so enticing—but he'd take any excuse to continue staring at her.

She picked up an empty glass at the head of the table and shot him a look. "Golly gee, Mr. Zac, you know just howta make a girl feel special."

Yes. I do. But that's beside the point. He was beginning to wonder if her way of dressing and demeanor were deliberate, almost as if she knew her prudishness was a turn-on.

"Tula, why do you wear camping tent frocks and undergarments that could provoke a perfectly healthy and virile man to take a vow of celibacy?"

Her head of blonde hair whipped in his direction, her blue eyes screaming foul, which shocked him, frankly; she was always smiling, always pleasant, no matter what he did.

Tula held up her frosty-pink fingernail. "First of all, Mr. Zac, it's not a tent, it's called a muumuu—it's hot out today, and I like being comfortable. Same goes for my underwear. Although, I am considering changing to a less itchy cotton bra. Polyester is not my L.A. friend." She held up two fingers. "Second of all, my fiancé doesn't care what I wear because he loves me for my kind heart and," she tapped the side of her head, "for what's up here. So I suggest you stop obsessing over women's exteriors, Mr. Zac. You might just find the girl of your dreams right under your nose."

Maybe I've already found her. Because Tula was spicier than a habañero Hot Pocket—a regular cheese Hot Pocket stuffed with fresh habaneros and the only thing he really knew how to cook.

Yes. I'm a stereotypical, immortal badass bachelor. So what?

Anyway, getting back to Tula... The issue was that Cimil had made it very clear: Tula was an employee and not fair game. Tula was also one hundred percent committed to some mortal shmuck, Gilbert. Not that Zac would ever believe anything Cimil said—his current predicament of being relieved of his powers, banished to L.A., and sentenced to find immortal love for one hundred couples was all her godsdamned fault. All because he'd followed his heart and made a play for Penelope, Kinich's mate. A very long story and all water under the bridge—*mostly.* What hadn't passed beneath that infamous proverbial bridge of no return, however, was how much he wanted Tula and how much she didn't want him back. Even when he'd been pursuing Penelope, prior to her full commitment to Kinich, he'd managed to get her interested. With Tula, though? Nada. He'd kissed her, held her, given her "the stare," which no woman on Earth could resist.

Yet she had.

"Are you sure your fiancé wants you for your mind?" he asked.

"Mr. Zac!" she snapped.

"Okay, but has he ever seen your underwear?" Because he fucking loved it. The giant granny panties especially. They just screamed *"I need temptation in my life!"* And he was here to serve.

She shook her head. "You already know I'm saving myself and don't believe in premarital sex."

Such a shame, because he would bet his favorite Bionic Man lunch pail—yes, it was a collector's item, so he had one—that Tula could drive a man crazy with her petite little body and wholesome goodness.

"You might want to show him the nunly goods before you tie the knot, baby, because your underwear is a crime against hum-*man*-ity." Zac mentally high-fived himself that time.

Tula huffed with indignation and then went about her business, completely ignoring him.

"What? I meant that as a compliment," he said defensively.

Suddenly, Tula set down her pitcher of water, planted both hands on the table, and began to sob.

Fuck. What did I do? Zac stood from his chair and rushed toward her. "Tula, I'm so sorry. Please don't cry." Did she not comprehend how human suffering, no matter where the deity landed on the asshole scale, impacted a god?

Tula covered her face with both hands and turned into Zac's chest, bawling her eyes out.

"Tula, I'm sorry. Please don't—"

"No. It's...not...you..." Sniffle, snort, sob. "We broke up."

"You and Gilbert?"

Sob, sob, sob. "Yes."

Yes! Is right. Zac smiled to himself and wrapped his arms around her small frame. This was the chance he'd been hoping for.

"What was it?" he asked. "The fact that you work for the sexiest male on the planet? Or his small penis?" Zac stroked the back of her head. "You can tell me anything."

"No," she snorted. "I really shouldn't. It's a private matter."

"No. You really should." *Because now I'm dying to hear why.* "It will make you feel better." *While indulging my thirst for superficial drama.*

A moment passed, and she pulled back enough to see his face, but remained wrapped in his arms, their bodies lightly touching.

Thank the gods for the confining strength of leather. She'd be halfway to pregnant already. But damned she felt amazing—warm and soft. Just the right size for cuddling.

Whoa! I am a god. Gods do not cuddle. We kick ass and fuck.

He took a small step back and dropped his arms. She was too busy sniffling and wiping the tears from under her eyes to notice.

"You're probably right," she whimpered. "I haven't told anyone, and it's tearing me apart."

Annoyingly, Zac felt his urge to help the poor

human kick in. *Dammit! Dammit! Dammit!*

Like rusty razor blades scraping their way up his throat, the words involuntarily bubbled out, "You...can...tell...me." *Aaagh...this is awful.* "I want to help."

"Really?" She looked up at him with her doey blue eyes. "This isn't some ploy to get me into bed?"

"No. Don't get me wrong; I mean, yes, I do want to get you into bed, but my need to comfort you is purely instinctual."

Her mouth dropped open with a huff. "So you're basically telling me that you don't really care and any kindness on your part is involuntary?"

Was this a trick question? "Uhhh...yeah. I'm a god. That's how it works."

She shook her head and stepped back, irritation flickering in her eyes. "And right there, Mr. Zac, is the reason you don't have a woman."

He frowned. "I have plenty of women. A new one every night." *I mean, look at me. I'm seven feet of hard lean muscle in sexy leather pants.* Had she not noticed?

She lifted her chin. "Has it ever occurred to you that you have a different woman every night because none of them want to stick around?"

Pfft! What...what...complete and total rubbish! "Women beg me to give them another go. All the time."

She shot him a look of doubt.

"Okay," he admitted, "perhaps they don't ask with their mouths, but they ask with their eyes."

She turned away, shaking her head, and then went back to filling glasses in silence.

"You doubt me?" he asked, thoroughly offended.

She made a little shrug. "Who am I to judge you? You're a god, after all. And I'm just Tula—little old mortal."

Of course, what she really meant was "You're just a stupid guy, like the rest."

"I bet the real reason you don't put out," he said, "is because deep in your heart you know that you'll be no good at it. Gotta hook him into marriage first before he runs. Am I right?"

Ha! Take that, you judgmental seductress!

Tula dropped the half-full glass in her hand and began to sob.

Oh no. Oh no. I made her cry again. "Tula, I'm so—"

She whipped around. "Fine, you win! I probably am bad in bed, and that *does* scare me. But he left me because I wouldn't sleep with him, so I lose either way! There. Are you happy?" she yelled. "You're all the same!" Tula turned and ran from the dining room.

"Now that was entertaining! Even Minky is clapping!" said his sister Cimil, who stood in the doorway leading out to the patio, her flaming red hair scooped up into two giant pigtails toward the top of her head.

"Shut up, Cimil, before I shove Minky up your ass."

She gasped with a snarky smile and placed her hand over her heart. Of course, her heart was covered with hot pink feathers since her entire blouse was made of them, making her look like one of those Troll things humans used to place over the eraser end of their pencils.

"You have offended my unicorn, and she is now challenging you to a duel."

He scoffed. "I'm not going to duel your invisible, blood-sucking unicorn. Don't be ridiculous."

Cimil looked over her shoulder at whatever was or wasn't there—who knew when Cimil was pretending or being serious? She then looked back at Zac. "Okay. Suit yourself. But that means you'll have to pay some other way, and Minky's been feeling quite randy since she got lucky at the mixer."

Zac made a sour face. *Disgusting.* "You really are bat-shit, Cimil."

"Yup." She nodded. "And now if you'll excuse me, I have to go pry Tula out of Kinich's coat closet, where she's crying hysterically and thinking of surrendering her virtue and living out her days as a harlot because *someone*—" her turquoise eyes bulged out in his direction like two giant spears "—has made her feel like she's worthless and undeserving of love. Thanks for that, asshole. Come, Minky." Cimil marched from the room, in the same direction as Tula.

"But I didn't do..." Zac's words faded as he realized that she was long gone and not interested in listening.

Gods, what's gotten into me? He really had

crossed the line and acted like a giant turd. He hadn't meant to, but what was a god to do? Pretend he was someone else? Someone kinder and deeper who actually gave a shit about others?

Pfft. Never. Only, he did care. Just a little. And now he was in a pissy mood.

He rubbed his face and groaned.

"Hi, Zac," said a soft female voice that sent his stomach spinning like a merry-go-round.

He slowly turned his head to find Penelope, who he'd been avoiding all morning since the summit started. She wore her long dark hair straight and looked lovelier than ever.

Zac dipped his head. "Nice to see you again." This meeting was the first time he'd seen her since his banishment to L.A.—a punishment for using his powers and trying to steal her away. All Cimil's bright idea. Sometimes it felt like Cimil was the true God, or Goddess, of Temptation. In any case, seeing Penelope now only confirmed what he'd suspected all along. He hadn't really felt anything genuine for her. It had been all about tempting her—an instinctual reflex he was only now just beginning to understand.

Penelope lifted her chin. "So I hear you've arrested Tommaso?"

"Yes. He's apparently turning into a Maaskab."

"Are you sure, because—"

Kinich, with his long blond-streaked hair, appeared at her side, still wearing his "Lover in the Kitchen. Warrior in Bed" apron.

"Brother." Kinich stiffly dipped his head.

"Brother," Zac replied.

Then the two just glared at each other. Zac didn't know what Kinich was thinking, but his mind was suddenly snatched away by an awareness of Tula having re-entered the room.

"Okay." Penelope clapped her hands together. "Let's get the meeting restarted." She began rounding up the other gods, who took their sweet time getting settled around the enormous limestone table chiseled with Mayan symbols and each of the gods' names. Zac moved to the far end, away from Penelope, who ran the show along with Kinich.

Penelope, who wore denim overalls and sandals, pulled out her tablet and began toggling through agenda topics. "Okay, everyone, a quick change of plans. Guy has asked that we add a topic..." Penelope suddenly looked up and noticed an empty chair. "Belch! Get your ass in here! The meeting's started!" she yelled over her shoulder toward the patio.

Shortly thereafter, wearing his usual loosey-whities (aka droopy underwear), a step up from his normal naked outfit, Belch staggered in, scratching his beer belly. "Sorry, fooolks," he slurred, "but I think I just saw a unicorn outside sharpening its horn. It looked really pissed." He pulled back his chair, but instead of sitting in it, he crawled on top of the table and proceeded to pass out, snoring like a congested lumberjack.

Penelope winced. "That's not going to be distracting."

Kinich sighed. "Well, at least he's here."

It was a requirement that all of the deities were present at summit meetings to vote, unless there were extenuating circumstances such as one turning evil. Or being captured by evil. Or under the spell of something evil. Or on vacay. The usual.

"Right you are." She checked off a box on her tablet. "Okay, so we need to take a vote on which strategy we're going to follow to deal with this issue of good immortals turning evil and evil ones turning good. Then Votan—sorry, I mean Guy—has also requested we vote to re-release Tommaso into his custody."

"Whatzzzz wrong with Tommazzoo?" asked Colel, the Mistress of Bees. She was blonde, tall, and wore a huge beehive on her head. Yes, a real one. And her little black and yellow soldiers were vicious little bastards with ninja-like reflexes. They were also jealous as hell. No man could get anywhere near her.

Gods, Zac thought, *I hope she never fills out an application to be matched at our agency.* He couldn't begin to imagine what man would want to date her—*she's anaphylactic shock waiting to happen.*

"Tommaso is turning into a Maaskab," Guy said.

The deities around the table all made *ewwww* sounds.

Poor Tommaso. He really wasn't such a bad guy. *But he will be.*

"I think we can still help him," Guy said. "Tommaso believes he's found his mate—some woman he met at the singles mixer last week."

"Okay." Penelope checked off another box on her tablet. "So that's added to the agenda for a vote. But first it's time for us to pick up where we left off before lunch." She took a quick breath, as if praying for patience. "Now, until we've figured out a permanent solution to the good and evil flip-flop, we're going to vote on a temporary solution. Those in favor of Ah Ciliz's recommendation of," she sighed and rolled her eyes, "killing ourselves, raise your hand."

The God of Eclipses, aka Ah Ciliz, aka A.C., aka dark motherfucker, raised his hand.

"Okay. That's one vote." Penelope checked the box, clearly trying not to roll her eyes again. "Option two: All in favor of Cimil's recommendation that all single immortals are to wed Minky—and no, Minky does not get a vote— raise your hands." Penelope looked right at Cimil, who was sitting frozen in her seat with her fingers laced together, completely motionless.

"Okaaaay. No votes—and let me just point out again what juvenile horse shit this is. You're all children. And moving on: Option three, my recommendation. We focus on the most powerful singles of the immortal community and get them mated up first, starting with the gods, in order to minimize the damage to the mortal community."

Everyone except for Belch and A.C. raised their hands.

Penelope shook her head. "I can't believe we have to waste so much time on this crap. Why don't you all just do me a favor and stop putting your idiotic solutions on the voting table? You just end up going for whatever I say anyway."

She had a point. But Penelope was only twentysomething years old. The rest of them were seventy. Thousand. One did what one could to make life more interesting.

Zac cleared his throat. "I think, Penelope, you forget that we're all immortal—no one really gives a crap about wasting time."

"Or about people's feelings," someone mumbled from the corner of the room. "Jackass."

Zac turned his head to see Tula glaring at him, her eyes puffy and red.

He was about to make a comment to censure the human, but then it dawned on him. He really was behaving like a cruel jackass. Uncharacteristically so.

Fuck. And I'm single.

Zac slowly raised his hand.

Penelope blew out a breath. "Yes, Zac?" she said with a bite.

"Can you put my name at the top of the list?" he asked.

Penelope tilted her head. "I guess. But...why?"

Because if that nagging feeling in the pit of his stomach was what he thought, his journey to evil had already begun.

"I uhh..." He made a little cough. "I think it would be in the best interest of everyone if those who are responsible for finding mates for our brethren are not at risk." Cimil, his partner, was already mated, so she was safe—if such a word could be used to describe a card-carrying member of the World's Most Awful People.

"Good point, Zac." Penelope made a note. "We'll make sure you get priority and—"

"Kill them all... I want to kill them all... Burn. Burn. Burn..." Belch mumbled between snorts and snores, still out like a light.

Penelope flicked her stylus at Belch. "And...adding Belch to the top of that list, too." She sighed. "Gosh, this is going to be a great rest of the year."

Of course, what she really meant was that they were all in for one hell of a shit storm. If the most powerful beings on earth turned evil, there'd be no stopping them. There weren't enough mated immortals—i.e., those who were good and not at risk of "infection"—to stand against so many unmated ones. Add to that, the gods who were still single—Bees, Belch, A.C., and himself, for example—were probably single for a reason.

Yep. We're fucked. This situation was going to get a whole lot worse before it got better. If it ever did.

CHAPTER FOUR

Tommaso glanced in the rearview mirror of his black Mercedes, unable to believe that this would be his life until further notice.

At least I'm a free bird. But this wasn't much better than Cimil's Tweety tank. There was a caravan behind him, containing Guy in a silver Pagani—a flashy and offensively expensive Italian sports car—and three very large black SUVs with tinted windows, containing a squad of Uchben, the gods' human army.

This was no way to win over a woman and convince her he was worth having. She'd either think he was a complete egocentric buffoon on top of being a violent criminal—if he had, in fact, tied her up—or that he was outrageously insecure and needed an entourage to make himself look more important.

He was neither. Yes, he was confident, to be sure. And handsome as hell—the ladies always said so—but looking like a Calvin Klein model with his black "I don't give a fuck" short hair and classic Italian features—lips like a sex god, jaw like a superhero, and perfectly straight nose—to him these were simply tools of survival. His six-two height and Mediterranean good looks made him stand out in a room and opened doors. They helped win people over even when he had been a soldier in the gods' army. "Always smile, son. Always walk into a room standing tall and let them know you are there," his father used to say. And that man knew how to own the room and lull people into submission with his mere presence. He had been a natural-born charmer and taught Tommaso at a young age that words were precious and to be used sparingly. Chivalry and good manners were to be doled out excessively. Both were very effective ways of controlling a situation because they subconsciously set a tone in the minds of others— even if one was in the midst of a crisis. If you were calm and confident, others would sense it. It was a philosophy he carried right down to his style of dress.

Set the tone.

Own the room.

Be a gentleman. (Except when talking to Guy— then be a prick.)

Because a gentleman was freer to break the rules and have it go unnoticed. Only now, his skills were definitely going to be put to the test.

He wouldn't be putting anyone at ease or presenting an air of total control by having these giant assholes on his tail. But these were the terms of his release. He had to be under twenty-four-hour surveillance and accompanied by Guy. Emma had stayed behind at Penelope and Kinich's house with...with...*oh, hell. What's the kid's name? Poochi? Pachi?*

Anyway, he needed to get to this woman fast. Because the moment he showed any signs of slipping further downhill—toward Evil Town—he would be sent away to immortal prison indefinitely.

Tommaso picked up his phone and dialed Guy, who answered immediately with, "You drive like a giant pussy with two left feet."

"I wasn't aware that pussies had feet—oh, wait. You mean an actual cat. Sorry, didn't realize you were speaking old man again. It's a bit difficult to understand."

"I might be seventy thousand years old, but I can beat you or any man with just my pinky."

Tommaso held back a chuckle. *Man, you just keep walking right into these.* "I'll pass. I've seen your pinkies and they look a little rough. But I think I saw a website once for men who enjoy that sort of thing."

A moment of silence passed as Tommaso waited for it to sink—

"Dear gods, you're so fucking juvenile," Guy grumbled.

"You mean young, virile, and relevant, unlike you? Why yes, I am."

"Shut up, you moron. What do you want?" Guy growled.

"I want what you want, which is for this to be

over quickly. So please do us both a favor and make sure you and your Uchben lie low."

"They know what they're doing, Tommaso. So leave the professionals to do their work; you just worry about begging this woman to give you the time of day."

She'll be begging all right—for more.

The other line on Tommaso's cell phone rang. "Gotta go," and he hit the answer button on his steering wheel. "Yes?"

"Hey, buddy, it's me, Andrus. What's this bullshit I hear about you getting arrested?"

Andrus, an immortal bad boy and his best friend, had just recently gotten married to a half succubus, of all "people"—just one more sign that the Universe was in fact flipping on its head. Thankfully though, Sadie was not your typical demon and was beautiful, kind, and smart—exactly what a guy like Andrus deserved. Which was why Andrus had done the impossible and forgone getting paired with his destined mate, some woman named Charlotte who was, ironically, Sadie's non-succubus cousin. Such a thing was unheard of—to turn your back on the Universe's will—but Andrus had always done things his way.

"So, how's the honeymoon going?" Tommaso asked.

"Fantastic. I'm enjoying keeping her succubus side well-fed—but never mind that. What the hell is going on? And tell me who's responsible so I can kill them. Slowly."

This was not going to be easy news to break, but

sooner or later, Andrus was going to hear the truth. "Do you want the good news or the bad news first?" Tommaso asked.

"Don't give a shit. Start talking."

"Bad it is. If you recall Cimil's big announcement about the Universe being out of whack—"

"How could I forget?" said Andrus.

"So, apparently, I am going to be one of the first to take a trip to the dark side."

"No," Andrus said. "You're fucking kidding me."

"Afraid not. My eyes have already turned black—Maaskab black." The standard was turquoise for anyone who carried the light of the gods.

"Oh shit. Don't tell me they're all red and bloody looking, too."

"Not yet. But probably soon. Which leads me to the good news; I think I've found her—my mate."

"Really? Who is she?"

Tommaso told him what he knew—not much—but included that he may have hunted her down and hurt her.

"This is not good, my friend. Where are you? I'm getting on a plane to come help."

"No. I insist you finish your honeymoon with Sadie. You deserve it." Hell, if anyone had gotten a bad draw of the life-straws, it was Andrus. Three hundred years ago, the man found true love only to discover his mate was the vampire queen, who was evil to the core. She basically sold Andrus off to be an indentured servant of the gods simply to save her own hide. She was killed eventually and Andrus was set free, but his return to happiness had been a long painful journey.

"I can't leave you by yourself," Andrus protested.

Tommaso glanced in the rearview mirror, finding a scowling Guy snarling in the car behind him. "Ah, but there's more good news. I'm not alone. Guy has decided to be my wingman."

There was an explosion of hacking on the other end of the phone, followed by hysterical laughter. "Votan? God of Death and War and the one deity on the planet who'd like nothing more than to rip off your balls?"

"Don't forget dismemberment—he's most certainly put that on his wish list." Guy made it no secret that he wished he had finished the job that day back in the jungle when Tommaso had been recruited involuntarily to Team Maaskab and had aided them in capturing Emma. Guy showed up with his gang of Uchben to rescue her and gutted Tommaso like a fish, leaving him for dead. It was that dark energy inside him that had kept him alive, and it was Emma who demanded that Guy make Tommaso immortal to hopefully cure him.

Andrus continued chuckling. "Well, then I'm definitely coming. I gotta see this."

"You're a true friend, Andrus."

Still chuckling, Andrus sputtered, "I'm sorry…it's just you and…Votan and…trying to pick up a woman."

"We are not picking up anyone. I am going to find her—*my mate*—and persuade her to give me another chance." And make sure she knew that he would never do anything to hurt her. *Not on purpose anyway. Gods, I'm such a fucking mess.*

"Well, if there's one thing you're good at," Andrus said, "it's impressing the ladies with your charm. So where is she?"

"Cimil said she's at some secluded hideout near Palm Springs."

"Uh-oh."

"Uh-oh, what?" Tommaso felt a cold chill crawl up his spine.

"Cimil knows who the woman is?"

Cimil was the *only* one who knew. "Yes, but she refused to give me or anyone else information aside from where to find her."

"Huge uh-oh. This reeks of a Cimil trick."

He was right. But... "Do you see any other options aside from letting this play out?" With any luck, tonight he could smooth things over with this woman, seduce her, and then that would be that. The Universe would take care of the rest and/or she would fall for him, as women often did. Then he would be cured.

"Are you sure you don't want me to fly there?" Andrus asked.

"Thank you, but I've got this under control. I'll be mated and cured before day's end."

There was a moment of awkward silence. Tommaso knew his friend worried, but he could be of no use. Besides, what could go wrong? Tommaso felt fine now—no more evil jitters—and this woman would have to forgive him—and love him. They were destined mates. Sexually driven toward one another. Magnets of desire.

"All right, man. Call me if you need anything," Andrus said.

"I will be just fine. And if anything comes up, I've got my wingman."

Andrus laughed. "Hysterical. Take care, bro. I'll call you tomorrow, and if you don't answer, I'm getting on a plane." Andrus ended the call, and Tommaso jerked his head to the side, giving his neck a little crack.

"Sorry, Andrus, but I'm going to be busy tomorrow." *Making breakfast in bed for my new mate after a long night of fucking.*

He totally had this.

CHAPTER FIVE

"This is not a hideaway." Tommaso stared at the enormous roundabout filled with luxury cars and scrambling valets in red vests. Off in the distance—beyond the manicured gardens and Italian-style reception building with natural stone façade, three-tiered fountain, and oversized potted red flowers—was a long stretch of golf course surrounded by rolling hills and villas.

Tommaso glanced down at the GPS on his console and then up again at the sign right in the middle of the roundabout. This was the spot, but Cimil had said nothing about "The Hideaway, Luxury Spa and Golf Resort." In fact, according to Guy, Cimil had said, "You can find your chicky boo at this hideaway..."

Realizing that Cimil had just told yet another one of her truthful lies, he rolled his eyes. *Cimil.* She was the most annoyingly insane deity he'd ever met—a wicked philanthropist. A psychotic peace-monger. A fairy hell-mother. Cimil's extra-special gift was making one's dreams come true while simultaneously forcing them to confront their worst nightmares. That last part was generally for her amusement.

Tommaso released a steady breath. *Fine. Bring it on.* He'd been through far worse. Of course, some of those "far worses" were moments when he'd been a pawn in one of the goddess's grand schemes. This time, however, he had the distinct impression that he was the soup du jour. But he could handle it. He merely needed to remain focused on the task— getting this woman to forgive him for whatever he'd done to her.

God, I hope I wasn't too horrible to her. Once again, he recalled the blurry image of her rage-filled eyes as she sat with a gag in her mouth.

It'll be fine. I'll explain what is happening and then let nature take its course. They were mates, and she would have an instinctual urge to want to help him.

Tommaso pulled up to the valet, noticing that only Guy's car remained behind him. The Uchben were probably off in some back parking lot, changing clothes to blend in and getting ready to follow him around.

The valet opened his car door. "Checking in, sir?"

"I am now." He was going to have to locate the woman, watch her carefully, and then pick the opportune moment to approach her and plead his case.

"But no luggage," Tommaso added.

The valet shrugged and handed him a ticket before Tommaso made his way inside to the reception area, which was quite nice. Indoor fountain, Italian cream marble, murals on the ceiling depicting tiny angels floating on their backs in very relaxed poses.

He walked up to the reception clerk—a young brunette in a burgundy vest—and offered up his most charming smile. "Hello, there."

She immediately lit up with warmth and wide receptive eyes. "Checking in, sir?"

"Why, yes. But I don't have a reservation." He leaned in, placing one elbow on the counter. "Hope that won't be an issue."

She batted her eyelashes. "Well, let me see here," she said sweetly. "Oh, look. There's one room left—our presidential suite."

Tommaso arched a brow. Only one room, huh? *Too bad for you, Guy. Guess you'll be bunking in your awesome car.* And the presidential suite? That would be perfect for him and his mate—once they worked through this little evil speed bump, of course.

He slid his wallet from his suit pocket and pulled out the Amex black card. "This should do the trick."

"Oh. Well, you certainly came to the right place to be pampered, Mr. Fierro.

Just as he handed over the card, he caught a glimpse of a woman—about five-five, creamy pale skin, and a dark bob—passing by, and he instantly knew. It was *her*. The woman from the mixer. His heart rate sped up. His skin began to tingle. He felt the gnawing urge to jump her bones.

Let the romance begin.

Her sweet scent permeated the space around him and left a lingering feeling of hard lust coursing through his veins. He turned and watched her walk away, enjoying the sway of her hips in her snug khaki shorts. She wore some sort of visor over her dark bob as if she were intending on doing some gardening. *Dear gods, she's so lovely.*

"Interested in golf lessons, sir?" said the clerk, snapping back his attention.

"Sorry?" he said to the receptionist.

"Golf. Are you interested?"

"Why do you ask?"

"She's the instructor." The clerk jerked her head in the direction of his mate, who'd disappeared around the corner.

"You mean...she teaches golf?" *How very human and boring.*

"Yeah. She's pretty popular with the men—for her lessons, of course." The clerk winked.

Dear gods. Had the clerk insinuated that his mate was a floozy? Tommaso's blood spiked with prickly anger. This he could not stand for. His mate being paid by various men, all of them looking at her sweet, sweet ass in those snug but despicably common shorts available at any Walmart or Target, teaching leisure sport for money! What the hell was the Universe thinking pairing him with someone so...so...so...ordinary?

You idiot. She's anything but ordinary. She was uniquely qualified to be his perfect match. In bed and in life. Not that he wanted the life part. Reality was that his past would not allow him to settle into any sort of traditional relationship. The people he loved always ended up, well…dead. And not just dead, dead, but violently murdered. The memory of his entire family, including his six-month-old nephew, little Antoni, would forever haunt him. Then there was Emma. No, she hadn't died, but it had been a close call. And, yeah, he'd loved her. She'd seen the good in him when he'd been in a place so dark that life had no meaning. But he couldn't keep her safe either. He'd handed her over to the Maaskab and enjoyed every dark moment while his heart had plummeted further into the abyss, unable to stand witness to what he was doing.

At best, the world he lived in could be described as dangerous, and nothing about his present or past lent itself to a traditional relationship. Nevertheless, his losses weren't merely his hell, they were his reason to fight. They were a wound that wasn't meant to heal and would always serve to remind him of his true north: *Some of us are born for pain. And if we're lucky, we'll be the ones giving it.* But seeing his parents, brothers and sisters, and their children, all lying facedown around their table, the floor a pool of blood, was a memory that would torment him until his last breath.

"Sir?" The clerk snapped her fingers. "She has a seven a.m. tee time. Should I book it?"

Tommaso narrowed his eyes in contemplation. "Book her for the entire month. Or year. However long your system allows."

The clerk frowned. "Sorry, sir?"

"You heard me. Block out her schedule completely." He flicked his finger at the card in her hand. "Go ahead. Whatever the cost."

"Oh-okay. As you like." The clerk tapped away on her keyboard and then handed him a set of key cards. "There's a complimentary wine tasting starting in just a few minutes, and breakfast starts at five thirty."

He dipped his head. "Thank you. Can you tell me where to find a clothing shop?" He still had on his gnarly biker outfit. *How does Andrus stand this?* The leather kept chafing his balls. "I...the airline lost my luggage," he lied, not wanting to explain why he'd shown up without extra clothes.

"Down the hall, to the right. There are several stores."

"Thank you." He turned around just in time to see Guy sauntering up, looking more irritated than ever. Likely due to the fact that he'd rather be at home with Emma and...and...and...*oh hell. I can't remember his name. Cookamonga? Ka-poy-poy? The baby.*

Tommaso ignored Guy, pretending they were strangers, but then slowed his walk as he reached the other side of the lobby just so he could hear...

"What!" Guy yelled. "What do you mean you have no rooms left? I will vanquish your soul and turn you into a steaming heap of dung if you do not rectify this at once!"

Tommaso smiled and kept on walking. Guy

could make all the noise he wanted, but he wasn't capable of turning humans into dung.

And I got the last room.

CHAPTER SIX

"No. This can't be your entire selection of clothing. It's inhumane." Tommaso leered at the neatly folded stacks of apple green and tangerine golf shirts, sherbet Bermudas, and plaid golf pants.

The salesperson, a young man in his twenties with spiky blond hair, pointed across the way to another clothing boutique next to the souvenir shop. "Have you explored the Sunshine Shack, sir?"

Tommaso almost vomited on his two-thousand-dollar Italian-leather, hand-stitched shoes that so, so did not go with the leather pants he still wore. "That store only carries swimwear." He'd be damned if he was going to show up to meet his mate and smooth things over wearing a Speedo. *Actually...that might not be such a bad idea. I am rather hun—*

Just then, he spotted his soon-to-be woman passing by, now wearing khaki slacks and a black golf tee. She'd changed clothing. *Dear gods, is that her version of evening wear?*

Do not panic. I'm sure this is just her work attire.

He noticed that she was walking with two older gentlemen who seemed a bit too happy and attentive, laughing and speaking with deep voices to impress her with their manliness.

Fuckers. Get away from my woman.

"I'll call my tailor in L.A.," Tommaso said to the salesperson and then quickly exited the shop to follow her and the two men. The three passed outside the main building, which housed the reception area, lounge and shops, and made their way toward what looked like the restaurant and private club for members. It was now dark outside, so he hoped she wouldn't notice him following behind and eavesdropping.

"Oh," said one of the men, "my swing is exceptionally hard. Har, har, haaaar."

"Well, mine is long," the other man said to her. "I'll show you later if you like? Har, har, haaar." He laughed like he had a club stuck up his ass.

Dear gods, no woman of mine is going to pander to a bunch of horny old men in order to make scratch.

Tommaso fought the urge to run up behind her and haul her back to his room right then and there. But there was the little matter of approaching her first and letting her know that whatever had happened between them in their last interaction was not a reflection of his true self. He was a gentleman. Deadly, but refined. Disciplined, yet quick on his feet. He was a trained guard in the gods' army who'd had a bad turn, and though he could never offer her picket fences, he could offer her mind-blowing sex and financial security. He could make her feel pampered like a princess. Hell, he'd even purchased a villa for her in the Hollywood hills, with a view any woman would approve of. *And a closet any woman would kill for.* He only hoped she wouldn't hold his behavior against the closet. It wasn't the closet's fault that he'd tied her up in it.

And it truly is a spectacular closet.

Tommaso entered the cocktail lounge with intimate lighting and velvety jazz playing in the background and realized that this was the wine tasting the clerk had just mentioned. The room, with a grand fireplace at the far end, was filled with couples, groups of older men harharhaaarrring, and wait staff who were busy filling glasses.

Tommaso scanned the space, looking for his target. *Why didn't I ask the receptionist for her name?* He'd been so distracted by her overwhelming curves and underwhelming clothing that it had slipped his mind.

"You must be looking for the steak house," said a soft feminine voice.

Tommaso turned and his brain immediately slammed into a wall that wasn't there. Nevertheless, the wall kept him from thinking, speaking, and acting like a basic human being.

"You okay?" she said, those warm brown eyes gazing up at him. A man could get lost in those eyes. Eyes that were giving him the death stare less than a day ago. *Wait. Why isn't she running or screaming at me?* Had she blocked out the incident?

Wanting to tread lightly, he asked, "Have we met before?"

She smiled with a pair of lips that were too sensual for words—slightly full, with a deeper than usual dip on the top lip. He instantly wanted to take those lips and run his tongue over every soft bit of them.

Abruptly, her smile melted away. "No. I think I would remember you," she said curtly.

How odd.

She added, "Especially since you're dressed for a Mad Max convention or biker rally—don't get a lot of people dressed like that coming to the resort."

Tommaso wasn't sure if she meant that as a compliment, insult, or if it was merely an observation.

Tommaso glanced down at his black leather pants and snug white T-shirt. He did look a little rude, but his appearance was best described as rock star a la Lenny Kravitz or classic James Dean sex-symbol-esque.

She definitely meant it as a compliment. But who the hell cares? Why isn't she running away screaming? Or yelling at me?

He leaned down a bit closer, staring into her eyes. *Dammit, she smells fantastic.* "Are you certain I don't look the least bit familiar?"

Her expression unreadable, she said, "You're a TV star, aren't you? Maybe I *have* seen you before."

Her pupils dilated for a fraction of a second. She

was lying. She had no clue who he was but didn't want to make him feel bad.

Okay, so this might be a blessing in disguise. But on the other hand...

What the fuck is going on?

He didn't remember much, but he recalled seeing her tied up and the poor woman running for her life. Yes, from him. Prior to that, he'd also seen her leaving the singles mixer in L.A. Of that, there was no question. They'd passed right by each other as she had been coming out and he had been going in. But there had been a moment when their eyes had met, and he just knew—as mates often did—that she was the one. He'd merely seen her for a moment, and it had done something to him. Made him want and feel and... *Fuck.* And need things. He never needed anything. Not anymore. And no, his comforts in life were not to be mistaken for needs. They were merely a way of life. A way to bring civility to his cursed existence. But make no mistake; when he had looked into her eyes at Cimil's mixer, he'd felt needs. A whole hell of a fucking lot of them. He had made it two steps inside the party before those needs were jerking him back by the collar of his organic cotton shirt, turning him right around, and tapping her on the shoulder as she waited for the valet to bring her car. She had turned to face him, and the world slowed to a glacial crawl. He didn't remember much after that.

But now, at this very moment, staring into her wide eyes, his world felt accelerated. Hummingbird, Indy 500, cha-cha-cha accelerated.

He cleared his throat, attempting to keep his deep voice steady, reflecting an image of control. Just like Dad taught him. "I'm sorry to say that I am not a celebrity. You merely seemed familiar, so I thought perhaps we'd met somewhere before," he lied.

"Oh. Sorry." She looked uncomfortable, and that was when it hit him; she didn't seem interested. Not even a little. "Well, if you're looking for the steak house, it's through that door, to your right, and down the walkway. Can't miss it." She pointed toward the exit and gave him a polite little smile before turning to mingle with the wine-tasting guests.

That's not possible. It's just not. "Excuse me." He grabbed her arm and gave it a gentle squeeze. "Would you like to have a drink with me?"

Her smile nonexistent, she tugged her arm back. "I don't date hotel guests. Bad for business. But I hope you have a nice stay at the resort. I do recommend the spa—our mud baths are to die for."

She turned away again and rejoined a group of five men with promiscuous gazes and fat wallets protruding from their back pockets.

How garish.

But worse than being rejected for some golf geezers was that she was supposed to want him. Him and only him from their first interaction. Sure, sometimes it took a little persuasion for an individual to give in to those wants, but it was akin to denying one's hunger. Sooner or later, you had to eat.

Scratching his manicured stubble, he watched her smiling and interacting with what had to be her clients.

So let me get this straight. I almost killed her, but she doesn't remember me. She'd rather speak with them than me. And I am pretty sure I'm into her. All right, I'm very much into her. She, on the other hand, had been polite for the first three seconds, but then threw up an icy wall so thick that it smelled suspiciously of a defense mechanism.

Running his hand through his hair, he turned and retreated, feeling the need to rethink the situation. It was clear that with this woman, something else was going on. But the clock was ticking, and at any moment, he would become a full-fledged Maaskab.

Once outside, he slipped his cell from his pocket and dialed. It immediately went into voicemail. "Cimil, it's Tommaso. You must tell me what you know about her. Tell me why I'm getting the feeling that she's not my mate."

CHAPTER SEVEN

Tommaso entered the presidential suite, still flustered from his interaction with... *Dammit. I forgot to ask her name again.* That wasn't like him to be lacking in the attention-to-detail department like that.

He walked down the small hallway and turned the corner where the suite opened up into an enormous living room with panoramic windows overlooking the golf course. A soft leather sofa faced a gas fireplace that ran through the wall into what had to be the master suite on the other side. This suite would surely impress any woman. *Specifically my woman—as soon as I figure out how to make her mine.* But once he did, he'd bet that the bathroom had a whirlpool tub for two and some relaxing lighting just perfect to set the mood for some hard hot fucking.

He went to go check out the amenities and nearly slammed into a giant tree stump.

"Can you call room service for green olives?

This martini tastes like crap," Guy said, pushing past him into the living room.

Tommaso turned with a scowl. "What the *fuck* are you doing in my room, Guy?"

Holding a martini glass to his lips, Guy shrugged, sipped, and made a sour face. "Yeah, definitely needs olives."

"Guy," Tommaso growled, "how did you get in here?"

Stopping in front of the small bar in the corner next to a giant potted palm, Guy replied with an obvious sadistic delight to his voice, "The lovely young woman at the front desk gave me a key since I will be sleeping with you."

Tommaso gnashed his teeth together. Had Guy seriously told the receptionist this? Obviously, he had meant "sleeping" in the platonic sense, but the A-hole made it sound otherwise.

What if she mentions something to my woman? He didn't need any additional hurdles. That included anyone presuming he was into men. *Idiot!*

Tommaso growled his words, "Sorry, Guy, I'm not into dating assholes nor does my cock find them pleasurable."

Guy made a sour face. "I am officially nauseous. And tread carefully or I might rescind my fucking offer to allow you the fucking couch."

Oh, how generous. The couch! "Once again, I will have to decline your offer of fucking on your fucking-couch. You really need to get past this obsession you have with me. I'm here to meet my mate—and if I have anything to do with it, the event will include lots of screwing. Using the proper hole found only on a woman."

Guy snarled, "You are a jackass." He then grabbed the martini shaker and refilled his glass. "I pity the poor woman who will have to endure an eternity of your delightful humor. But as you have already planned to make her wildest dreams come true this evening with your impressive manliness, you can do so in her room. I'm sleeping in that nice big bed, as a deity of my size should."

Damn him. On the other hand, did it even matter? Tonight was pretty much shot with his woman. He needed to regroup and think through his next steps carefully given something was going on with her and things had not gone his way. *Or you could go back to that wine tasting and try again.* After all, this was a life-or-death situation. Perhaps he'd retreated too quickly or misread her somehow?

Tommaso sighed. "Guy, you must leave. And let me remind you that if I don't get lucky, I'll turn into a Maaskab and get thrown in jail. You will join me, and then who will be there to protect Emma and…and…"

"Kaz. My son's name is Kaz. And Emma would not be left alone. I have an army of well-trained soldiers to look after her."

Tommaso tsked. "All right. If that's the card you want to play. But if it were my woman, I wouldn't leave my beautiful mate in the hands of a group of extremely fit men who'd be happy to 'look after her,' as you stated. Especially when you could be locked up for years and a passionate woman like her is bound to have needs." Tommaso knew that would get under Guy's skin.

Guy set his glass down on the bar. "Your taunting tactics won't work on me, Tommy. And you will *not* fail at securing your mate's affection and commitment."

That wasn't exactly true. So far, she seemed indifferent toward him. "And if I don't?"

"I will kill you." Guy smiled, but he wasn't joking. "And that will solve my problem of going to prison with you." He shrugged his broad shoulders. "Can't hold me accountable for a dead man's actions, now can they?"

Tommaso snarled. "You're a bastard, Guy."

"I am the God of Death and War. I think the term bastard falls short when attempting to articulate the magnitude of my unpleasant side." He grinned. "But what can I say? I'm gifted."

"Fucker."

"Yes, I am that, too. And now you should go and order my olives—and practice being grateful for my having given you this chance to save your life."

"Order your own godsdamned olives." Tommaso turned and headed outside. Who the hell did this guy—no pun intended—think he was? *I'd rather sleep in my own car than share a room—or a presidential suite—with that son of a bitch.* The truth was, Guy—Votan—whatever—had saved him from rotting in prison, but only because Emma had forced him to do it. But had Guy or the other gods ever once acknowledged the fact that Tommaso had been one of their best soldiers, holding the record for most Maaskab killed? He'd served loyally and fought hard for them because he'd wanted to be a part of something good in this world. And in exchange for his service, his family had been murdered, he'd been tortured and brainwashed, and then blamed for the crimes he'd committed while under the Maaskab's control. No one, except for Emma, had ever recognized all he'd sacrificed or done. Not that he wanted or needed praise. Hell no. But for these bastards to run around, behaving as if they'd all done him some glorious favor, well…they could all piss the hell off. Honestly, if it weren't for the fact that he loathed the Maaskab with every drop of blood in his body, he'd simply let himself turn evil just so he could be on another team. "Team Good" was fucking torture.

He slid his cell phone from his pocket, dialed his tailor's personal cell and asked for him to send a few outfits overnight. With such short notice, the clothes would be off-the-rack, but his tailor at least knew his sizes and could make him look better than if he just ran out to some local shop.

Now that his clothing situation was taken care of, Tommaso dialed Emma.

While waiting for her to pick up, and standing outside next to a big fountain in a large garden, Tommaso watched a shooting star blaze across the Palm Springs' sky.

Amazing. It was one of the things he enjoyed, aside from his gentlemanly comforts: The exquisite beauty of nature. He'd been raised by his parents to appreciate beauty—fine art, the emotional depth of classical music, and good food, ranging from his mother's homemade pesto gnocchi to a filet mignon seared in hand-churned butter and chives. But some of the most beautiful things in this world weren't man-made or complicated. They were simple and there for all to see. The quartz veining in a garden rock, the way the afternoon sunlight danced on the ripples of a pond. *And...*

"Hello?" Emma's sweet voice chirped through his earpiece.

And...sweet revenge.

"Hey, Emma, it's Tommaso. I hate to ask for your help again, but your husband—"

"Dear gods, please don't tell me he's getting on your case and acting all jealous again. I keep telling him to let it go, but he won't."

What was Emma talking about? "Won't let what go?"

Emma sighed with exasperation. "Nothing. Never mind. I'll talk to him."

"Emma, you can talk to *me*. What's wrong?" He would kick the crap out of Guy if he was mistreating her in any way. Emma was special. She was a good, good person with a big heart. "Emma?" he pushed.

"It's just..." She sighed again. "He keeps saying that I have feelings for you—that I talk about you all the time. But that's because I'm worried and you're my friend. But he won't let it go."

Leave it to Guy to be such a giant, self-centered prick that he couldn't comprehend what he had. Emma loved him and had almost her entire life.

"He's an insecure moron, Emma. Because anyone with eyes can see the way you look at him." He'd give anything to have a woman look at him like that, like she would walk through the fires of hell just to be by his side. And Emma had. She had gone through the worst possible nightmare to be with Guy. It was so much more than simple love, and if Tommaso ever found a woman who'd risk everything, give everything, as Emma had given to Guy, he'd never let that woman go.

"I'm sorry I brought it up, Tommaso," Emma said quietly. "But he just doesn't understand and he won't let it go, and I refuse to give into his insecurities by giving up our friendship."

Guy really was such a prick. "I will speak with him—make him see that—"

"No. I will. I don't want you getting in the middle."

Poor woman. He wanted to intervene, but he'd honor her wishes. That was far more important because if there was one thing he knew about Emma, she hated when people tried to step in or treat her like a child. "Very well. But I'm here if you need anything."

"Thanks, Tommaso. And if there's anything I can do, say the word."

He was about to ask her to get Guy the hell out of his room, but at that moment he turned around, finding two large men standing behind him. "Thank you, Emma. Give my regards to...the baby. I must go now." *Why can't I remember the darn baby's name? Kalulu? Kavortis?*

He ended the call, maintaining his gaze on the two snarling men. They were Uchben, and his guess was that they were the ones assigned to keep an eye on him.

"Good evening, brothers," Tommaso said.

"We are not your brothers," said the blond man on the right, dressed in casual khakis and a dress shirt. "You are a fucking Scab—and a traitor."

Tommaso's blood began to boil. He was anything but a "Scab" and he was most certainly not a traitor.

Tommaso began to loosen his tie. "Come a little closer and say that to my face."

≈≈≈

The next morning, lying in his king-sized bed, Tommaso woke up to a ringing phone on the nightstand, his head a soupy mess of vagueness. He sat up and scrubbed his face with his hands, groaning from a blunt ache in his brow.

Damn, I feel like I have a hangover. And now that he thought about it... He winced as he placed his hand over his right rib cage. Fuck. He lifted his shirt, and there was a big bruise in the shape of a shoe print.

What the hell? Snippets of memories flashed through his head. Fists flying, bones cracking, and blood.

The still-ringing phone brought him back to the moment. He reached for it and answered. "Yeah?"

"Hello, sir. This is Jenny from the front desk.

Your instructor is waiting on the course and wondering if you'll be attending your lesson this morning?"

Oh shit! He glanced at his watch. It was seven-o-five. He hadn't planned on going to any of these lessons; he'd planned to be in bed with his mate and waking up to having his cock sucked. But that wasn't about to happen, obviously.

"Yeah." He cleared his throat. "I'll be there in five minutes."

He got up from the bed and went into the bathroom, where he caught a glimpse of himself in the mirror. "Holy hell." His T-shirt was torn on the shoulder and had blood on it. His leather pants were smeared with sticky syrup. He dabbed his pants and gave his finger a whiff. *Strawberry? What the hell happened last night?* The last thing he remembered were those two Uchben guards—the ones who were supposed to be monitoring him from afar—throwing an insult at him. Then he'd gotten angry, and the rest was a blur.

Shit. No time to figure that one out right now. He had to go meet his woman.

He quickly brushed with the complimentary toothbrush and washed his face before wetting his hands and giving his hair a tousle so it would fill out on the flat side where he'd slept.

He rushed from the room and realized his new clothes hadn't arrived. *And while I'm thinking about it, how did I arrive at the room?* And where was Guy?

Tommaso heard a muffle in the closet. He pulled

the doors open and jumped back. "Fuck!"

Inside were the two Uchben guards from last night, gagged, sitting with their backs pressed together and hands tied behind them.

The men didn't say a word, but their silence and the startled look in their eyes said it all. As did the bruises on their faces.

Holy shit. Did I do that? Tommaso was about to ask as he pulled the gag from the blond man's mouth, but one guard quickly started blathering, "We won't tell anyone. We promise. Please let us go." The man looked like he might piss himself.

"Uhhh...okay. But, what exactly is it that you won't tell anyone?"

The guy began to stutter. "Don't fuck with us. We made a deal, and we'll keep it. Just don't send that video to anyone. Please, man. We said we're sorry."

Video? Tommaso looked at his watch. *Crap.* He had to get to the golf course. "Fine. Okay. You can go now." He untied them and shooed them out the door. He then quickly slid his cell from his pant pocket and pulled up his videos. It took all of five seconds of watching the two men spanking each other and weeping to understand that he'd had another Maaskab episode last night. That was the only explanation.

I'm like the goddamned Hulk. Only...not green. And much better looking.

Thankfully, he hadn't killed the men. He'd simply knocked them around a bit and then proceeded to make them film a rather unmanly, kinky video. Why would he do that? He played it again and listened. Yes, mixed in with the sounds of grunts and slaps as the two guards spanked each other was the distinctive sound of his own deep voice chuckling.

Man, I'm one sadistic bastard. And he was clearly a risk to everyone around him. Especially anyone who upset him. Which was why he needed to hustle.

He left his room and hurried toward the main building, regretting with every step the fact that he'd ruined his clothes last night, but feeling a small twinge of satisfaction. He hadn't murdered those guards and they would never call him a traitor again.

At least, not to my face.

CHAPTER EIGHT

Tommaso stepped out on to the green, cringing that this was how he'd have to spend the day with his mate. *I look like a complete shmuck.* Lime green golf shirt and orange and white plaid shorts. But all of the plain, more subdued colors were small or mediums. He was a large, well-built man, more on the lean side like a swimmer, with very broad shoulders. He wasn't seven feet tall like the gods, but he was still six-two, and his workout regimen made his legs and thighs a little more muscular than the average guy. In short, the only clothing in the sports shop that had a chance of fitting were these…

Humiliating. As he approached the woman, his abhorrence for his outfit seemed to fade into the background. All he could see were her brown eyes sizzling with irritation. She was not happy.

He glanced at his watch. "Sorry about the time," he called, approaching her with his most charming smile, "but there was an issue with my luggage, and my replacement clothing didn't arrive as planned."

Her anger dialed down from pissed to mildly peeved. "Oh. Well, I'm sorry to hear that. I hope they find your things." Her eyes swept over his outfit. "Those clothes will work just..." Her eyes lingered on his crotch for a moment and then snapped up to his face. "Fine."

If I were applying for clown school.

"The shorts are a bit tight," he admitted with false confidence, which was the only way to deal with a situation where one had no other option but to go with the flow. "But it was either this or risk the extra-large size, which would probably fall off and expose my bare ass. And cock." He gave her a wink.

She blinked at him. "Sorry?"

"I am a commando sort of man."

She gave him a look. "Uh. Okay. That's good to know?"

"For you, yes, it is." He flashed another charming grin.

Void of any interest, she frowned.

Not even a hint of desire? Now this was humiliating. What was going on?

"Wait. Didn't I meet you yesterday?" she said.

She doesn't remember me?

Before he had a chance to say a word, she added, "Oh, I know. We met at the group golf lesson in the afternoon."

This was becoming stranger by the second. First, she had no recollection of him having gone evil on her, and now she didn't remember meeting him last night. Had someone put the whammy on her to make her forget? It was the only logical answer. *But if yes, then who?*

"We met at the wine tasting last evening," he said. "Do you not recall?" *You were about as friendly as a cucumber.*

She gave him a sideways glance. "I can't say that I do."

"You thought I was someone famous, in leather pants," he added, "looking for the steak house."

She snapped her fingers. "I remember now. Sorry, it was a long day. Welp, let's get started, then." Her tone was even and professional—not overly icy, but not overly friendly either. "I'm Char, your golf instructor for the entire day since I hear you've booked up all of my slots—let me guess, you're hoping to impress the boss at a new job with your swing."

"No. I, uh…"

"Ah, wait. Don't tell me." She snapped her fingers again and then pointed at him. "You're finally going to pop the question to the woman of your dreams, and you want to ask for her father's blessing. And he's a big golfer."

Her guess was partially correct. "You're fairly close, but I—"

"Well, congratulations," she said, and gave him a swat on the arm as if they were just two dudes, hanging. "We'll have you putting and swinging like a PGA all-star in no time. Dear old dad won't be able to turn you down. Let's start over here and get a look at your swing. We'll go from there. Or as I like to say, golf from there." She made a little snort.

It was kind of...well, adorable. "Oh, and my apologies. We'll be walking the course today—someone vandalized the golf carts last night—covered them with some gooey strawberry gel—so strange. But they're all getting a wash down."

Strawberry? Like the stuff on his pants this morning? *Nahhhh... Must be a coincidence.*

"Some people have no respect." He shook his head.

"You should see what they did to the course. The garden crew was up at five, pulling out chunks of steak from the holes. Probably just some bored teenagers."

"They should be found and disemboweled, the little fuckers."

"Uhhh. Okay." She gave him a look. "Let's get started." She headed toward the driving range.

As she walked ahead of him, he stared at her apple-shaped bottom. Despite the unflattering cut of her khaki shorts, it was the kind of ass a man liked to squeeze while having his dick ridden hard—

No. Don't you dare get hard. Don't you dare. Kittens. Crying babies. Maaskab. In these tight shorts, his lower half would look like a circus tent, sans colorful flag.

Char turned and started walking backwards, pointing off to the side of the course where they had the multistory practice platforms. "We'll go up to the second level, okay?" As she pointed, he noticed how her plump and nicely round breasts jiggled at little. *Shit. Don't look at her breasts. Think about...golf shirts. Off-the-rack plaid shorts. Me looking like a complete asshole with my dick sticking out.* He felt his shaft going limp again. *Thank gods...*

This was going to be a very long morning. But there was no getting around this lesson. He had to spend time with her and try to understand what was going on. Something was not right.

After five long hours of putting, chipping, and swinging, Tommaso was ready to call it quits and head back to L.A. to strangle the hell out of Cimil. On the other hand, Cimil hadn't been the one to suggest that Char was his mate; she'd merely said that he would meet her at the party. So had he made a mistake in assuming that Char was his? She wasn't remotely interested in him, and his attempts to ascertain any personal information were getting him nowhere.

That woman had a wall so thick around her that even a wrecking ball wouldn't get through. Every question he'd asked was met with the shortest possible answer. For example, when he'd asked where she was from, she replied, "I live around here." Not quite an answer. He'd asked what brought her to Palm Springs and then what got her into golf, but she'd only replied, "The usual," to both questions.

That said, her golfing and ability to teach were solid. He loathed the sport—not nearly physical or lethal enough to satisfy his tastes—yet he'd enjoyed his morning. She had a quiet patience and kindness he genuinely connected with. Unfortunately, he wasn't there to enjoy himself. Not that way. He was there to get mated and stop his evil cancer from taking over his body before he did something truly heinous. *If I haven't already.*

Maybe he should go back to L.A. and find Cimil and strangle the truth out of her.

"Char," he said, placing his club into the golf bag, "I'm afraid that I'll need to cut this lesson—"

"Would you like to have lunch with me?" she blurted out. "My treat?"

"Sorry?" he asked, unsure his ears had heard her correctly. This was the first sign of warmth she'd shown all morning.

"You know, lunch?" she clarified. "I'm starved, and since you paid for the entire day, it's the least I could do. That and you haven't hit on me today, which is really a breath of fresh air."

Huh? Tommaso frowned. That was why she was being nice to him all of a sudden? Because he wasn't hitting on her? "Your clients frequently make passes at you?"

She shrugged. "Well...yeah. They do."

"How does your boyfriend feel about that?" he asked, probing for some personal information.

The reaction on her face was instantly glum. "I don't have a boyfriend." She looked down at her feet.

The way she'd said it made him think she'd recently had her heart broken. Could this be why she wasn't opening up? The heart was more than simply a muscle. It reflected one's internal state, like the thermometer of the soul. He knew this because his soul had been shattered to pieces a long time ago, and his heart, as much as he wanted it to beat with joy, simply couldn't. Not that he needed to heal. His pain was a reminder of why he had to be strong, in control, and never allow anyone to get too close. Caring for others was simply opening up one's self to weakness. And it was opening them up to danger.

"Tommaso?"

Her soft voice jarred him from his dark thoughts. "Yes?"

"My offer for lunch? I mean—I understand if you need to go take care of some business or whatnot before we continue on with our lessons for the day, but—"

Tommaso's cell phone rang, and he reached into his pocket to silence it, but the caller ID said "Bat-shit Crazy."

"One moment, Char." He held up his finger. "I have to take this. It's urgent."

"Sure." She gave him the scoot-scoot gesture with her hand.

He turned and started walking away so Char wouldn't hear. "Cimil? You better tell me what the hell is going on, or so help me!"

"Whoa, whoa, whoa, big Tommy. But I've got a rule to never answer serious questions before noon."

"It's one o'clock."

"Not in Hawaii. And everyone knows I go on Hawaiian time."

"Since when?"

"Since...noon today. But now it's only eleven in the morning in Maui, so I'm afraid you'll have to wait another hour."

Fucking Cimil. "I'm not calling you back in an hour, Cimil. The clock is ticking, and this is serious."

"Oh, I know it's serious. That's why I keep changing time zones. It's the only way to slow everything down."

What the hell? "You can't be serious, Cimil. That's too stupid, even for you."

"Sorry. You'll have to call back in an hour if you want the answer to that."

Godsdammit! She was so frustrating. "Cimil, please, I'm begging you. Can't you for once answer a question like a normal person? I need to know if Char is really my mate. Will she cure me?"

"Absolutely not."

Huh? "To which question?"

"Can you ask the questions again? I forgot them."

Fucking shit. Someone needs to end her. "Is she my mate or not?" he snarled.

"I don't know. Why does everyone think I know everything? I'm not a godsdamned unicorn."

I'm going to kill her.

"Do you at least know if she can cure me?" he asked.

"Hold on. Let me ask Minky," Cimil replied. "Hey! Bitchface! Tommy wants to know if this chick he's after will keep him from turning into a horrible monster." There was a long pause and Tommaso almost imploded. "What! No!" Cimil began cracking up. "I don't believe you! That's too funny."

"What? What's too funny?" he growled into the phone, but Cimil kept wailing on the other end of the line. "Cimil!"

"Hello? This is Cimil. Leave a message at the tone. Beeeeeep."

"Cimil," he snarled, "I know it's you. Stop this juvenile behavior at once, and tell me what you know. Is Char going to cure me?"

"Tommy? Is that you?" Cimil chirped.

"Yes!"

"What the hell are you doing calling me? You're supposed to be at lunch with your future mate! Hurry or the window will close!"

Son of a... He turned and Char was no longer on the course. She must've walked off while he'd been busy dealing with Jedi Master Fuck-Tard.

"I'll call you back in an hour," Tommaso said, and was about to hang up when Cimil yelled.

"I'll be out of town! You'll have to call when I get back!" The call dropped.

You just spoke to me on your cell phone, you horrible, insane deity! Of course, he understood that though Cimil had put him through the wringer, she'd also answered his question. He rushed toward the main building to find Char.

He hoped he would find her there.

❧∼❧

After doing several laps around the large restaurant, Tommaso finally spotted Char sitting next to an older man with hungry eyes and a wolfish smile. Tommaso could see the look on her face—polite, closed off, and weary.

He's hitting on her! Dammit. He didn't want to be rude and make a public scene, but this was his "window" and he couldn't afford to let it close. Not now. Not when he was so close to becoming something he'd be so ashamed of.

Tommaso weaved through the dining room and approached the small table near the window overlooking the outdoor patio seating.

"Char, honey," he said in a deep confident tone, "I'm sorry that my business call took longer than expected." He dipped down and kissed her on the cheek. "It won't happen again. I promise."

There was a moment, just a small one, where she seemed confused, but then she caught on. "No problem, honey. Oh, Tommaso, may I introduce you to Mr. Lenox. I gave him a lesson yesterday. He's here on a boys' golf retreat weekend."

Tommaso turned to the man, who wore a peach-colored sweater-vest and white slacks, his thinning silver hair neatly combed back. "Nice to meet you, Mr. Lenox. And thank you for keeping my seat warm. Char is far too precious to be left alone for even a moment around here. You'd be surprised how many men—married men—try to pick her up."

Mr. Lenox smoothly slid his left hand with a wedding ring under the table. "Well, I will leave you two to your lunch, then." He rose from the table. "Nice meeting you, Tommaso. And Char, I'd say that I'd see you for another lesson, but you're all booked up for the weekend."

For the rest of her life, actually.

"See you next time, Mr. Lenox," Char said.

The man scurried away, and Tommaso triumphantly took the empty seat and sat back, crossing his arms over his chest.

"Thank you. That was very kind," Char said, stirring her red straw around in her glass of what looked like Sprite or some other clear fizzy soda.

"Don't mention it."

The waiter showed up and took Tommaso's drink order. He asked for a martini. No olive.

"So," he said, thinking carefully about his next words and knowing there was much at stake, "I know this seems very forward, but—"

A panicked look took over her face and her eyes widened.

He held out his hand in a "stop right there" gesture. "Before you get the wrong impression, I'm not going to hit on you."

Not today, anyway. Okay—maybe.

"Oh." She suddenly looked guilty. "I'm sorry. I just assumed that…"

"Don't worry. I understand. You are, after all, a very beautiful woman, and it's only natural that any man with a sex drive takes a swing." *Oh. That was a good one. A golf pun.* He mentally patted himself on the back. "But what I was about to say was that you don't seem like the type who's intimidated easily. So why are you offended when a man shows interest?"

She nodded and stared at her glass, but didn't reply. There was a quiet yet mysterious serenity in her gaze that he found alluring. *This woman is filled with many secrets.* Not so dissimilar to himself.

"I apologize," he finally said after a few moments of enduring her silence and trying not to look at the soft-looking breasts pressing against her shirt. *Godsdammit. I just looked at them. Maaskab. Baby spiders. Puss.* "That was not very gentlemanly of me to pry."

He suddenly realized she hadn't heard a word he'd said. She was off somewhere else.

"Char?" He rapped his knuckles on the table, jolting her in her seat.

"Oh," she said. "I'm sorry. I'm not myself lately."

"Because of the recent breakup with your boyfriend?" Tommaso guessed.

"What gives you the idea that I've gone through a breakup?"

"Anyone who's paying attention can tell you've recently had your heart trampled."

She reached for her glass and squeezed her fingers around it tightly—too tightly—as she sipped. Tommaso couldn't help imagining how those fingers might feel wrapped around something else that was also nice and thick.

Dammit! Golf pants. Plastic silverware. The God of Death and War. Tommaso had successfully headed off another boner.

"He didn't break up with me," she said stiffly, setting down her drink. "We never started because he didn't want me." Her eyes glossed over a bit.

But how dare this prick make her feel less than beautiful and lovely? He'd kill him! Then he'd send him a thank you card.

"Whoa." She shook her head and blew out a breath. "This is so not like me to blubber and whine to a stranger, let alone a client. My apologies."

"No, please do not apologize. I don't mind at all." She was beginning to open up. This was exactly what he needed—to break through that wall.

Tommaso slid his hand across the white tablecloth and gave her wrist a little squeeze. "Obviously, this man didn't know what he was giving up, Char. Anyone can see you're a special lady."

"Oh no, he knew. He even said I was perfect for his soul, but his heart belonged to her—my cousin." She swept away an escaped tear. "It's probably for the best; he hung out with all of these crazy people who called themselves vampires and wore bright turquoise contacts. Seriously, L.A. has the craziest people."

Uh-oh. Wait a second. This sounded familiar. This sounded like…

"Hey, Charlotte. How's it going?" A redheaded waitress strolled by, flashing a quick smile at Char.

Charlotte…Charlotte… "Your name is Charlotte?" Tommaso felt like a brick of cement had rammed down his throat.

"Yes. Charlotte Meyer."

Tommaso bolted to his feet, almost knocking over the table and its contents onto Charlotte's lap. "And this man who rejected you, his name wouldn't happen to be Andrus, would it?"

Her brown eyes widened. "Oh, God. Please don't tell me you know him? Please don't tell me that you're one of his freaky friends who wear those contacts and—"

He held out his hands. "I don't know him," he lied. "I know *of* him. We, uhhh—go to the same tailor." *Gods, what the hell is going on?*

"But then how did you guess?" she asked.

How did I guess? How did I guess? He came up empty.

Then the only thing that popped into his head was another fib. "We go to the same tailor. I was getting fitted for a new suit and...overheard him talking about some wild singles party and a woman named Charlotte. And her cousin—yes, I think it was his cousin, a...Betsy or Bambi...or..."

"Her name is Sadie. We haven't spoken or seen each other since we were little. Then this woman, Cimil, tracked me down and—"

"Cimil," he whispered to himself, realizing that this was just one of her giant cluster-drama-mind-fucks. *I'm going to kill you for putting me in this position.*

"You know Cimil, too?" Charlotte asked.

"Oh, uh...she also goes to my tailor," he lied again. Gods, he hated deceiving this woman. She deserved his honesty and utmost loyalty.

She looked at him suspiciously. "It's a bit of a

coincidence, don't you think?"

"Absolutely." He had to think quickly. *Oh gods. Charlotte even looks like Sadie. Why didn't I notice before?* They looked like sisters. *Cimil. Cimil did something to me!*

He had been trapped in her basement for half a day. She could've easily had the Goddess of Forgetfulness whip up one of her famous Faghetta Boutit concoctions and slip it into his water.

"Tommaso?" Charlotte said. "How do you really know Cimil?"

Crap. Ummm... "My tailor. Like I said. She came in with Andrus that day. She was the one he was talking to." *Phew.*

She gave him a look and then shook her head. "I don't know what those two were on, but it had to be something powerful."

Still standing, he dipped his head. "If you'll excuse me for one moment, Charlotte, I must make a call. I won't be long."

He turned and tried to conceal the fact that his innards now felt like tofu scramble—an unnaturally squishy mess that had no business being in his manly stomach. Emma had made it for him once when she was on one of her many health kicks.

Fuck. Fuck. Fuck. Charlotte's in love with Andrus, he said to himself while strolling through the restaurant with a blank expression. As soon as he turned the corner, he blacked out.

CHAPTER NINE

"Tommaso? Are you all right?"

Tommaso found himself sitting in front of an uneaten shaved steak sandwich and an empty martini glass, with Charlotte snapping her fingers across the table.

What the hell? His eyes moved around the room, his brain now feeling like that tofu scramble he'd been thinking of moments earlier.

"What happened?" he asked himself aloud.

"I don't know," Charlotte replied. "You just sat down, started smiling, and chugged your martini. Are you all right?"

Tommaso frowned, feeling completely discombobulated. "How long have I been sitting for?"

"About five minu—"

"Excuse me, but there's an urgent call for Mr. Fierro." The tall waiter with a dark crew cut, large biceps, and a perfectly straight back loomed over the table like a death threat.

He was not their waiter. He wasn't a waiter at all. The man's name was Brutus and he was one of the elite Uchben he used to work with.

Tommaso offered a calm, collected smile to Charlotte, as he'd been trained to do in stressful situations. "One moment, Charlotte. I'm afraid this urgent business matter has me losing my mind."

"Go right ahead," she said, her eyes tinged with annoyance. Tommaso would not win points leaving like this, but what could he do? Tell Brutus to pound sand? That would likely end with Brutus trying to take him out by force and Tommaso beating the crap out of him.

Just then his phone went off—it was Andrus, calling to check in, no doubt.

Fuck! Andrus! The shocking memory jolted his nervous system back to the shittastic cluster fuck he'd landed in.

Charlotte was Andrus's mate, godsdammit. The mate Andrus had tossed aside—an unprecedented move—to be with Sadie, Charlotte's half-human, half-incubus cousin. Their human mothers were twin sisters, and Charlotte completely human, but none of that mattered. If Charlotte was meant to be with Andrus, then she could not possibly be Tommaso's special someone. And that meant his attraction for her was just that: an attraction. She probably couldn't save his soul any more than a good jerk-off. Sure, it might feel good, but it lacked a deep connection. And without that, there would be no way to counteract the evil vacuum slowly syphoning off his soul. He'd be lost to the darkness that represented the murder of his family.

Tommaso silenced his phone and followed the "waiter" outside and around the corner to a narrow, flower-lined walkway where Guy stood, arms crossed, feet apart, looking like he was going to kill something.

"Nice shirt," Tommaso said, commenting on Guy's very tight white T-shirt. "Love how it accents your nipples."

Guy narrowed his turquoise eyes. "Shut up, pretty boy, or I'll crack you in two like a wishbone."

Tommaso stopped right in front of Guy and was about to tell him that he'd gladly fight any day—the seven-foot deity didn't frighten him. Nothing did. Well, except turning into a Maaskab—but Guy cut him off.

"Speaking of outfits," Guy said, suddenly noticing Tommaso's unsophisticated, popsicle-colored clothing, "I see you've turned over a new fashion leaf. Let me guess, it's called '80s kindergarten chic?" Guy let out a self-congratulatory chuckle.

Tommaso shook his head. "What do you want, Guy? Besides to grow up. Oh, wait. Is it to yell at Emma some more?"

"What did Emma tell you?" Guy snarled.

Sadly, he'd promised Emma he wouldn't intervene. Otherwise, he'd be tearing into Guy about what a giant prick he was for not getting up every morning and thanking the good Universe for giving him such a wonderful mate.

"Never mind. What do you want?" Tommaso crossed his arms over his chest.

"I want to know why you were just in the kitchen, spitting in the soup of the day."

"What?" Tommaso frowned.

"Do you not recall strolling in there while the staff was not looking and hocking a loogy into the clam chowder?"

"I did no such thing."

"Oh really?" Guy slipped his cell from his pocket, hit the screen, and then held it up. A tiny video played of Tommaso strolling into the kitchen, sucking back a ball of phlegm, and then coughing it out into the soup.

"Holy fuck." Tommaso let out a breath and then scrubbed his hands over his face. "I don't remember a thing. I just blanked out." But why the hell would he do something so...so...*so horribly rude?* "It's happening. I'm turning evil." He looked up at Guy. "I'm fucked. Completely fucked."

"Yes, yes, you are. In the head. But we already knew that."

Ass. "This isn't a joke, Guy. The woman sitting at the table, the one who I was certain was my mate, is actually Andrus's mate. She's not going to be able to help me."

Guy's jaw went slack. "You mean she's the woman Andrus rejected for Sadie the succubus?" His tone indicated he already knew the answer.

Great. Here it comes in three, two—

Guy burst out laughing hysterically.

Tommaso crossed his arms. "Go ahead and

laugh, but if I end up in jail, so will you."

Guy jerked his head and pff'd. "You really think I'll go to jail? I'm the only god who gets his hands dirty, and my brethren have no desire to fill in for me should I be indisposed. I thought we covered this."

"Perhaps they won't jail you, but what will Emma say if I end up rotting in prison?"

"She'll get over it," he snarled.

"No. She won't. She's too good a person. Which is exactly why she's never given up hope that you'll act like a grown-up someday. And it's why you love her."

Guy's turquoise eyes flickered with irritation. "Don't drag her into this. Besides, what do you propose I do? Wave a magic wand and make this woman fall in love with you?"

"That's not a bad thought." It was just an idea and a long shot, but time was almost out. He felt an attraction to Charlotte—a very strong one. And Cimil had said that Charlotte was his mate. The point being that if Andrus could pick a mate by choice, why couldn't he? The only hurdle was getting Charlotte to reciprocate the interest.

How about getting her to open up? That might be a good place to start.

"I'm the God of Death and War," Guy said, "not love."

"Funny. I thought you were the God of Teeny Tiny Man Tees."

"Tommaso, do not mock me," Guy growled.

But you make it so easy. "I'll make you a deal.

You bring me the Goddess of Love and I promise that whatever happens, I'll make sure Emma knows how hard you tried to save me."

Guy mulled it over for a moment. "If I do this for you, then we're even. No more threats. No more trying to make me look bad in front of my wife. Deal?"

"Will you apologize for ripping a hole in my stomach and leaving me for dead when I'd been mind-fucked by the Maaskab and my entire family murdered?"

Guy stared at him for a slow, strained moment. "Yes. I will apologize. Just as you will for leaving Emma for dead on the Maaskab altar to be bled out as a sacrifice because you were too weak to fight the darkness."

"Fucker," Tommaso proclaimed.

"Right back at you. Do we have a deal?" Guy snarled.

"Deal." Tommaso held out his hand and Guy gave it a shake. "Now, fuck off."

"You first."

Tommaso dipped his head. "With pleasure." He needed to get back to Charlotte and start groveling ASAP. "Call my cell and let me know when Ashli arrives." Ashli was the human wife of Máax, the God of Time Travel. And in a very strange turn of events—another very, very long story—she ended up inheriting some of his powers which, unbeknownst to Máax, because he was too busy running around trying to save everyone, included the gift of Love. But the moment Ashli met Máax, she began to change as their souls began bonding. Now the woman was the full-blown Goddess of Love. She merely walked into a room and everyone instantly felt like writing poetry or singing sappy songs. Cimil and Zac had been begging her to come on full time to the matchmaking agency to help out, but Ashli had a new baby. She was only game to help out on very specific cases.

"And, by the way, where did you go last night?" Guy had not stayed in the suite, thank gods.

Guy shrugged his brows. "Wouldn't you like to know." He strolled off as if making a dramatic exit from a stage.

"Idiot," Tommaso mumbled and then headed back inside to face Charlotte.

࿓ஓ

Charlotte had left the table the moment Tommaso returned, telling him with a sharp tone that she'd see him back out on the golf course after he was done eating. "And I paid the bill," she had snapped.

Too distracted by the room full of people eating delicious phlegm chowder—*Dear gods, the horror!*—Tommaso didn't stop Char from walking out. After seeing her very unwelcoming expression, he realized he needed a few moments to reformulate his plan of attack. At least until Ashli, the Goddess of Love, arrived to save the day.

In the meantime, though, what the hell could he do? Charlotte wasn't the least bit interested in him and seemed to value the fact that he wasn't making any moves.

Annnnd, lest you forget that she's brokenhearted over being rejected by your best friend and you're now having evil blackouts. That last part was cause for concern, but at least his act of defiling the soup had been harmless.

He left the restaurant, shaking his head at himself. Until Ashli arrived, he would have to try to make some headway with her. On his own.

If she doesn't like being chased, perhaps she will enjoy chasing. It might make her feel in control, being in the driver's seat, pursuing a man.

The only problem was that he was a man. A man who was used to going after what he wanted and being in control. He'd have to get her interested in him, enough that she'd do the pursuing.

But this breed of subtle seduction was a skill women excelled at, not men.

What have you got to lose, man?

CHAPTER TEN

Matchmakers, Inc., Headquarters.

"Dear gods, woman! How you torture me!" From his desk on the fourteenth floor in downtown L.A., Zac stared across the stretch of gray carpet at Tula as she emptied the contents of her file cart into the new cabinets they'd installed this morning. What started out with a few hundred immortals looking for their special someone had turned into thousands overnight. Most of them hopeless cases. They had everything from ancient cantankerous vampires to lonely sex fairies to a crusty putrid Maaskab who'd already flipped teams. *Dear gods—do they think I'm a mate-magician?* There were limits to even the Universe's powers when it came to finding love for the truly unlovable. In either case, Immortal Matchmakers, Inc., was officially over its head in work. They'd have to hire more help and start throwing a hell of a lot more singles parties. The good news was, however, that his and Cimil's punishment would be over much faster. The moment they matched one hundred immortals with mates, they'd be given back their powers and allowed to return to their realm.

Tula ignored Zac's comment as usual and continued with her wholesome filing work, in her long wholesome flowery pink skirt and long-sleeve pink blouse that blocked every bit of delicious cleavage he knew she had hiding underneath.

Zac groaned as she did absolutely nothing provocative or sexy. "Can't you at least pretend to be completely slutty and into me?" That might temper his urge to seduce her. "After all, I am shirtless—for your pleasure, of course—so it's only natural for you to want to show your gratitude."

"Eww...no." She shot him a look. "And I already stripped down to my undergarments on Friday—a humiliating experience, by the way—just to get you off my back. It didn't do squat, as you pointed out."

"Yes, but I also suggested you get naked. There's still hope it could work." Although, he doubted that would quell his urge to tempt her either, now that he thought about it. Merely seeing the petite woman in her giant granny panties had given him cause for an emergency jerk-off in the men's room.

"No," she snapped, continuing with her duties. "And shouldn't you be focusing on finding your mate? 'Cause she's not me. That's for sure." Yes, Tula had been sitting in the summit meeting when he'd had that brief moment of panic, wondering if he wasn't beginning the journey to evil himself.

He felt all better now.

Zac leaned back in his black leather ex chair. "What if I give you Sundays off? To get off. With me, of course." They worked seven days a week in this office because when you were immortal and serving a work sentence, who gave a fuck about weekends?

Tula mumbled something that sounded unpleasant beneath her breath and continued sliding beige folders into their alphabetical slots.

"Sorry? Didn't catch that," Zac said. "Were you saying that you're finally coming to your senses and want me to deflower you?" He crossed his big awesome arms over his very chiseled bare chest, which women found irresistible. "My large cock and I can go all night, in case you were wondering." He smiled, waiting for her to blush as usual. "In fact, consider yourself lucky your boyfriend dumped you before you handed over your virginity—his little weenie would've lasted all of a minute and then you'd be living your life with that wondrously underwhelming memory."

"That's it!" Tula threw down the pile of folders in her arms. "I've had enough, Mr. Zac." She stomped over to her desk, which was only a few feet from his, right in the middle of the large room. She opened her desk drawer, grabbed her extremely large flowery purse, and marched toward the elevator doors.

"Where are you going?" he asked.

She repeatedly jabbed the call button before

turning around. "I'm quitting. That's where I'm going!"

"Quitting?" He stood from his desk. "Why the hell would you do that?" He'd hired her after she'd begged him for a job. Okay, technically Cimil hired her, but he'd agreed to let her stay because she'd said she needed the money to finish college. And if there was one thing he couldn't resist, besides tempting people, it was helping them. The gods were hardwired that way. Assisting humanity, deploying their divine gifts, trying not to go crazy because the world was such a fucked-up place and so were they—that was a deity's gig.

Tula stared at him, her big innocent blue eyes tearing up. "You think I am just some *thing*—a toy—for you to play around with? You think that my broken heart is a *joke*? Well...well...fuck *you!* Mr. Badass God!"

Zac's jaw dropped. "Did you actually just use the F-word?" She never cussed.

"Uh-huh. That's right," Tula continued. "Fuck. Fuck. Fuck! You've ruined me. Turned me into a dirty-mouthed, disrespectable woman who will never be able to face her mother again! Are you happy now?"

"Uhhh...is this another trick question?" Of course he wasn't happy. He didn't like seeing her upset one little bit, actually. A total shocker. He never cared.

Tula opened her mouth to speak, but then snapped it shut and huffed. The elevator chimed and the doors slid open.

"Tula, wait! Don't leave."

She stepped inside and then turned and faced him. "You're the worst god on the planet. I hope they never give you back your powers," she said as the doors closed.

Words failed Zac. But what shocked him more than the fact that she'd used a bad word, wished him ill, and quit was how much her anger towards him stung. He felt...he felt...well, frankly like he'd lost something important.

What? You're a jackass. She's just a human. A tiny insignificant human who prides herself on things that do not matter. Purity, goodness, those were things only fools believed in. He'd seen seventy thousand years of human evolution to know that. Sooner or later, mortals grew up. They had sex—some for love, some to satisfy hormonal needs, some for survival or procreation—and through the course of their lives, they became intimately familiar with joy and triumph, failure and pain. Mostly pain. Things, such as cuss words or maintaining one's public image, became irrelevant, fading away as the human began to grasp the pure and simple fact that being alive was a messy affair. As it was meant to be. Like a giant puzzle where if one was lucky, a few precious pieces fit together. The rest was...well, chaos. Random. Different paths colliding as billions of people played out their lives in this world.

Those who remained fixed and rigid in their ways, who denied themselves the simple pleasures and moments of joy offered to them, including fucking—okay, and chocolate—were missing out. Because for humans, life was short. And certainly too short to worry about making the entire world happy or trying to make others think one was respectable. Hell, he'd never once heard a person proclaim on their deathbed that they wished they'd fucked less or used less profanity. Hell no. It was the other way around. Humans always said that they wished they'd been braver and said what was truly on their minds. They wished for more time with the people they loved. As for romance, one Scotsman he'd watched die over a hundred years ago said it all with his final breath, "I wish I had plucked every one o' mi dear Betsy's feathers. But nay. I gathered but a handful. No' even enough to stuff a pincushion."

Zac sighed. *Ah yes. Words to live by.* And he couldn't waste his time trying to make mortals like Tula see the light. Waste of godsdamned time.

Then why are you so fucking upset?

The cell phone on his desk rang, disrupting his very important and divine epiphany. "What!" he barked into his phone.

"Don't 'what' me, you giant twat," said the deep voice on the other end of the phone.

"Votan, always a displeasure," Zac said.

"Shut it. I need a favor—and stop calling me Votan."

"I'll start calling you Guy when you stop acting like a two-thousand-year-old." *Such a juvenile.*

"Just remember, Zac, you need my vote when it comes time to lift your banishment."

Bastard. "What do you want?"

"I need you to track down Ashli."

"Ha! I knew it was only a question of time before Emma lost interest in you."

"Idiot. It's not for me; Tommaso needs help with his woman."

"Tommaso? Why didn't you say so?" Just because Zac had had to put Tommy into jail didn't mean he'd pass up the chance to help the man; putting Tommaso in jail yesterday morning really had been for the poor guy's benefit anyway. He didn't want Tommaso turning into a full-blown Maaskab and running off and killing people. Then the gods would've had to execute him. Now at least he had a chance at getting his life back.

Whoa. What's happening to me? It wasn't like him to be so compassionate.

"Make sure Ashli gets to Palm Springs by tomorrow," Guy demanded.

"Tomorrow? No can do. Last time I spoke to her, she said she'd be 'unplugging' and spending time with Máax and her baby. No deity business unless it was a matter of, and I quote, 'the world is fucking blowing up. Again.' This is not that."

"Convince her. You are, after all, the God of Temptation, so fucking tempt her."

"Although I thoroughly enjoy the tempting game since it's part of my nature, may I remind you that I do not actually possess any powers at the moment. And why do you even care what happens to Tommaso? The last time you spoke of him, you were cursing the Universe because he still lived."

Yes, yes. Zac had heard the spiel at the last summit meeting about Guy helping Tommaso because he'd vowed to be his guardian, his very own freedom being the collateral. But Zac didn't buy one word of it.

There was a long pause before Guy replied, "My interests in Tommaso are none of your business."

"Of course they're not. I simply enjoy knowing about anything that causes you angst. It gives me great pleasure." And if he had to guess, Guy was only doing this to appease his mate, Emma. *Gods, this has to be killing him.* Guy hated Tommaso with a passion.

"Fuck you, brother. Find Ashli. Get her to Palm Springs by tomorrow. Make sure she knows she is to help Tommaso capture Charlotte's heart."

Zac nearly choked on his tongue. "Did you say Charlotte?"

"Yes."

"Andrus's Charlotte?"

"Now you are catching on."

What the hell was happening? Good turning evil, evil turning good, immortals rejecting mates, and now this?

Zac ran his hands over his very silky head of awesome black hair. "Fuck."

"This is what we are hoping for," Guy pointed out.

"Indeed. I will call you if anything comes up."

"Excellent. And brother?" Guy asked.

"Yes?"

"You're still an epic asshole for what you did to

Kinich and Penelope. But if Emma had belonged to someone else, even one of my brothers, I am finally beginning to understand that I would've turned the world upside down to have her."

In other words, he understood that Zac had done everything in his power to win the woman he loved, including playing dirty.

Only now, Zac knew he never truly loved Penelope. He could only remember the want, the desire, the need to make her cross the line and want him.

It wasn't like that with Tula. *I want...I want...I want her to see the good in me.*

Fuck! "I gotta go," he said in a panic, ending the call and running for the elevator. "Tula!"

CHAPTER ELEVEN

While making his way to the eighth hole, Tommaso carefully rehearsed what he would say to Charlotte. First, he'd have to do a little groveling for continuously cutting out on her. Second, he'd need her to start seeing him as a sexual object, one to be exploited and used and sucked and ridden hard, day and night, and...

Who the fuck are you kidding? That was his fantasy. And thinking about doing those things to Charlotte instantly sent blood rushing to his cock.

He looked down at his orange and white plaid shorts. *Well, that's not obvious.* He pulled his shirt hem over his enormous bulge and started thinking about unsexy things such as Cimil. And her horrible unicorn. And that basement full of moaning clowns.

His dick began flagging. *There, that's better.* But the moment he spotted Charlotte's sweet womanly figure off in the distance, her back to him, he couldn't help but get excited again. *Godsdammit!*

He was about to stop walking to try to deflate the

randy bastard again when something struck him as odd. Or, more accurately stated: wrong. It wasn't so much the way Charlotte stood, but something about the rigidity of her posture. Almost like, almost like when a small animal realizes it's been spotted by a wolf. There's this moment of stillness where it can't decide if it should run or remain perfectly still, hoping it was mistaken about being seen.

That was exactly how Charlotte stood. She even had her fists balled as if readying to fight.

"Charlotte!"

She didn't move, and whatever she was looking at, just up over the ridge, was out of his line of sight.

Fuck. His bodyguard slash military training kicked in, and he started running as fast as he could, all the while his brain going into defensive planning mode. There were no weapons anywhere nearby, but Charlotte had the golf bag about thirty feet from her, containing a whole hell of a lot of nice heavy clubs. *Shit.* Did he go for her or for the clubs first?

"Charlotte! Run!" he screamed. He hoped she might turn around, see him sprinting in a raw panic, and then give him a look—a scowl or a frown or something to indicate that his imagination had gotten the best of him.

But that wasn't what happened.

He screamed her name again, but she remained frozen about fifty yards away, staring off at something that clearly terrified her. And yes, she was most definitely within earshot because a small group of golfers up ahead and off to the right had all looked in his direction when he'd yelled.

The soft grass making it impossible to run any faster, Tommaso yelled once more. Useless.

I'll go for her first, he decided. Ten yards. Nine. Eight. Seven. Six. Five... He grabbed her from behind and was about to shove his body in front of hers, but she yelled and twisted her body in such a way that their feet became entangled. They both went down in a mess of arms, legs, and a loud crack, with Tommaso landing right on top of her.

Charlotte's body went limp, and he immediately scrambled off her. He got to his feet and looked around, searching the horizon for whatever had immobilized her. There was nothing there. Not that he could see.

He glanced down at Charlotte, who lay there unconscious, a bloody rock about the size of his fist to the side of her head.

"No, no, no!" He kneeled down to discover a wound on the back of her head. How had this happened? He'd been trying to protect her.

But from what?

With my luck she was just daydreaming. And then he'd tripped on top of her and cracked her skull open.

Two men in white golf shirts and baseball caps came running over. One of them screamed back to their caddy to call for help.

Tommaso had already removed his shirt and began applying pressure to the wound.

"What happened?" one of the men asked.

"She fell," Tommaso said.

"But we saw you running for her," one guy said.

"And then you tackled her," added his companion.

Just then, three more men came up, all wearing blue jumpers with the resort's logo on the front. They were supposed to be gardeners, but Tommaso knew those straight backs and clean cuts.

Uchben.

They started herding the men away, saying that they'd already called for medical assistance.

One of the golfers protested, "But someone should call the police—"

"Go back to your games, gentlemen, nothing to see here," said the largest "gardener," who was in fact, Brutus, the same man who'd posed as a waiter earlier.

"Thanks," Tommaso said. "But she needs to get to a hospital and—"

Charlotte let out a soft groan.

"Charlotte? Are you all right? Can you hear me?"

"Owww…" She reached for the top of her head. "What happened?"

"Don't move," he commanded. "You hit your head on a rock."

Her eyes still closed, she mumbled, "Why did you tackle me like that?"

He brushed the hair back from her forehead, still applying pressure to the wound. "Tell me what you saw, Charlotte. What scared you out there?"

"I felt him watching me," she muttered.

"Who? Who was watching you?" he demanded,

angry as hell that someone would torment her like this.

"The monster."

CHAPTER TWELVE

It wasn't long before the paramedics arrived and checked Charlotte out, determining she would not have to be hospitalized or require stitches. The cut, though deep, was only half an inch long.

"She needs a cold compress, but other than that, she'll be fine," said the female paramedic.

They moved Charlotte into a sterile-looking, bright white first aid room on site at the resort, and Tommaso stayed with her.

The moment the "garden staff" and paramedics left the room, Tommaso was doing his best not to sound alarmed.

"Charlotte, I need to ask you something. And please don't think that I'm judging you, because I'm not. But what did you mean when you said there was a monster watching you?"

Charlotte, who was stretched out on a gurney, sitting up with a bag of ice on the back of her head, went rigid from head to toe. Tommaso was fairly certain she'd even stopped breathing.

"Charlotte?" he pushed, standing over her with his arms crossed.

"I don't know what you're talking about." She sounded defensive.

"I saw you standing at the top of that hill, looking like you couldn't move your feet."

"I-I was just standing there, watching some golfers."

Bullshit. "I called your name, and you didn't respond."

She looked away, toward some Heimlich poster on the wall as if suddenly fascinated by the thing.

"Charlotte," he said sternly, "tell me what happened."

She didn't reply, but her body did. Her breath quickened, her nostrils flared, her face turned tomato red.

He sat down next to her in one of those plastic molded chairs and reached out, laying his hand on her thigh. Dammit, touching her felt way better than he imagined. "You can trust me, Charlotte. I won't think you're crazy."

She let out a slow breath and then looked at him, conflict and turmoil stewing in her brown eyes. "If I think I'm crazy, then you sure as hell will."

Was that what was bothering her? "Don't be so quick to judge. Appearances can be deceiving." *I'm certified fucked in the head. In fact, if you cracked open my skull, tiny sour jellybeans would fall out.*

"So, if I told you that I've been having nightmares—the kind that feel so real I wake up and run to the kitchen for a knife or call 9-1-1, hysterical and convinced something is in my house, or that I'm afraid to go to sleep anymore because I think I might never wake up, what would you say then?"

Her words sickened his heart. Had he done this to her? Hurt her like this? He wished he knew what was happening.

"How long has this been going on?" he asked.

"A very long time. But I'm afraid to get help. They'll lock me up."

Shit. A very long time? He'd only seen Charlotte for the first time a few days ago. Was something else or someone else tormenting her?

"But just now," he said, "when you were on the golf course, you said that you saw the monster." She had not been asleep.

"I was just having a daydream."

He knew she was lying. *Fuck. Was it me she sensed?* "In your dream, what happens? What does the monster do to you?"

"It's silly," she groaned. "Please, I'm fine. Just go and enjoy the rest of your day."

"Uh-uh. No you don't."

She flashed a small frown at him.

As if that's really going to scare a guy like me off. He leaned back in his chair and crossed his arms over his chest. "I'm not going anywhere, dear woman. Not until you tell me what really happened and I'm convinced you're all right."

"There's blood all over your shirt. You should go back to your room and change."

He shook his head. "Nope. Not leaving. Besides,

the blood makes me look edgy." It actually made him look psycho, like he perhaps took the sport of golf a little too seriously and had beaten someone to death at the ninth hole.

"Please," he said, "I am only trying to help."

Charlotte sighed. "Fine. In my dreams, at first the monster seems like it wants me to help it. Then when I can't, because I'm too afraid, it turns on me. It drags me out of bed and tries to kill me."

Tommaso ran his hands through his hair. What was happening? Had he dreamed of attacking her or somehow shared one of her nightmares? In the immortal world, it wasn't unheard of for couples who shared a powerful connection to share emotions, thoughts, and sometimes even speak with one another telepathically.

Only, she and I don't have a powerful connection. Their relationship was more like a one-way ticket on a lusty train, and he was the only one riding. He needed to rectify that immediately.

That aside, she'd been having problems before they'd met. Now he wasn't sure of what was real—or happening—but he no longer had the option to simply tell Charlotte the truth: He was turning into a real live, grade A horror film creature and needed her help, just like the thing in her nightmares. She'd be terrified of him.

So what next? He still had a shot at saving himself if he could get her to like him. *I need to get her to trust me, to let her guard down.* If he could do that, then she might feel something for him and end his transformation. It was worth a try at this point, as there were no other options and no other women to fall madly in love with. She was it. And he wasn't complaining.

"The nightmares are bad enough," she muttered, "but I wake up feeling like the dream hasn't ended..." Charlotte groaned.

"You simply need a good night's sleep, that's all," he assured her. "Things always look different when you're well rested." Not exactly so simple, but it couldn't hurt.

"Funny. Sleep is the one thing I'm not getting."

He nodded, rubbing his stubbly chin. "You trusted me just now to tell me something very personal. I want you to trust me again."

"Why?" She blinked her beautiful brown eyes at him and he noticed how they had flecks of orange. Not gold, but orange. They were lovely.

"I have a proposal for you, Charlotte."

"Oh no." She held out her hands.

Damn her. Such a thick wall. Well, he'd have to bring out his finest chisel. "Don't flatter yourself, woman. There are no strings attached; I merely want to ask you to trust me and answer a few more questions."

"Why?"

He could see the despair in her eyes. She wanted someone to trust. She was tired and feeling alone.

"What if I told you," he said, "that someone once helped me when I truly needed it, that she was the only thing in this world that kept me sane when everything in my life was crumbling? Would you believe that I have been waiting for the opportunity to pay back that debt?"

"So it's a karma thing."

"Yes." In a way, he supposed it was. But nothing in his world was that simple, and trying to explain the complicated truth to her wasn't an option.

"Fine," she said. "If you really want to help, then spend the night with me."

PART TWO

CHARLOTTE

CHAPTER THIRTEEN

Please don't say no. Please spend the night. But would he say yes or simply think I was crazy? I'd never been so forward with a man. Or with anyone, for that matter. But I was at the end of my rope. My dreams now haunted me in the daylight, seeping into the world I'd worked so hard to build around me, all to protect myself from the things that had driven my poor mother mad.

She claimed the monsters were everywhere. She claimed that they masked themselves as everyday people, befriended us, made us trust them only to feed on us.

I didn't believe her when I was younger. But now I did and had for a long time. Which was why I suspected that the ordinary things in this world— stoplights, TV shows, days in the park, and bedtimes—were some sort of self-perpetuated hoax. Order, routines, and activities meant to distract us from the real world. A world filled with monsters.

I looked up at this beautiful man, Tommaso, hovering over my gurney. He made me feel so safe, though I didn't know why. Or particularly care at this point. The simple fact that he gave me relief was enough for me. I couldn't remember the last time I'd really slept, and my endeavor to keep afloat with caffeine, vitamins, protein shakes and anything else I could buy legally was no longer doing the trick.

My legs stretched across the gurney, I set the bag of ice down on my lap and ran my hands over my bob. I used to wear it long, like my mother, but cut it off a few years ago. I had done everything within my power not to draw unnecessary attention to myself and to feel safe, while not giving up my life.

Sadly, I wasn't winning that battle. That was why I finally had to accept help. *Tommaso.* He was like an angel sent to answer my pleas for help.

But, oh God, what would this man say if he knew what I was thinking? Still, I didn't want him to leave, not when he made me feel other things, too. Those dark brown eyes—almost black—that piercing gaze, and those lips… Damn. Those lips. They were like signposts that told a woman exactly what to expect from a guy like him: dirty nights in clean sheets. He wasn't a slob or a tomcat. He was the sort of man who took care of himself and took pride in perfection—including pleasing a woman in bed.

Okay, yes. That last part was just an impression. But my fear of monsters hiding among us had made me acutely aware of people's behaviors—when they lied, when they were afraid, and most importantly, when they were dangerous.

Tommaso was dangerous. But in a good way. I could tell by the way he carried himself that he protected what was his, which was just another reason I felt so attracted to him. *But God, if I ever told him the truth*—about my fears, about what really went on inside my head—he'd run for the hills.

His dark, menacing gaze locked with mine. "Did you just say that you want me to...to..." He spoke with a hint of an Italian accent that so frequently had me distracted. Just like last night when we met at the wine tasting and he had on those sexy leather pants. For the first time in my life, I hadn't been able to stop myself. I hit on a man. Yes, me. Then he began to speak in that deep sensual tone laced with that seductive accent, and I quickly realized he was way, waaay out of my league. Nobody was more shocked than me to see him this morning on the green. My pupil for the entire day? Him? The hottest man I'd ever seen. Yeah, right—like I'd forget meeting *him*. But that was what I'd told Tommaso, like a complete imbecile. I couldn't spend the entire day with him, trying to maintain a professional demeanor, if he knew that I hadn't been able to get him out of my head all night.

Now, however, I was beginning to see that Tommaso was so much more than just a pretty face. He gave me something I so desperately needed.

"Spend the night with me," I repeated. "But not the way you think." *Or the way I want.* "I'm asking you to watch over me while I sleep."

He lifted both delicious dark brows, and his sensual lips puckered, as if hoping for a kiss to persuade him.

I resisted the urge to deliver. "Well?" I prodded.

"I-I have—"

"Oh. Your girlfriend." I shook my head, feeling like an idiot for having forgotten about the reason he'd come for lessons. But of course he'd be taken. He was so goddamned hot that every time I looked at him, I had to pretend he was one of my horrific monsters simply not to drool. Still, I couldn't help appreciating those broad shoulders or the way the muscles on his exposed forearms and calves hardened with even the slightest movement, like he was built from steel cables underneath that olive skin. On this man, tacky golf shorts looked like male lingerie. It was obvious that his attention to his physical appearance didn't stop at his sexy fucked-all-night hairdo.

I was jealous of whichever woman had won him over.

"No. I don't have a fiancée," he confessed.

What? My heart did a flip. *Stay calm. Staaay calm.* "But you said—"

He held up his large hand—with those thick fingers that made me think of something else altogether—to shush me. "*You* said I was engaged. Or trying to impress the new boss. I never confirmed."

"You didn't correct me either."

He dipped his head of messy black hair. "And

for that, I offer my apologies. But the truth as to why I wanted golf lessons from you puts me in an awkward position."

My pulse accelerated as a look of raw lust radiated from his eyes.

Lust. Lust. Lust! He's giving me the sexy eyes. I hardly knew what to do. I was used to just ignoring men's advances or telling them to take a hike. But actually enjoying a man hitting on me was completely novel. I hadn't even had a date since my first year in college. Community college for the first two years and then Cal State Long Beach for years three and four, where I obtained a useless degree in athletics training. Golf was something I just did on the side that turned into something more.

He continued, "I hope this doesn't rub you the wrong way, but I wanted to spend time with you— not to bed you or make you mine for one night—but to get to know you."

My breath hitched. His words felt so, so good. *Wait. Why would he want someone like me?* I was such a mess. Couldn't he see that?

"Because you want to learn a perfect swing?" I asked.

A subtle, seductive smile crept across his full lips. "Aside from the fact that you love to play, I couldn't give a fuck about golf."

"Really?" My heart ballooned with elation. Okay, I knew that might sound silly—to get so excited about him wanting to spend time with me, but anyone who understood my past—what I'd gone through and how hard it was to feel anything for anyone—well, they'd comprehend why my connection with this strange man was a big deal. Oddly, he was exactly what I'd hoped to find when that really strange woman, Cimil, told me that I'd meet my soul mate at her mixer. *Ugh*—that party had been like a horrific freak show.

Tommaso cocked his head. "Men throw themselves at you by the truckload. Why's it so hard to believe I want to get to know you?"

"I have my reasons." And they were pretty damned scary ones.

"Do tell."

Hell no. He'd think I was damaged goods and mad like my poor mother. "Are *you* ready to tell me everything about yourself, even your darkest secrets or most painful moments?"

"Hell no," he scoffed.

Ha. Exactly. "Then we're on the same page."

He dipped his head. "Indeed, we are."

"So will you spend the night?" I hoped he'd say yes, because I hadn't slept more than a few hours a night for the last month, and even those hours were shoddy. Any more of this, and I would drop dead from exhaustion. And while I didn't have children or any human beings dependent upon me, I did have a mortgage and some very strange but loving animals no one would ever want except me. Yeah, four of them were chickens with only a few feathers to their names and one cat who completely hated me. But so what? They were my kids. My best friends, Mike and Susan, who ran a vegan café, never stopped giving me a hard time about how I was even worse than they were with my animal causes.

Rubbing the bit of black scruff on his chin, Tommaso leaned back in the brown plastic molded chair beside my gurney. It was the strangest thing about this man, but on the outside he was so sleek and polished, like an elegant luxury car. But that look in his eyes and the way he carried himself said he was not to be fucked with. Not even a little.

That's why I feel safe around him.

"If I spend the night," he finally said, staring with a wolfish gaze, making me fidget on the creaky metal gurney, "I want something in return."

Sure, I'll totally have sex with you. In fact, you can bend me over right now on this bed and... The space between my legs tingled with the thought. And my skin began longing for those large hands of his to touch every soft inch.

Regardless, I blurted out, "I'm not sleeping with you," knowing I was far too messed up to invite him or any man into my life. Still, I was allowed to have my fantasies.

He smirked with his eyes. "Ouch. You're a cold, cold woman, Charlotte."

I offered him a quick smile. "Sorry. It's not that you're not a handsome man. Because you are. It's just that I'm—"

"You don't owe me any explanations."

I mentally phewed because I didn't have one. I had been planning to pull something out of my ass that would've been complete nincompoopery, like... *"Hey, the kitty isn't really trimmed for visitors. Not a good time."*

He went on, "I was going to point out that I paid for golf lessons for the week."

"And?"

"And I've already confessed that I did so simply because I wanted to get to know you."

"And?" I repeated, awaiting his demand.

"I will spend the night, but you will have to answer ten questions."

Pfft. Okay! That would be easy.

"Truthfully," he added.

Dammit! That would not. "What about you? Do I get to ask anything I like?"

He leaned in and rubbed his thumb over my chin, just below my lower lip. I resisted the urge to moan or whimper or suck on that thumb—all seemed like appropriate responses to a man like this touching me.

"You, my dear Charlotte, may ask me anything you like." He flashed a cocky little half smile.

Meaning, I could ask, but he wouldn't necessarily answer.

"Do we have a deal?" he added.

Sleep. I needed to sleep. Just one night of peace and safety. I would go insane if I didn't get it. And the thought of this beautiful man keeping me safe and sound while I did it, well... "Deal. Thank you, Tommaso."

CHAPTER FOURTEEN

Tommaso insisted on driving me home, which, after I hit my head, wasn't a surprise. Neither was his hundred-thousand-dollar car—black, sleek, sexy, just like the suit he now wore. He'd changed somewhere between the time he left me in the first aid room and checked out of his room.

"So, uh..." I ran my hands through my hair, self-consciously patting the knot on the back of my head to make sure it wasn't actually the size of a basketball.

"Are you feeling all right?" he asked.

"Oh. Yeah, feeling fine. I just..." *I'm at a loss for words.* Why had he changed? Now he looked even hotter, and I was questioning my decision to let him in my front door along with my ability to keep my hands to myself.

"Yes?" he said, his voice deep and low, filled with masculine confidence.

"So this is the real you?" I swept my hand through the air in his general direction.

"Yes."

"And the preppy golf clothes you've been wearing around the resort or the leather pants from last night?" I asked.

"I was making do until my own clothes arrived."

"Oh." I bobbed my head. It made sense. From the moment I saw him, I thought he looked out of place. His sherbet clothes reminded me of a Batman doll that had been dressed in a My Little Pony tutu. And I wasn't talking about the doughy '70s Batman in the blue underwear with the awesome yellow utility belt. No, sir. I was talking Superman-assassin. Rusty-bucket-of-nails-voiced Batman.

"So, what exactly do you do for a living again?" I asked, my tone unintentionally critical.

"I thought I was the one asking all of the questions?"

"You said I could ask anything I liked."

"Indeed, I did," he admitted.

I waited, but he kept his eyes glued to the road, saying nothing.

"Fine." I let out a little breath. "Don't answer, but just know that maybe you're not the only one who's interested." Why had I said that? I needed to keep my flirty urges in check, but it was so damned difficult.

He flashed a glance my way, quickly returning his eyes to the road and then checking his mirrors like he was watching for something. *Or someone?* I already felt safe enough to take a nap.

"What kind of interested?" he asked.

"Is this one of your ten questions?"

"No."

"Then I'm afraid I can't answer." I smiled and looked away. Did he have any clue what he did to me? My stomach felt crazy inside—flutters and rolling waves. And dammit, did he have to smell so good? His Mercedes—completely showroom-floor immaculate, by the way—smelled like a delicious mixture of spice and leather, male and new car.

He was silent for several long moments. "All right, Charlotte, here's my first question: Why the big wall around you, metaphorically speaking of course?"

"You think I'm closed off?"

He continued, "It's obvious that you don't lack confidence in yourself, and you're friendly enough, but you keep everyone at arm's length. You don't share anything personal, do you?"

He sure didn't waste time with the big questions, but I wasn't ready to answer. It was too complicated and... "Can I table that question?"

"We had a deal."

"I didn't say I wouldn't answer. I just prefer us to work up to the more difficult topics." I pointed to the left, toward the stretch of road leading out of town. "Turn here."

"You live pretty far out of the way," he said, taking in the barren desert surroundings.

"I like my privacy," I lied. What I really liked was living in my fortress—it was the only way I could relax at night.

You mean, it used to be the only way you could relax. Nothing seemed to help anymore. Mainly because I couldn't shake the feeling that something bad, something evil was coming for me. Again.

God, please don't let me end up like my mother. Not that I didn't love her—I did. More than anything. But I hadn't been able to save her. No one had.

Twenty minutes later, we turned down a dirt road and came upon my chain-link fence.

"Well, this certainly is...private," he said, checking out the open desert surrounded by rocky hills off in the distance. He then noticed the barbed wire at the top of the fence, too. "A woman's touch?"

"I live alone out here and there are a lot of animals." He was onto me and my crazy.

I got out of his car to unlock the thick chain holding the gate together.

"Must be some very big animals," he yelled through his window as I rolled back the gate.

"Huge!"

He smirked at me, a sign that he knew I was lying, and then drove in, waiting for me to lock the gate behind us.

As I walked toward his car, a cold chill swept over me. *Shit.* I swiveled on my heels and looked through the gate toward one of the hills off in the distance. Someone or something was watching. I could feel it.

"Charlotte?"

I turned my head and saw Tommaso standing just outside of his open car door, looking at me with concern.

"Uh…it's nothing. I just thought I—never mind." I marched toward his car and got inside.

He slid back into the driver's seat. "What did you see, Charlotte?"

"Is this one of your ten questions?"

"Should it be?"

I didn't want to tell him the truth about why he was really here. But another part of me felt like he might understand. In fact, I found myself wishing he might. My two best friends, Mike and Susan, had moved away to San Diego a few years back to start their vegan café. We still spoke at least once a month, but even so, I never told them what happened to me. Only my mother knew, and I sometimes felt like that was her ultimate mental demise—she hadn't been able to protect me.

"Maybe," I replied, feeling discombobulated in his presence. Everything about him made me feel all messy inside and unlike myself. Possibly a good thing.

"Then I'll put it on the list." He closed his door, hit the gas, and we continued down the dirt road that led to my house.

శారా

"I think I'm going to have to change my profession," Tommaso said as we entered my two-story, modernist home with a smooth poured-cement exterior, sharp angles, and stone façade on the first floor to hide the steel shutter inserts.

"And your profession again is…?" I waited for

him to fill in the blank as I lugged in my golf clubs I'd insisted on carrying myself, setting them against the wall next to the front door.

"A little of this. A little of that," he said casually, standing in the steel-reinforced doorway, checking out my foyer and living room just off to the right—limestone-colored tile, a few indoor palms, and two soft beige couches facing an extra-large glass brick fireplace.

All right, so he's not going to answer. But it had to be something interesting, I guessed. He had an air about him that screamed investor slash James Bond slash...*Buffy the Vampire Slayer.*

Weird. Why the hell did that come to mind?

"It's beautiful," he said.

He stepped all the way inside, and I closed the front door, locking it with the heavy bolt. "I inherited some money after my mother died. She was a financial analyst and invested well." With the money, I'd made my home into my modern fortress.

"Why so dark, though?" he asked.

"Oh. Sorry." I headed into the living room and pushed the button on the wall. The sound of motors churning filled the room, so did the light. "Security blinds." I smiled awkwardly.

Tommaso cocked a brow and then walked into my living room to get a better look. "I would ask about the apocalyptic-bunker motif, but I'd hate to prematurely spend one of my ten questions."

I flicked my index finger at him. "Good call."

With his hands on his waist, he spun around, taking everything in. There wasn't much. On the other side of the living room was an open doorway leading to a small dining room with a steel-framed skylight above my solid granite dining table. To the other side of that room was my kitchen—cement countertops, commercial-grade appliances. Simple. Sturdy. Clean. The upstairs was just as sterile, but I liked it that way: uncomplicated. So unlike my life.

"I like your paintings," Tommaso said. "Reminds me of Napoli, my home."

On the wall beside the fireplace were the only two things in the house that didn't really belong to my sterile decorating style. They were large paintings of the Italian countryside I'd found at a gallery in San Diego while visiting my friends Mike and Susan. I'd known Mike as long as I could remember—my best friend since kindergarten. Susan I'd met in high school—we both waited tables at a local coffee shop. Ironically, the two were my best friends, but we never hung out all together. Not even at school. Then one day, Mike invited me to a party, and I brought Susan along. The two of them were inseparable ever since and now had two kids. As for the paintings, I had no clue what possessed me to buy them—I wasn't into art—but I hadn't been able to resist. I'd felt drawn to them, like I knew I'd go to that place someday. Yes, I was beginning to wonder if I would go with this man.

"So that's where your accent is from," I said. "I couldn't place it."

"I'm from a small village near Napoli, but my family is deceased now."

I wasn't sure I understood. "You mean your parents?"

He spun around slowly, inspecting the ceiling and windows as if memorizing the lay of the land. "No. My family—brothers, sisters, their children—every last one of them."

He'd said it so casually, I wondered if I misheard him. "Everyone?"

"Everyone," he confirmed.

Jesus. "What happened?" I knew I shouldn't ask, but I couldn't help it.

Still standing in the center of my sparsely decorated living room, he gave the side of his mouth a little scratch, possibly debating how much to share. "A very tragic event, one that's probably best to talk about another time."

And...no sharing. Okay. I didn't want to push, so I dropped it. I could very much understand not wanting to relive painful old memories.

"So, now what?" he asked.

A loud hiss echoed through the room.

Tommaso's eyes toggled back and forth. "What was that?"

"My cat, Bitch Pants."

His brows pulled together. "You named your cat 'Bitch Pants'?"

What else? I rescued her from certain death. She hated me with every hair on her cantankerous body. "It's complicated. But my chickens are pretty friendly. Would you like to meet them?"

"Do they hiss like a demon from hell?"

"No. They cluck—really, it's more of a 'gaaawk,

gaaawk' rather than a cluck. I think because they're cold all the time."

"Should I ask why?"

No. He really shouldn't because then I'd have to explain how they were featherless due to a stress condition caused by inhumane treatment. And how I had tried to knit them sweaters and heat their coop, but they only picked the sweaters apart, and the space heaters freaked them out. My next big project was to build them a little house with central heat and AC.

"Maybe I should finish showing you around," I said. "Then we can head upstairs to my bedroom."

He gave me a look. A sexy look. Of course, everything he did was sexy. Even the way he just stood there doing absolutely nothing in his elegant black suit, with his messy black hair, olive skin, and "don't fuck with me" posture. Such a turn-on.

Maybe inviting him here was a mistake. I already liked the feel of him in my home, like he belonged in my life somehow. But that would be silly. We'd just met.

Yet you invited him to watch you sleep at your house. That's not at all strange.

Shut it, I told myself. *He said yes.*

"I meant so I can sleep," I finally clarified.

He nodded his head. "Yes. Sleep is lovely. But you hit your head today and haven't eaten since lunchtime. Let me prepare you dinner before you go into hibernation."

He offered to cook for me. Considering his very refined, masculine vibe and very expensive clothing, I hadn't chalked him up for a cooking man. *Hot!*

"I'm fine. I promise. Oh—but you," I rolled my eyes at myself, "you're probably hungry. Let me make you something."

"I am not about to allow a tired, injured woman, who's asked for my assistance, to wait on me."

"But you're a guest. It would be wrong to…" My voice trailed off as he removed his blazer and tie and threw them both over the back of my beige couch before rolling up the sleeves of his dark blue shirt. I swallowed down the lusty-lump in my throat, taking in the view of his muscular forearms.

"Or I could let," I croaked, "you cook."

He smiled. "Just show me to the kitchen."

"Right th-this wa-way…"

He followed me through the dining room, and I was hit by a strange woozy sensation. Then, for just a moment, I felt his eyes on me, like we were touching, yet…we weren't.

What the hell? I stopped, unable to breathe, and then turned and looked up at him. The sensation hit me again, more intense this time. He stood three feet away, but he might as well have been naked, pressing himself against my body.

"Are you all right?" he asked.

I shook my head no.

"What's the matter?" He flashed an alerted glance over his shoulder, then the other, before turning back to me.

"Who are you, Tommaso?"

"What do you mean?"

"Why do I have the feeling that you're not at all who you seem?"

"Because I'm not."

I waited for more.

He shook his head disapprovingly. "You ask me to tell you everything, my dear Charlotte, yet you haven't exactly been forthcoming."

True. Fine. Let's do this. I lifted my chin and sucked in a fortifying breath. It was crazy to want to open myself to this man I didn't know, but something inside kept gnawing at me: *Do it. Do it!* "I keep people at a distance because I'm afraid."

"Afraid?"

"Not of people. Of the…the…"

He reached out and squeezed my arm. "Charlotte?" he pushed.

"I'm afraid of the monsters." God, I sounded like a fucking child who'd watched too many scary movies. Totally laughable. Only, he wasn't laughing.

"You mean your nightmares," he said.

"I think I dream about them so much because they're real." I *knew* they were real.

His expression didn't change. Not one little bit. "Perhaps they are."

"So-so you believe they exist?" I asked.

"Indeed, I do."

I couldn't believe this.

"They're called Republicans," he added.

"What!" I huffed and pushed him.

Laughing, he held up his hands. "Sorry. I meant Democrats?"

"Ohmygod." I turned and headed for the kitchen. "What an ass."

"Charlotte, I was merely joking to lighten the mood and help you relax. But I believe you. I truly do."

"Right." I entered the kitchen, trying not to lose my cool. "You know, for a moment there, I thought I could trust you. But clearly my sleep deprivation is getting to me."

"You *can* trust me. I, too, have encountered my fair share of challenges and pain that haunt me. And like you, I wish to overcome them. Maybe that's what's brought us together."

There wasn't an ounce of fear, whininess, or despair in his tone. He spoke about his past like it was a mountain he wanted to scale with his manly arms and legs, and when he got to the top, he'd beat the fuck out of that mountain and call it his bitch. Whereas...

"I'm just trying to survive here, Tommaso." And not feel like a moron for admitting the truth about what really scared me.

He smiled. "Then let me cook you dinner, Charlotte. It's as good as any place to start."

Dang, he was good. Such a charmer.

"Do you always get your way?" I asked.

"Not frequently enough." He stepped around me and headed for my fridge, leaving me hanging onto his words. "Now let's see what Charlotte has in her fridge."

CHAPTER FIFTEEN

"This. Is. Amazing," I said, spearing a piece of prosciutto—normally my favorite for sandwiches—mixed into the creamiest spaghetti I'd ever tried in my life. It was so decadent that I felt like I should be wearing a sequin evening gown and have my hair up in a fancy twist. Instead, I still wore my unflattering khaki golf slacks and white golf shirt.

Wowwy, glamorous me. The funny part was, I didn't actually feel uncomfortable like this. I'd given up primping or making myself girly nice years ago. Yeah, I bathed and brushed my hair and everything, but I did what I could to tone down the sexy. Sadly, it made very little difference. The men at work still hit on me, which was odd. I was a normal-looking woman. Not ugly, not raging hot either. Just...normal.

"It's an improvised version of my mother's recipe," Tommaso said, watching me intently from across the charcoal gray granite table.

"Were you close to her?" I took another bite and

washed it down with a sip of Cab—one I'd been saving for a special occasion. In my world, having dinner with an unfathomably gorgeous man like Tommaso qualified. He felt like a breath of fresh air mixed with sunshine.

He nodded, but didn't elaborate.

"I lost my mother about two years ago," I said. "She died in a car accident." Really, she was crazy and never should've been behind the wheel. She drove her car right into a telephone pole while going ninety. To this day, I wondered if she was running from something or just unaware of how fast she was going.

"I'm sorry to hear that," he said quietly. "Do you have any other family? And before you ask, yes, this is one of my ten questions."

Question number two. "I have two cousins from Cleveland."

"That's it? No siblings? No—not part of my ten questions."

"Honestly, there's just Sadie and Nell, my cousins."

"And their parents?" he asked.

"Technically, Aunt Claire—who was my mother's twin—is missing, but she's presumed dead. Sadie's dad, Uncle Chuck, was a lunatic—some violent criminal or something, so my aunt Claire ran away. The horrible part was how she left Sadie and Nell behind." Oddly, my mother once showed me a picture of Sadie, and we actually looked alike. So much so that when I was younger, I fantasized that she was my twin sister. Not that being an only child was bad—my mother, who had been a financial analyst for a big bank in town before she went off the deep end, definitely overcompensated with the toys and clothes. But family was the one thing I never had much of.

"How tragic for your cousins. Do you ever speak to them?" he asked.

I shook my head. "I want to. I really do, but I'm afraid."

"That they'll be like their father," he guessed correctly.

"Yes. But I recently found out Sadie moved to L.A. I got invited to some big party she was supposed to be at, and I wasn't planning to attend until this crazy woman, Cimil, tracked me down and convinced me if I went, I'd meet the perfect man, too. She claimed to be some famous matchmaker." Honestly, repeating the story aloud made me realize how bonkers it sounded. It was as if I'd been under some strange mind control after speaking to that woman.

I expected Tommaso to laugh at me, but he simply looked intrigued. "This is the party that Andrus attended."

"Yes." I still thought it was pretty strange that they knew each other, but the one thing I'd learned was that this world was full of strange.

"Well, I for one am happy you did not end up with him. You deserve a man who's completely committed to you and only you."

I stared for a moment, imagining Tommaso being that man—vacations in Tuscany or, even better, on some secluded virgin beach with white sand and glassy turquoise water. Him lying next to me in an oversized hammock while we sipped piña coladas—*no, wait, make that ice-cold beers with a slice of lime*—gazing out at the ocean.

I mentally sighed. *Who the hell am I kidding?* "I'd be happy with a man who's close to my age, unmarried, debt-free, and reasonably good in the sack." I slapped my hands over my mouth. "I sed dat outloud, di'in I?"

Tommaso laughed with that hypnotically deep, masculine voice of his, and it felt like being covered in warm gooey caramel. So delicious.

"Yes. I think you did," he said, circling his finger on the rim of his wineglass. "But a woman like you really shouldn't set her bar so low."

Flattery will get you everywhere, sir. "So you think I should set my bar up here?" I held my hand up above my head.

"Higher."

I reached a little higher. "Here?"

He pointed straight up toward the sky. "A little higher, honey."

I gave him a sideways glance. "You wouldn't happen to be up there somewhere, would you?"

He grinned. "Now you're catching on."

"Someone has an ego." I cracked a big smile. I just couldn't help loving the way he seemed so comfortable in his own skin. Like his strength and masculinity radiated from somewhere deep inside him.

He shrugged playfully and took a sip of his wine.

As for me, my heart felt like it was flittering around inside my chest. What was it about this man that had me feeling so unlike myself—bold, lusty, and unafraid?

"So, Tommaso, tell me, aside from thinking you're the ultimate catch, how do you enjoy spending your time?"

"The typical." He stared hungrily from across the table. I had the impression his mind was on other things: me.

My pulse rate accelerated while my muscles relaxed from the wine, my inhibitions fading with the sunlight outside.

"What's...typical?" I asked, my voice low and reflecting all the suggestive thoughts of ways I'd like to see him spending his time. Most involved him being naked. One may have involved him touching his hard cock while I watched.

"I spend my time working, *playing*, doing the things that most do. But by far, I enjoy playing the most. As long as I'm in good company." His words were charged with sexual innuendo, and I felt my panties steaming up. I wanted to reach across the table, pull his mouth to mine, and maul him with my tongue.

"Aren't you getting tired of this?" I asked.

"Of what?"

"This. Of us dancing around what's really on our minds." I couldn't believe I was being so bold, but this man...this man...he was driving me crazy. I felt like I had to have him or I would die.

"That depends." He gave me a look so carnal

that it made my toes curl in my tennis shoes.

I took a sip of wine so my words wouldn't stick in my throat. It didn't work. "Depends on wha-what?"

"Charlotte, are you really ready for us to take things to that level? The level where we're being honest?"

Feeling my c-spot tingling and my nipples pearling up, my mind started to zero in on exactly what it was ready for: Him. Me. Naked on top of this table.

I bet he's packing something impressive down there, too. The way he carried himself was like a bold advertisement that said, "I've got nothing to hide."

I finished off my glass of wine and carefully set it down in front of me. "Yes. I am."

He leaned back in the chair, and from the way he sat, I could see a knee popping out from underneath the table. He had his legs wide open. Whether it was consciously done or not didn't matter. It made me think that he was hard as a rock under this table, his shaft straining against those black slacks.

"Prove it." His voice dropped into a raw seductive tone.

I pressed my thighs tightly together. "What would you like me to do?" I hoped he'd ask me to crawl over and help him out of those pants.

An image of sucking him while he sat in that chair flashed in my mind.

I had to stop torturing myself. I wasn't really going to do this. It wouldn't be fair to him.

"Answer a question," he said.

"What do I get if I do?"

"Anything you like," he replied.

I simply stared, trying to keep it together. "Anything" comprised a very long list of possibilities.

"Tell me why you really brought me here," he said.

The honest answer was different from the reason I now wanted him to stay.

"Okay." I cleared my throat, ready to tell him a small part of the truth, but not everything. "Ever since I could remember, my mother talked about these creatures who fed on us—humans. I think that got me started on being paranoid at a young age."

His emotional temperature didn't waver. "And how exactly do they feed?"

"She said they'd seduce a person and then somehow suck the life from them." Personally, I believed there was another sort of creature lurking out there that fed on fear.

"Like a demon of sorts."

"I sound crazy, don't I?" I asked.

He hesitated before answering, which wasn't a good sign. It meant that he likely wanted to think over his reply because he didn't want to insult me.

He leaned forward, his eyes intense and locked on my face. "I promised that I would help you, Charlotte. So whatever's out there, I will ensure you remain safe."

I believed him. Right down to the marrow in my bones. Which made me want him even more.

He went on. "And I thank you for answering my question honestly. Now," he rose from the chair, "let's get you tucked into bed. I understand that I am quite skilled at the fucking part."

My breath stuck in my throat. *Holy shit. This man is so damned...*

Our eyes locked and, as if he'd just read my thoughts, we rushed toward each other—me pushing up from my chair and it crashing to the floor; him bolting around the table, rushing toward me.

Our bodies slammed together and our mouths collided in a carnal combustion of lips mashing, tongues thrusting, breaths mixing into one giant mess of lust.

He spun us both around and popped my ass onto my dining table, pushing himself between my legs while his hands roamed wildly—my waist, ribcage, and breasts.

"Gods, you're so fucking sexy, Charlotte," he panted.

My arms locked around his neck, and I parted my thighs that extra inch to get him extra close.

Oh shit. Oh shit. I felt his hard, thick shaft press against my throbbing c-spot. I'm going to...*oh Godddd.*

He pushed his hard cock into me, through my pants, sending a spike of sensual shock waves through my core.

I reached for his belt buckle, intent on removing those few pesky layers of horrible fabric between us.

He gripped the hem of my shirt and pulled up, me only too happy to lift my arms and assist any way I could. I was generous like that.

The moment my shirt came off, he pulled his head away and forcefully yanked down the front of my bra, exposing my breasts to make way for— *ohhh...*

His lips parted, and my sensitive nipple entered the heat of his wet mouth as he sucked hard.

"Oh, God. That feels so good," I panted my words. The way his tongue massaged and lapped at the sensitive skin while his other hand—a lot rougher than I would've imagined—kneaded and pinched the other breast.

I ran my hands through that damned sexy hair of his, enjoying the softness as I held him to my chest.

The moment was over way faster than I wanted, but like me, he was not in leisurely lovemaking mode. He was on a mission.

He pulled back and started unbuttoning his shirt, staring at me with a hungry, unapologetic gaze as if to say he wasn't sorry for what he was about to do: fuck me hard.

His shirt dropped to the ground, and my jaw dropped right along with it.

Crap. I gasped in awe. *That's just not right.* Olive skin, lean ropes of hard muscles down his thick arms, well-defined pecs, and chiseled ripples covering his stomach that looked like two sets of stepping-stones leading down to the giant bulge in his pants. *Wait, what are all of those scars?*

It looked like he'd once been branded or sliced across his chest.

I would have to ask him about it later, because right now, I wanted him and he wanted me. Nothing else mattered.

He reached for the waistband of my pants, popped the top button and peeled them down quickly, my panties going along.

He took a quick look at the throbbing space between my legs and made a deep masculine groan. "Very nice."

I felt a little self-conscious having this man stare at a place I rarely saw myself, but thankfully, he looked excited by whatever was down there because he shoved his body between my thighs.

Oh, hell. My legs! I hadn't shaved them in weeks. "Sorry about the stubble," I panted.

"I fucking love stubble." He then pushed me back while reaching to free his cock from his pants. "On a woman, I mean. Specifically you."

Phew. "Thanks for clarifying."

"Any time."

His body leaning over me, his mouth now returning to mine, I felt the tip of his warm shaft pushing against my wet entrance.

Ohgod. He felt so good. I couldn't think or speak. I just needed him inside, pushing and sliding and grinding and cumming and—

My doorbell rang, and we both froze. My blood pressure hit the floor, and panic washed over me, extinguishing my brainless sexual urges.

He was still holding his rock-hard dick in his

hand, hovering over me and readying to thrust. He looked me in the eyes. "Does anyone have the key to your front gate?"

I shook my head no. But had my answer been "yes," this moment would've been welcomed; fate stepping in to stop me from what would've been a huge mistake. Seriously. What was wrong with me, almost getting it on with this man right here on my table? (A) I was old enough to know better than to have unprotected sex—even if Tommaso completely sucked all rational thought from my mind. (B) I did not want to get involved with anyone. My life was…it was…it was complicated. And I refused to let someone watch me go crazy like I had to watch my mother.

Anyway, getting back to the unknown person or persons at the door, my answer had been "no." No one but me had a key, so this was time to panic in lieu of berating myself for coming ridiculously close to getting fucked on my dining room table.

Speaking of fucking…

"Fucking hell," Tommaso said and quickly backed off, tucking himself away and zipping up, but not before I got a look at his equipment.

Holy crap. It was thick and long and I already felt its absence.

He looked at my naked body and the exposed flesh between my thighs, which I snapped closed, before he let out a quick sigh of regret and turned away.

"You stay right there," he barked, heading for the front door.

"Wait!" I called out, sliding from the table and reaching for my pants and shirt. "Don't open that!" Whoever it was had broken through the gate. I didn't even receive mail or packages here; it all went to my P.O. box downtown.

"Stay there, Charlotte," he commanded.

Like hell I will! I threw on my clothes inside out. Normally, I would've been running for the hills or my bedroom with the reinforced steel door and barred windows, but I felt uncharacteristically braver, stronger, and...well, protective. I didn't want whatever was out there to hurt him. But before I could get to that door and make sure he didn't open it, the thing swung wide open, the door itself blocking my view of whoever or whatever was there.

"Tommaso, no!" I yelled.

Still within view, he looked at me and held out his hand. "It's all right. It's for me."

Huh? "But who would—"

"It slipped my mind," he said hurriedly. "I told my colleague where to find me. I'll be right back." He disappeared outside, slamming the front door behind him.

What in the...? So they broke through my gate? I went to the window and pulled back the curtain.

Shirtless and looking very annoyed, Tommaso stood in my front yard—a rock garden with a few lonely palm trees—facing a man about his height who wore black cargo pants, a black tee, combat boots, and black baseball cap. Dark shades covered his eyes.

"Who the hell is that?" I whispered aloud. The man looked like some sort of special ops gangsta. And down my driveway was a black SUV pulled to the side. I could see someone in the passenger seat, but couldn't make out more than a large shadow.

Okay, so now I *really* was beginning to wonder what Tommaso did for a living.

I watched as Tommaso started yelling at the guy, and of course, I had to listen in, so I cracked open my window just in time to catch him saying, "We had a deal."

The man shook his head no and said something else, but I couldn't hear.

Whatever it was, though, Tommaso exploded. "That's bullshit! I need more time! And what about Ashli? She was supposed to be here. What about your side of the deal?"

The man shook his head no.

Tommaso did not look happy. He then flipped his middle finger at whomever was in the SUV. From my window, all I could see was a large hand coming out of the car, flipping the bird right back.

Tommaso turned away and headed back toward me. I expected the special ops guy to return to his vehicle, but he followed Tommaso right up to the porch, turned, and faced away like he was guarding the president.

What the hell?

Tommaso burst through the front door, his face a bitchy red. "You should go upstairs."

Now dressed, albeit sloppily, I jerked my head back. "Excuuuuse me?"

He snapped his fingers and pointed up the stairs. "You. Upstairs. Now," he repeated.

"Hell no."

He marched towards me, and I was too stunned to do much more than throw up my arms to keep him back. "What's wrong with you?"

"I can't catch a break. That's what's fucking wrong with me. As for you, I'm sure your interest in me is superficially grounded or due to the fact that you're tired."

Not true, but what was his point? "Meaning?"

"Meaning, I will watch over you as promised, and then we will go our separate ways."

Why had he turned on me like this? It made absolutely no sense. None whatsoever.

"Tommaso," I reached for his arm and squeezed, "what's going on? Who are those men outside?"

He blew out a long, angry breath that sounded more like a growl, looking embittered as hell. "They are not colleagues. These men are here to take me away."

I blinked at him. "Take you? Where?"

"To prison."

I stepped back. "You mean they're cops?"

He shook his head no. "Think of them like a very secret branch of the military."

Ohmygod. I covered my mouth. "So that guy is standing on my porch to make sure you don't run."

"More or less. Yes."

"Are you going, then?" I asked. I didn't want him to leave because... *Shit. Maybe he was right.* It suddenly dawned on me that maybe the attraction I felt for him was "superficially grounded" because he made me feel safe.

"I'm staying the night," he replied. "As promised so you can sleep. I'll be gone in the morning."

"Oh." I nodded with my eyes glued to the floor.

"And...my apologies for the way I spoke to you just now. This situation is not your fault."

"But what did you do?" I asked, wondering if he was dangerous in other ways I hadn't thought of. Bad ways. Like Uncle Chuck, Sadie's dad, kind of ways.

"The nature of this group—to which the men outside belong—is confidential. So I'll simply say that their rules are very rigid, and I've broken one. One that is fully outside of my control, but nevertheless, I have broken it."

I couldn't believe this. "There must be something you can do?"

He gave me a strange, almost hurt look before pasting on a superficial, charming smile and tilting his head to the side. "Sadly," he said, his voice filled with regret, "*I* am unable to do anything. My fate lies in the hands of another." He reached out and ran his thumb over my bottom lip. "And she is not ready to help."

"You mean Ashli?"

He dropped his hand and gave me a quizzical look.

I shrugged. "I may have been listening to some of your conversation outside."

He frowned. "Ashli is not your concern. Neither is my problem. Your only focus is going upstairs to sleep—it's the least I can do for you, and I'd like to do it."

Now realizing how tense my body was, I let my shoulders fall. It was sad, the two of us. It seemed that we both had huge ugly shadows lurking over our heads, poisoning our lives, but neither was great at trusting others to help. Me especially. I'd become so accustomed to thinking that anyone, anywhere, at any time could be one of those monsters. (Crazy, I know.) Tommaso was the first person I'd ever met who I knew for sure wasn't. The moment he looked at me, I thought, *This man would do anything to protect the people he cared about.*

But now it seemed our secret little worlds were about to separate us before we'd ever really started. Unfortunately, neither of us seemed ready to go to the next level. We just…weren't.

I drew a deep breath. "Thank you, Tommaso. I appreciate you doing this. Especially given your circumstances."

He bowed his head. "It's my pleasure, Charlotte." He then gestured up the stairs, and I obeyed, my brain already fading into a state of sleepless delirium. Today had been straw day. As in, camel's back.

With each creak of my blond-wood stairs leading up to the second story of my house, I again became acutely aware of Tommaso's strong, sensual presence and of how close we would be to a great place to utilize it. A few handful of minutes earlier, we'd been naked, our brains saturated with potent hormones, our bodies sizzling with need. Just thinking about it made me all tingly again.

No. No. Nooo... You and I already had this discussion, I said to myself. You are not going to drag some poor guy into your life. On the other hand, he was going to prison—so crazy. *Maybe he needs a good last romp?*

No! You put your dick back in your pants, Char! Put it. Back.

I don't have a dick.

You know what I mean.

Yes. And you're bonkers. Which explains why you're having a conversation with yourself.

"Charlotte?"

I realized I had stopped in my bedroom doorway and was staring into the abyss, but probably looked like I was staring at my bed in a dreamy fashion. I rolled my eyes at myself, cringing. *I must look desperate.*

"Yes?" I replied.

"I will stay downstairs."

"No. I mean—whatever makes you more comfortable."

He didn't respond, so I turned around to see his face. Though it was beautiful, no doubt, there was a strange ugliness shimmering in his eyes.

"Sure you don't want to tell me what happened?" I asked.

He lifted a brow. "I do not."

"Okay. I understand," I said dejectedly, too tired to fight anymore. I turned to head into my bedroom, and he grabbed my arm.

"Charlotte, it's not that I don't trust you; it's that

there are rules, and what sort of man would I be if I got you mixed up in something that would ultimately make your life more complicated?"

I bobbed my head. "You'd be a giant asshole."

He smiled shallowly. "Exactly."

"Well, thank you for not being one of those. Not a fan." I raised my hand a little.

"You're most welcome." He drew a breath. "And now, I think it's best if you get some rest. I will be right outside."

"Don't you want to sit here?" I pointed to a small white armchair in front of the fireplace in my minimally decorated room—light gray carpet, glass nightstands, white comforter on the queen-sized bed. The windows had French-style unbreakable security glass to let in the light but keep me safe.

"I think I've endured enough temptation for one night," he said. And it was the nicest rejection I'd ever heard. He was such a gentleman.

He continued, "Besides, there is a lovely chair in your hallway here, and I'd like to sit and enjoy my last evening as a man."

"Sorry?" I said.

"I meant *free* man."

God, this was awful. I understood that we were both in situations where being together was not possible, but I still wanted to help him. Okay, and wanted him too, as impractical as it was.

"Okay, then. I'll see you in the morning." He didn't look at me as he closed the door and left me standing in my bedroom all alone.

Jesus. I scrubbed my hands over my face. The

emotional roller coaster he put me on was unlike anything I'd ever experienced. We were like a bottle rocket, shooting high into the sky and then falling fast. Then repeating the maneuver once again with a wild wiggle in our trajectory.

I can't believe he's being taken to jail in the morning. And now that I thought about it, if he'd broken some big rule of this very "secret" group, why let him stay? Why not take him immediately? Something about all this was extremely suspicious.

He's definitely hiding something.

I walked over to my bed and sat, squeezing the edge of the mattress with an angry death grip, thinking how I wanted to finish what we'd started on that table downstairs. And I wanted to get him to open up. But the truth was, I was more of a danger to him—a train wreck waiting to happen—than anything else. Then there was the fact that in the morning, he'd be gone to some secret prison. The two of us equaled a zero-sum game.

I flopped back on my bed and laced my fingers over my stomach, staring at the ceiling.

Man, this is going to be a long nighhht... I felt my eyes slamming closed. My body had reached the end of its rope.

෴

Sometime in the middle of the night, I heard a rustling downstairs and then the pipes running water. I popped up from my bed, listening some more, it taking a moment for my brain to recall I had a man in my house.

Tommaso. I'd fallen asleep—so blissfully and completely nightmare-free, I might add—but now the facts were taking another run through my head, this time with a fresh brain. I couldn't believe that I wasn't fighting to help him. Must've been my fatigue. Because I was very much attracted to him, and I felt like we had a connection. More importantly, I felt like I could trust him. Then there was the fact that he was insanely beautiful. Maybe I didn't love him, but the right ingredients were there if we simply had more time together.

Not wanting to offend this gorgeous man and knowing I had a lot to say, I scrambled to my bathroom to rinse with mouthwash. I checked myself in the mirror—*oh, hair, why must you be so difficult?*—and decided to run a brush through my lopsided brown bob. It did no good.

Oh well.

Still wearing my inside-out golf polo from the club and khaki pants, I decided to peel those off and throw on this long red nightgown I had. It wasn't frilly or anything, but the knit fabric hugged my body all the way down to my calves and the spaghetti straps showed off plenty of neck and shoulders.

I tugged down the gown to show a little cleavage and then hurried down the stairs to find Tommaso. After hearing the running water, I figured he'd be in the kitchen, getting a glass of water or something, but that room was empty.

"Tommaso?" I stood in my kitchen, listening for

noises or his response. Nothing. *Where is he?* "Tommaso?"

Had he left already? *Oh, God. Please no.* I suddenly heard a small clank in the room behind the kitchen. It was my laundry slash storage room.

I headed straight for it and then flipped on the lights.

I really wished I hadn't.

CHAPTER SIXTEEN

Run faster, Char. Faster! I leaped up the stairs two at a time, the sound of heavy footsteps closing in on me. I got to my room, slammed the door shut, and then twisted the dead bolts. Yes, bolts, as in plural. Nothing except for a tank could get through that door.

Still, I couldn't take my eyes from it, feeling afraid that that...*thing* might still find a way inside.

Ohmygod. Ohmygod. I can't believe this. The air around that thing had been like... *Fuck. I don't know.* Some sort of dark cloud hugging its body. And the smell—dear God. It was like someone had sprayed eau de death in my laundry room. And when it turned its head, the eyes were like pits of blood red mixed with black. It was scarier than I remembered. So much scarier.

And the weirdest part of all? I could swear it was doing a load of laundry. Yes. Fucking laundry!

I pushed the heels of my palms into my eyes,

shaking my head. *That can't be right. It can't be.* But I wasn't dreaming. And I knew what I saw: That monster was shoving a giant bundle of whites—dirty towels and such that I'd left in a basket there—inside the machine.

Okay. This is real. This is happening. But what do I do? Tommaso was in the house somewhere, or... *Shit. He left.* They took him away, and now I was all alone.

"Charlotte?" There was a loud knock on the door. "Charlotte! Are you all right?"

"Tommaso?"

"Yes," he yelled through the thick door. I could barely hear him. "Why did you run into your room?"

"The monster is out there! Be careful."

"Char, there's no monster."

"Yes! There is. I just saw it in the laundry room."

"That was me. Open the door."

Him? But no, I knew what I saw.

"You were washing a load of..." My question faded away while my brain started to spin, like a teenager with a really fast car and nowhere to go, making little doughnuts in the dirt. Finally, it stopped and landed on "Duh!" Monsters didn't do laundry. I had been dreaming or sleepwalking or something.

I unlatched the door and Tommaso's tall, masculine frame filled the space, his dark eyes flickering with worry.

Oh, hell. That's definitely not a monster. Look at

him. He still had on his deep blue shirt. He looked sexy and immaculate and…

"Wait. Why were you doing laundry?" I asked.

He shrugged. "I don't actually know. Guess I needed something to do."

"Your last night as a free man, and you're washing my dirty towels. Strange."

"I cleaned your fridge, too."

"Wow. You really are perfect. And strange," I added.

"You think I'm perfect?"

"Maybe. Okay, yes. Even those scars on your chest are hot, because I'd argue that those made you who you are." Now more than ever, I wanted to know how he'd gotten them. I wanted to know everything.

He looked confused all of a sudden.

"What?" I asked.

He tilted his head just a little, studying me. "I'm wondering what would've happened if we'd met sooner."

I wasn't sure. The only thing I knew was that if things had been different and we had "worked out," he would've had to watch me slowly go mad—completely shitty for him. That said, "I wish I could have more time with you."

"Me too," he said, looking down at his perfectly polished, expensive-looking, black leather shoes. Probably Italian, like their owner.

God, what was it about this man that made me ache so hard? Sadness, longing, desire, and so many other things I couldn't articulate. I glanced at the clock over on my nightstand. "We have a few more hours until the sun comes up."

"And?" he asked.

"And I believe I owe you eight more answers." What I was really saying was that I did want to take things to the next level.

He flashed a subtle smile, and it was the first time I noticed that he had a dimple hiding underneath his manicured patch of black scruff.

"I would love to share these final hours with you."

CHAPTER SEVENTEEN

Stretched out by my side, my head resting on his arm, I snuggled into his chest and listened to the deep, melodic sound of his voice. He'd said he wanted to ask me questions, but instead, he began telling me about his life. He'd grown up in a small village in Italy near Napoli and had several brothers and sisters. They spent summers living in a dream—playing hide-and-seek in an olive grove, helping their grandmother and mother tend their grapevines, swimming in the pond by the house that had been in their family for ten generations. The house had survived every war, every political movement, every drought, and neighborly feud.

"Our land had history," he said, gazing up at the ceiling as we spoke. "It was drenched in my family's sweat, tears, and sometimes blood, but above all, it was filled with our love. Fifty acres, four hundred years, over one hundred and eighty Fierros were born on that land, worked that land, and died on that land."

That was a lot of Fierros. And the timber in his tone echoed a deep sense of pride in where he came from.

"Do you visit home anymore?" I asked, knowing that his family had all been tragically killed.

"No. Though I own and care for the estate, I can't go back. There are too many memories."

"And you're unable to sell it," I surmised. The land was too precious, filled with too much history.

"Yes."

"I understand."

There was a solemn moment that passed, and I wondered—selfishly—if he was feeling truly comfortable telling me all this. Because I wanted to hear it.

I inhaled deeply, savoring the spicy sweet scent of him passing into my lungs. "Will you ever go back?" I asked.

"I thought to someday, but now I might never be free again."

I looked up at him. Or his square jawline, really, and it made me want to pet his bristly stubble. *And his chiseled abs. And his... Focus, Char. Focus.* "They can't keep you forever."

He chuckled. "They can, actually. This is the disturbing part."

"What did you do?" Murder, treason, terrorism? To sentence someone to life imprisonment was a big deal.

"As I said, I broke a rule."

All right. "What kind of rule?"

"I'm not at liberty to say."

I sat up and looked down at the beautiful man stretched out on my bed, his dress shirt unbuttoned just enough to allow me to see a smattering of dark hair on his upper chest. I resisted reaching down to pet that, too. Because from there, it was a slippery slope, and I really wanted this: getting to know him. *Really* know him.

"How many people did you kill?" I asked, hoping he'd say none.

His forehead and dark brows crinkled. "Why would you say that?"

"You said you've been sentenced to life."

"Yes, but not for murder."

"Then?" I asked.

I could see him debating, but then he gave in. "After my family was murdered, I lost it. I decided to go out alone—without my team or any backup— to hunt a group of very dangerous men—these sort of religious fanatics. Only their religion is death and evil. We'd been tracking them for months, and I knew better than to break our protocols, but all I could think of was how I needed to take out my rage. Maybe what I really wanted was to die—I don't know. But after my family's funeral, I flew to Mexico alone—didn't tell anyone where I was going. And I was captured."

"Oh God. You must've been terrified," I said, trying to imagine what he went through.

"I wasn't. I was too angry to see straight. But had I stopped for a moment and thought about what I was doing, I wouldn't have simply gone running off on my own like that. But I did, and I thought I'd gotten lucky when I spotted one of these men in the jungle—not too far from where we'd caught a few of them one month prior. I tracked him to this strange temple covered in stone masks. And just when I thought that I finally had him, I realized it was me who was being hunted."

It was a trap. How horrifying.

Tommaso continued, "They took me to their caverns beneath the ruins, and they tortured me. Then they brainwashed me and made me do a lot of things I am not proud of."

I covered my mouth. "Crap. How awful."

"It was. Mostly because I was semiconscious when I acted on their behalf."

"So you *did* kill people?"

"I tried. And one of them was a woman I cared very deeply for and still consider a friend to this day."

"Wait. So your brain was hijacked. You tried to kill someone, but didn't. And you're going to prison forever because…?"

"It's complicated."

"So what? They can't do that to you. You're the most honorable, nicest, straightforward man I've ever met. And might I add, totally sexy. And gentlemanly. And you have excellent taste in clothes and cars."

He grinned. "I like you, Char."

"Well, good. Because I like you, too." He was the first person I'd ever met that made me feel everything good all at once—calm, safe, exhilarated, sexy, horny, nervous, and excited.

I added, "And if those ass-fritters don't see the truth about you, then they're the ones who deserve to go to jail."

"I do not disagree."

I crossed my arms over my chest. "Then?"

"Then what?"

"Then why aren't you fighting? Get a lawyer. Start an e-petition. Rally the masses to bring attention to these assholes."

"Dear gods, no. That would only make things worse."

How funny. He'd said "gods." I wondered what religion he belonged to.

"Tell me what would work, then, and I'll help you, Tommaso." And I meant it. I'd spend every dime I had.

A very strange expression swept over his face. It wasn't pain or hurt, or joy or happiness. If I had to guess, I'd say it was humility. As if my desire to help truly touched him.

"You okay?" I asked.

He nodded and reached both arms behind his head, staring up at the ceiling fan.

If he was okay, then why wasn't he speaking?

"Tommaso? Talk to me."

He didn't respond, and I so badly wanted him to. This conversation was more than just words—we were both taking a leap of faith, letting down our guards for just a few hours. It wasn't much, but it was something.

"Please?" I asked.

He pushed the heels of his large hands into his

eyes and then made a deep groan. "What you and I have is special, Charlotte. But it's a connection that will take time to nurture and grow. And not only am I an impatient man, I'm almost out of time. Which is why I'm struggling not to tear off your clothes and fuck you."

His bold but honest words made me choke on a nonexistent something in my throat. "I'm not sure I see the problem." About the fucking part, I meant.

He sat up and pummeled me with his intense gaze. "I do. Because it won't be enough. I'll have this memory of you and me. And missing what we could have had will turn my prison sentence into torture."

Goddammit. This couldn't be our path. I had to get him to see this little spark between us could grow into a flame or a giant bonfire or something really bright and possibly very, very hot, that it might actually heal the horrible pasts that haunted us.

"Ask me," I demanded.

"Ask you what?"

"Question number three or four—whatever. Make it anything you want."

"Charlo—"

"No. We had a deal. You help me sleep, and I answer. I've rested and you have no right to turn me into some welsher."

He laughed. "Anything I want?"

I nodded eagerly, hoping one of his questions would help him see that I might be worth fighting for.

"Yes."

"Okaaay. You asked for it."

"I did." I smiled, and his smile faded into a look that could only be described as lust. Pure unfiltered lust.

He reached behind my neck and pulled me to his mouth. I closed my eyes, savoring the warmth of his sensual mouth touching mine, and I had to keep myself from gasping. It was so unlike any kiss I'd ever had. This one felt...felt...fucking awesome! A drink of ice-cold lemonade on a hot summer day awesome. Crème brûlée that was perfectly creamy with a delicate crisp sugar crust awesome. Running on the beach with the wind whipping through your hair awesome. Perfect dress on sale that made you look ten pounds lighter, ten years younger awesome. Only this kiss was way better.

I threw my arms around his neck and poured my heart into it, hoping and praying that he would feel what I felt: We really needed to figure this out. What we had was just too good.

His tongue met mine and the soft heat of its strokes reached down inside me, touching every erotic inch. His breath whooshed out and entered my nostrils, the particles mixing in my lungs and entering my bloodstream. His warm hand gripped my bare shoulder and the heat of his skin absorbed into mine.

I never knew that one kiss could join two people like this. But in an instant, it had. He was now pulsing inside me, living and breathing.

Trying hard not to cry from the emotional

tsunami flooding every inch of my body, I pulled back and looked into his espresso-colored eyes, now noticing how they had flecks of turquoise. How strange. I'd never notice that before.

"Please tell me this is all a dream," I said.

He gave me a strange look. "Why, Charlotte?"

"Because if I find out in the morning that this is real, and it ends, it will be my worst nightmare ever."

He looked up at the ceiling again. "So close. Yet so, so far."

What the hell did that mean? "Tommaso? Please tell me what's going on." Because this thing between us was powerful. *I can't be imagining it.*

"No. Because you can't help me, Charlotte."

I laughed bitterly. "How the hell do you know that if you haven't let me try?"

He looked down at my hand and slid his into mine. "You're amazing. Completely and utterly amazing."

I didn't know about that. I only knew I was feeling a sense of clarity that had escaped me my entire life.

"Ask me another question," I pushed.

He glanced my way for a moment and smiled. "All right. Why golf?"

"It made me feel safer carrying a weapon at all times, and I didn't think a loaded gun was a good idea. But holding a nine iron? Hard to misfire a golf club."

"Why do you need to feel safe at all times?" he asked, quickly catching on to the real issue that plagued me.

I swallowed hard. This wasn't going to be easy, but if confronting my demonic memories would change our fates, then so be it. "I watched my mother beat a monster—this tall thing covered in black muck with ropes for hair. She beat it to death from that very window." I nodded toward the window to my right. "Her boyfriend at the time played golf, so she was really into it. I guess a club was the only thing she had handy. But then more came—I couldn't see how many, but they seemed to pop right out of thin air. And just as they began closing in on her, something came out of the dark and attacked one of them. It was this...*thing* with glowing orange eyes. They disappeared and haven't been back since—but they're always here." I pointed to my head. "Always."

Tommaso's face turned into a mess of turmoil. "Did the monster hurt you, Charlotte?" he asked, his voice so deep and low that I felt like it was vibrating my bones. "Did it?"

I drew a breath. "Yes."

"What did it do to you?" he sounded angry. Furious, in fact.

"It...it—"

"Tell me, godsdammit!" he yelled. "What did those evil fucking bastards do to you?"

My eyes teared up. I wanted to tell him. I did. But the truth was too ugly. Too horrific. And I couldn't understand why he was getting so damned angry.

He gripped me hard on my shoulders. "I'm not

asking. I'm demanding. You tell me, Charlotte. Or so help me!"

My head jerked up. How dare he?

"Or what?" I barked.

"Don't push me, Charlotte. Not now. Not after you opened the fucking can. Tell me!" he yelled.

"Or what? You'll do what they did? You'll hold me down and cut me and make me scream? You'll violate my body and kill everything inside me?"

He pulled back his head and stared with horror. "Please tell me that was just another dream. Please, Charlotte."

This was why I could never get close to a man. Or anyone. Not because I hated or blamed myself, but because I feared the way people might see me. Of course, if I did tell anyone, they'd only think I was insane.

Well, they can go fuck themselves. Because I wasn't crazy.

"It wasn't a dream," I said.

His eyes filled with so much rage, I had to wonder if I'd gone too far. Shared too much. He looked beyond pained. He looked like he wanted to tear the world apart.

"I am truly sorry, Charlotte, for what was done to you."

"Thank you, but I'm okay." Or I would be with time.

"I promise that this will never happen again." He stood.

"Where are you going?" I asked.

"To settle a few scores."

"Tommaso?" This made no sense. How would he know who to settle scores with? "What aren't you telling me?"

He reached down and stroked my cheek, looking into my eyes.

Holy shit! His eyes are turquoise. What in the…?

"Everything," he said. "I'm not telling you everything. Because I can't. But just know I will make sure this never happens again."

He turned and headed for the bedroom door. I sprang from the bed, following him. "Wait!" But he was already down the stairs, almost to the front door. "Tommaso! Please don't go."

He stopped with his hand on the doorknob, breathing heavily, but then jerked the door open and stepped into the darkness.

I then heard loud grunts and groans of a struggle. "Crap!" He was fighting with that soldier guy on the porch.

I ran down the rest of the stairs and flipped on the porch light, only to find no sign of him and an unconscious man on the ground.

Shit. Shit. Shit. What did I do?

CHAPTER EIGHTEEN

Lying in his extra-long, king-sized bed, Zac played a mental game of Pong where on one side of the net was Miss Grovel telling him he should go to Tula's apartment again—as he'd done yesterday after she'd quit—and beg her to open the door so he could administer the proper groveling. On the other side of the court was Mr. Idon'tgiveashitorneedanyonebecauseI'manawesome god.

Both players were scoring equal amounts of points, which made his dilemma all the more frustrating. *Oh, balls!* It was so unlike him to be on the fence. He was a deity. Strong. All-knowing. Deity.

Nevertheless, with Tula, he had no idea what to do. She'd gotten under his skin in a significant way, and the thought of her leaving him—*I mean, our agency*—upset him. Worse yet? It pissed him off that she thought so little of him. *Damned human!*

How dare she make me care about her opinion! What sort of womanly witchery was this? Huh?

He looked at his cell phone on his very manly stainless steel nightstand—*Godsdammit!*—and grabbed the thing. Yes, it was three thirty in the morning, but he would call her and set her straight. She had to come back to work. She had to stop making his life so difficult. Yes, that was what he would do! He would demand—as a god was entitled to do—that she stop making him feel all…miffed.

And squishy inside.

Above all, she had to cease making him care. How could he be expected to do his job and match couples, in order to end his banishment, if he was too busy worrying what one little lowly human female thought?

The nerve of her!

As Zac spewed his mental stream, phone in hand, it started to ring. He looked at the caller ID. *Ugh. Votan. The God of Whininess.*

"What?" Zac answered.

"Nice to speak to you, too, brother. Did I interrupt your nightly jerk-off marathon?"

"I wasn't jerking off, you jerk-off." He wasn't in the mood for that tonight.

"Well, I know how lonely you get since you're unable to keep a woman for more than five seconds—the approximate amount of time it takes for them to discover your pre-ejaculation issue."

What? Asshat. If fucking a woman for five hours straight and giving her ten or more orgasms in a row was considered an "early arrival," then so be it.

"Well," Zac said, "since I'm not a needy little bastard like you, and prefer to stay single, I'll be putting you at the top of my list when my switch flips to evil. I'm thinking I'll hog-tie you and throw you into a volcano. Twenty or thirty times."

Guy made an exaggerated sigh. "It's so cute when you have hopes and dreams and believe you've got a chance in hell of achieving them. Kind of like with Tula; I hear she won't even spit in your direction."

Okay! He crossed the line. Note to awesome deity self: smite Votan at earliest possible convenience. "What do you want, Votan?"

"Guy. My name is Guy, asshole."

"Okay, Guy Asshole. What do you want?"

"Shut your stink hole. We've got a situation with Tommaso. He took down my guard Brutus and ran off. I'm in pursuit, but his car disappeared once we got onto the highway. He was heading your way, back to L.A."

I knew this would happen. Why do they never listen? The gods had held an emergency conference call late last evening to discuss Tommaso's conditional parole situation. The original deal being that as long as Tommaso remained in control and wasn't a threat to anyone, Tommaso would remain free so he could track down his mate. He apparently found her, thanks to Cimil, but hadn't made an instant connection with this woman, Charlotte. Probably because she was Andrus's intended mate. Only Andrus had fallen in love with Sadie, Charlotte's cousin. The two women even looked alike. It was all very strange. However, if Andrus could hit the reset button and choose his own mate, then why couldn't Tommaso? *Stranger things are happening in the Universe.*

In any case, Tommaso had engaged with Charlotte at a small wine-tasting event last evening, but she did not appear to have any interest, which meant his transformation would not be halting. Then, according to the Uchben surveillance team, they witnessed Tommaso wandering off last night at the resort and plugging up quite a few holes on the golf course. With raw meat. Then he'd put shampoo in the resort's fountain and coated the steering wheels of all of the golf carts with strawberry lube.

Hehehe. Where did that man get so much lube? Zac would have to ask.

Anyway, Votan—*I mean Guy Asshole*—had called a meeting via telephone late last night after following Tommaso around and witnessing his behavior, to plead with everyone to give the demigod another day to save himself. It ended up being a debate that lasted until morning with Guy putting his foot down. "I am the God of Fucking Death and War, and Tommaso is *my* responsibility. And as such, I am accepting full responsibility and standing behind my commitment to endure any fate that may be handed down to him."

The point was, Guy had really stuck his neck out to help the one man who made him feel threatened—the only other man Guy's wife cared for.

Crazy. Because everyone knew that Guy only

did it for Emma, his wife. *He must love her a whole hell of a lot.*

But now, Tommaso had spent the entire day with Charlotte and had not shown signs of reverting back to normal—eyes were still black.

The leeway had expired. Tommaso had to be brought in before he truly hurt someone.

"So you want me to do what, exactly?" Zac asked Guy.

"I need you to call Andrus. He's the likeliest person Tommaso will run to for help."

Idiot. "Yeah, but Tommaso will know that we know that. And he wouldn't dare drag his friend into this." Zac might be an insensitive prick, but he knew enough to deduce that Tommaso was a guy with a very decent soul. *Poor bastard can't help what's happening to him.*

What! Who the fuck are you, man? Zac never felt sorry for people. Sympathy was for pussies. Zac punched himself in the face and cried out. *Damn, that hurt.*

"Zac? Are you tugging too hard? Remember, it's the only dick you've got unless you're counting your entire self." Guy chuckled.

"Fuck off, you wanker."

"No. You're the wanker. They should make a spinoff of that *Naked and Afraid* show, dedicated specifically to you. They'd call it Naked and Alone Again." Guy burst out laughing.

"Well, at least if I were married, I wouldn't allow my wife to pussy-whip me to death and make me run around saving her lover. What a moron."

"Tommaso is *not* her lover; they are friends," Guy growled.

Zac felt the surge of delicious satisfaction. He'd most definitely won this pissing match. *Only five hundred billion more to go*! That corresponded to the amount of time it would take for the Universe to end, by his own calculations.

"As always, it's been a pleasure, brother," Zac said, feeling Guy's anger radiate through the galaxy. "I will be sure to reach out to Andrus and warn him not to assist Tommaso should he come calling."

"Thank you. Have a good evening."

"I love you, too." Zac was just about to hang up, but Guy began ranting about how he did not love him. "Oh, but you do. Because I'm an awesome deity. You cannot help but worship—" Zac's phone had another call coming in. *Tula!* "Gotta go." He switched over to the incoming call. "Well, hello there, Tula. Come to grovel for your job back?"

"Mr. Zac, I think I messed up." Her voice sounded frantic.

"Now, now. I know you miss me, but—"

Tula broke in, "That Tommaso man called the agency's emergency hotline, sounding all upset and telling me it was a matter of life and death."

Uh-oh. "What did you do?"

"I gave him money. All of my cash for tuition."

"What? Why would you do that?" Zac scolded.

"Because he sounded so desperate, and he needed help."

Of course she would do that. She was too kind

not to help others, even when she shouldn't. He'd have to work on that with her.

"Do you have any idea where he went?" he asked.

"No, sir. He said he didn't want to be tracked. That he was going to die and take them sons of bitches down with him."

Zac pinched the bridge of his nose. "Great. Just great."

"Zac?"

"Yesss," he groaned.

"I'm sorry. I mean about earlier." Her voice was filled with a tenderness that made his heart ache.

"I'm sorry, too, Tula. Will you come back to work?" He thought that asking her the question might hurt his ego, but it didn't. It gave him a strange sort of satisfaction to let her know that he missed her.

"Yes, Mr. Zac. I will."

"Will you come naked?" Didn't hurt to ask.

"What? No! Goodnight, you giant…you giant god of pigs."

"See you bright and early." He grinned.

"See you bright and early."

The call ended and Zac felt absolutely glowy and gushy. *Damned human.* He smiled again. He so liked her.

He then quickly remembered Tommaso. *Crap.* He called Andrus and hoped the damned man would answer.

And for once, listen to me!

CHAPTER NINETEEN

My moment of hysterics was silenced by a loud knock at the front door. Tommaso was gone. Just...gone. And though I had no clue where he went or what making sure this "never happened again" really meant, I knew the situation was bad. Worse, there was no one for me to call. Nobody to ask for help.

I stumbled to the door and checked the peephole. *Please be Tommaso. Please be Tommaso. Please...I don't believe it.*

I jerked open the door. "Andrus?"

"Charlotte." He dipped his head of spiky black hair as I looked him over. His black leather pants looked like the centerpiece to a bouquet of weapons—multiple daggers, machetes, and other stuff—fixed to his waistband. *He looks like some giant deadly charm bracelet.*

"Where's Tommaso? He hasn't been answering my calls! Did those fuckers take him?" Andrus stormed past me inside, immediately spotting the huge man laid out on my couch. I had brought the soldier inside after telling him I was going to call 9-1-1. He'd groaned and insisted I just help him to his feet, which I did. But then he started flagging again, and I got him over to the couch. I sort of hoped he might wake up and tell me where to find Tommaso. Then the doorbell rang.

Andrus began shaking the soldier like a ragdoll. "Brutus! Where the fuck is he?"

Andrus knew this man?

Andrus slapped the man so hard that blood started dribbling from his lip.

The man moaned, but didn't wake.

Andrus continued, "You think you can take him, Brutus? Fuck him over like that and not have to answer?" Andrus drew his dagger and pressed it to the man's throat.

"Andrus! Put that down this minute or I swear I'll go demonic on your ass!" said a female voice.

I looked in the doorway and spotted...and spotted...a woman with long auburn hair whose face looked just like mine.

"Sadie?" I gasped her name.

She sighed with exasperation. "I'm so, so sorry, Charlotte. This is not how I wanted our reunion to go."

"You're really here," I muttered.

"Yes. And it's about twenty years overdue." She looked at Andrus, who still gripped the soldier in his hands. "Oh, for fuck's sake. Let poor Brutus go."

Andrus grumbled something in a foreign language—*Russian?*—and then let the man fall back onto the couch.

"What are you," I pointed to Sadie, "doing here with him?" I pointed to Andrus.

Sadie, who wore plum-colored leather pants and a black tank, looked down at her booted feet. "Charlotte." She drew a breath and looked at me. "I have so much to tell you. So much to say—I don't even know where to start."

Well, I knew exactly where to start! My mother told me that Uncle Chuck, Sadie and Nell's father, was a violent and "deadly" man. Then, after going to that party in L.A., with Sadie's crazy, wannabe vampire friends…well, no thank you! "I'm not interested in hearing about your depraved lifestyle and monster worshiping."

"I don't worship monsters, Charlotte. I *am* one of those monsters. But I don't prey on the innocent."

I stepped back. "This isn't funny. Get out."

Sadie crossed her arms over her chest, and I watched as her eyes turned a bright orange.

"Fuck!" I stepped back. Words could not describe how I felt.

I was about to make a dash for my clubs, but Andrus stepped in the way, blocking me from getting near them or the front door.

Sadie sighed. "We didn't cut our honeymoon short and fly thousands of miles just to come and hurt you, Charlotte. I promise."

"What are you?" I asked.

"I am a succubus. And before you laugh because

the name is so comical, I will tell you that my father is an incubus."

"You mean Uncle Chuck? The violent criminal?" I said.

"Char, he's not a violent man—"

"But then why did your mother run?" I asked.

"He loved my mother with all his heart. He tried to convince her he would never hurt her, but when she threatened to leave with me and Nell, he wouldn't have it. She then realized we were half-breeds and gladly left us behind."

Somewhere, beyond the present shock, the harshness of what she said was sinking in.

Sadie went on, "He and my very human and loving stepmother raised me and my sister, Nell, who has stayed human, by the way. But my father hurts no one—he's a dentist now."

"You *kill* people," I said, unable to believe this wild story.

"Sometimes, but mostly I dine on Andrus now. He's immortal."

"Immortal? Like vampires?" *Oh god. Those people at the party weren't pretending?* It was time to hit the "freak the hell out" button. "Then you're a monster." I looked at Andrus. "You're both monsters!"

"Charlotte," Andrus barked at me, "you may call *me* anything you like, but do not speak to my wife in such a manner."

Who did this guy think he was? "This is my house and you can shove—"

Sadie held out her hand. "It's okay, Andrus."

"No." He stepped toward me. "You may be my mate, Charlotte. But she is the love of my life."

"Mate? What are you talking..." I looked at him. Then I looked at her. Then I looked at him again. For some god-awful reason, I felt connected to him, but it was completely against my will. Almost like feeling hungry for something you knew might make you sick. That was the only way to describe it.

Ohmygod. He means "mate" just like in those crazy romance books I read! It dawned on me that something had been off when I'd first met him at that mixer. The moment I set eyes on him, I felt like I'd been drugged or hypnotized or entranced by him. I hadn't been able to explain it.

This is real. This is really happening. I walked over to my empty khaki couch by the fireplace and plunked down, my head spinning with so many questions.

"Charlotte? Say something." Sadie walked over and sat down next to me.

I instinctively wanted to move away, but then I caught a whiff of something. It was sweet and delicious and made me want to stay close to her.

Whoa! I jumped up. "You're doing some sort of voodoo crap on me." I made the symbol of the cross with my two fingers. "Stay back."

Sadie gave me a strange look with her big brown eyes. "Honey, I'm not going to hurt you. I promise. Otherwise the gods wouldn't let me roam free. Or my father for that matter."

"She speaks the truth," Andrus said. "I keep my woman well fed so she's never tempted." He flashed a flirty smirk at Sadie.

"Gods?" I looked at them both.

Andrus's gaze fell on his black leather biker boots for a moment as if debating.

"Well, if you're not going to tell her, then I will," Sadie said. "She has to know what's going on."

Andrus held out his palm and looked up at me. "No, I will tell you. I don't want the gods having any reason to punish you, Sadie."

"Punish her for what?" I asked, slightly panicked.

"It's on a need-to-know basis, but I agree. You need to know," Andrus said.

I waited to hear what other sort of bizarre crap would come out of their mouths next. "Well?"

He drew a breath. "There are fourteen gods and a host of other immortals—demigods, vampires, fairies, and such—that make up our community, so to speak. And it seems that something happened during the last near apocalypse."

Apocalypse?

He continued, "We are seeing cases of good immortals turning evil. Evil immortals are turning good. We don't know why. We don't know if this is permanent. All we know is that anyone who is mated seems to be immune."

"But you said I'm your mate—and we're not together," I pointed out.

"Yes. You are the woman the Universe chose for me. But my heart was already taken. Either way, Sadie is my soul mate, and we are safe. Tommaso, however, is not. And we must help him."

Tommaso. In all of this, I'd forgotten about him for a moment. "He lied to me, didn't he? You do know each other."

Andrus made a weird face, somewhere between a wince and a cringe.

"Yes," Sadie jumped in. "They're best friends."

I felt the room spinning. "And he knows about all of you and these...these...these gods?"

"Yes," Andrus said.

He lied to me. This entire time, he lied to me. "What is he? Some sort of demon or..."

"He is a demigod, like myself. A human infused with the light of the gods to make us immortal. But don't let the name fool you. We have no powers. Aside from our awesome manliness."

"Tommaso is a demigod?" I said aloud as the idea tried to sink in.

Andrus pointed to his eyes. "The turquoise eyes are a giveaway. Tommaso's eyes are dark brown because he's already turning into a Maaskab."

"What the hell is that?" I asked, forgetting to mention that I'd seen Tommaso's eyes turn a bluish green right before he bolted from my house on some mad revenge spree.

Andrus explained that Maaskab were some horribly evil sect of priests who worshiped the dark arts, descendants of the Mayans. Tommaso had been captured by them, brainwashed with their dark energy crap, and then cured by the light of the gods. Only his cure was reversing itself.

"They look a bit like those monsters from the Predator movies," Sadie added. "And they smell like roadkill."

Those were the men he told me about. The ones who'd captured him in the jungle. And he used to be one? And he was turning into one again? My blood pressure dropped so low, I felt like a vacuum had been created inside my body. Hollow. I felt hollow.

"He's...he's..." I shook my head from side to side. This entire time, I'd had the monster inside my house. He'd been in my goddamned bed! I almost slept with him! He'd washed a load of my laundry!

Oh, God. Oh, God.

"Out!" I screamed, popping up from the couch. "Both of you out! And take that guy with you!" I pointed to the unconscious man on my sofa.

"Charlotte, please," said Sadie. "Tommaso is like a brother to Andrus. We understand if you don't love him—that can't be helped—but at least tell us where he went or what happened."

"Love him? Love him? Wait—you weren't— he's wasn't—did everyone think I'd be his special someone?"

Andrus and Sadie just kind of stared at me.

"I could never love him. Never," I growled. "He's everything I loathe in this world—a monster—not to mention, he's a liar and completely untrustworthy."

God, I just couldn't believe this. The entire time, I'd been seeing only what I wanted to see: a beautiful man, perfect in every way, coming to rescue me from my misery. All the while, I had ignored what I already knew. He was dangerous. He was one of those things who'd come into my home and hurt me.

"Charlotte," Andrus said, his voice low and stern, "Tommaso is not a monster. And he needs our help. Where did he go?"

"If I tell you what I know, will you leave and promise never to come back?"

There was a long moment of silence. Finally, "If that's truly what you want, Charlotte," Sadie said with a sadness in her eyes.

But there was no one sadder than me. My mother had gone crazy because of "people" like Sadie. And now, to learn there were real live gods on the planet? Where were they when she needed help? Where were they when I'd been attacked? I wanted nothing to do with any of this.

"I've never wanted anything more," I replied, pointing at the front door, urging them to leave.

"Okay. But if you ever change your mind—"

"I won't. I was attacked when I was nineteen by one of those things. I told Tommaso about it and he ran off, saying he wanted to settle a score." Now I knew he was simply going to be united with his flock of rotten, evil bastards.

Andrus whooshed out a breath and scratched the back of his head.

"What?" Sadie asked Andrus.

"The Maaskab were basically exterminated," he replied. "Cimil said they'd only left a couple alive in case they ever needed help with dark energy. But since the whole postapocalyptic-good-versus-evil mishmash, I know one of the surviving Maaskab is now her nanny. Still disgusting and smelly, of course, but incredibly nice. Who knows where the other one is or where Tommaso went?"

What in the... "Out! Leave. All of you. Go figure out your Satanic Scooby mystery somewhere else."

Sadie stood from the couch and was about to speak but snapped her mouth closed. Good choice. Because there wasn't anything she had to say that I wanted to hear.

I watched the two leave, Andrus carrying out the soldier by throwing him over his shoulder as if he weighed nothing. *Muscly show-off!* Part of me wondered why I'd ever felt so hurt when he'd rejected me at first sight, but now I didn't seem to care. All I could think of was Tommaso. How I'd trusted him implicitly. How he'd lied to me. How I couldn't see that he was one of those despicable creatures inside.

I slammed the door shut and turned to head to my kitchen. *Vodka. I needed vodka.*

My doorbell suddenly rang, stopping me in my tracks. *Seriously? What part of "go away and never come back" don't they understand?*

I returned to the door and yanked. "I wasn't joking when I said—oh shit! No, not you!"

CHAPTER TWENTY

The moment my mind registered the fiery redheaded nut bag standing on my porch, wearing shiny pink Spandex pants and a "Let's Poke the Bear" shirt—with a picture of a bear bending over—I tried to slam the door shut. "Oh, hell no!"

But her pink, jewel-encrusted platform flip-flop wedged into the door. "Ow!" she yelped, "That was my foot, you tart!"

"Go! Leave! You are *not* welcome here," I grunted as she pushed the door open with her body, and I tried to keep her out.

"Fine. But I wouldn't recommend staying in there alone with Minky. She hasn't fed yet."

"Who's...Minky?" I continued pushing and grunting.

"My unicorn. She's invisible, but trust me, that doesn't make her any less dangerous."

What the fuck? "Okay, Crazy Face, you're definitely not coming in!" I almost had the door shut. The little five-foot woman was no match for me—five-five of solid golfing athlete, emphasis on the solid.

"Minky, bite her!" Cimil commanded through the door.

Suddenly, I felt a puff of hot air on the back of my neck. "Gah!" I let go of the door and jumped back, stumbling toward my clubs. I quickly grabbed the putter and started swinging it from side to side. "Stay away!"

Something grabbed the club and then it disappeared into thin air.

"Oh! Just great!" Cimil spouted from the doorway. "Now I'm probably going to have to take her to the vet again. And, of course, it will have to be a new one because she ate the last poor woman. Minky, what did I say about eating sports equipment? Huh?"

I heard a little huff and a neigh.

With my back pressed against the wall, my eyes frantically searching the room for...well...I didn't know, it began to sink in: There was a fucking invisible unicorn in my house.

Like someone had pulled a black curtain over my eyes, I felt my body going limp.

"Hey, Char-Char! Waky, waky!" said a voice and then something warm and wet slithered over my cheek.

I felt too dizzy to open my eyes.

"Okay, Minky. I heard you," said the woman.

"But you may not nibble on her toes. Or cheeks. On either side of her body. Go outside and forage. I think I heard some clucking out there."

Chickens. My chickens. I cracked my eyes open, only vaguely aware that I was lying on my tile floor in the foyer. With my shoes off. And my pants off.

"Don't you dare touch my chickens," I grumbled. "And where the hell are my pants?"

"Under your head, silly. I had to put something there to stop the bleeding. Looks like you had a boo-boo that reopened when you fainted and fell. BTW, nice tile. Not even a crack." Standing over me, Cimil batted her big turquoise eyes at me.

Turquoise. They're turquoise. That means she's one of them! I popped up, feeling woozy, but lucid enough to run. And defend my chickens. From invisible unicorns.

Unfortunately, the throbbing in my head had its own plans. Bad ones.

I threw my hands over my eyes. "Owww...shit. I think my brain is dented."

"Oh, you shut up. And get up. We have some serious bull-cocky to chew."

I looked up at her, my head pounding away. "Are all immortals as mental as you?"

"Fuck no! I'm seventy Gs old and counting. Even my pubes are wacky. All curly 'n' stuff. It's downright irritating."

I cringed as my mind produced an unwanted image of the curly carpet to match her crazy red drapes. *God, please kill me now. Runaway boulder. Swarm of African bees. Misdirected arrow from*

Daryl's bow. Anything!

"Please stop talking," I groaned my words.

Before I could blink, Cimil plucked me from the floor by my upper arms and stood me up with my toes barely touching the ground. I quickly realized that the earlier battle at my front door had been a show.

"All right, missy," she said, "you need to listen close and listen good, or you will spend the next eternity scraping gum off of the bottom of tables in a federal penitentiary. I'll let you know which one after I decide, but there are many with gum problems. And the eternity after that will be served cleaning Minky's room, and let me assure you, the task puts hair on your chest!"

She glanced down at her cleavage, and I noticed a few little red hairs sticking out.

"Dear Lord, what or who are you?" *Aside from completely bat-shit crazy.*

She released me, and I leaned against the wall, thinking about making a run for it.

"Take one step toward that door, and I stop playing nice god. Get it?" she growled, guessing my thoughts.

Oh shit. "You're a god?"

"Goddess of the Underworld," she dipped her head, "at your service. Actually, I'm in hot water for nearly ending the world and constantly lying to my brethren, so my powers and title have been given a time out while I pay penance. Anywhoodles, the dead still speak to me and give me makeup tips and cookie recipes and the like, but without my powers, it's difficult to sort through all of the noise."

She was a goddess. A real live goddess. With a freaking unicorn. And she was standing in my foyer, rambling about…well…I wasn't sure. I only knew I really, really wanted this interaction to end. Despite being beautiful in a very surreal sort of way, she was scary as hell. And frankly, I wasn't one hundred percent sure I wasn't dreaming again.

"Oh, okay." I nodded my throbbing head. *Ow.*

"Good. Glad we got that all straightened…" Her voice trailed off, and she looked up at the ceiling. And then she just sorta kinda stared at it, almost like she was watching a tennis table match, her big turquoise eyes darting back and forth.

"Umm…are you all right?" I asked, thinking that if she didn't reply, it might be a good time to make my exit: grab my cat and chickens and then haul ass.

Some pants would be good, too.

"Oh yeah…" she said with a dirty, phone-sex voice tone. "Auntie Cimi is doin' great. Yes. Get it right there. That's the spot. Harder. Slap it harder!" Her eyes continued toggling. It was so, so disturbing.

I sidestepped toward the front door, and her head snapped down in my direction.

"Hey. Where do ya think you're goin'? Huh? Huh?" She leaned in and popped up on her tippy toes, putting us nose to nose. "Huuuuh?"

I held up my hands in surrender. "Nowhere. I'm going absolutely nowhere."

"Good. Because despite what Tommy thinks, I like the kid. I mean, yeah, he has his disgustingly good side, but don't we all?"

I shrugged. "I-I really can't sa-say."

She poked her index finger into my breastbone. "Take your Uncle Chuckie, the incubus, for example; did you know he started turning good decades ago? All on his own? Now," she dropped her finger and perched her fist on her bony hip, "do you have any idea why a thousand-year-old demon who enjoys killing women by orgasm would hang up the old handcuffs—and rope, whips, ticklers, and lubes—to become a dentist and loving father?"

Huh? "Uh. No. Can't say that I do."

"Love, chicky. He fell in love."

"How lovely?" I said, still completely unsure of where this was all going.

"Yes. It truly is. Because if there's hope for a selfish demonic fucker like him—get it? Fucker? He's an incubus who likes to…" Cimil noticed I wasn't laughing. "Never mind. My point is: If there's hope for him, there's hope for anyone."

I nodded slowly. "How lovely…again?"

"Yes!" Her finger shot up. "It is. Because even after Chuckie's first human wife—his mate—ran out on him and his daughters, rejecting him when he finally told her what he was, trampling on his poor sulfuric-smelling demonic heart, he made a choice. He wasn't going to give up on the life he dreamed of. He wasn't going to let anyone but himself define who he was. Not genetics, not his dark and very kinky triple-X urges, and most certainly not his dietary preferences. He took the bull by the dangly, sticky bits and found a woman who loved him for who he was and wanted to share his dream."

I had no idea if her story was completely made up about Uncle Chuck, but it didn't feel real. None of this did.

"That's a very nice story. May I go now?" I asked.

"Not even close, chica. Oh, and by the way, you should thank Uncle Chuckie. He's watched over you since the day that Maaskab attacked you."

"He's watched over me," I repeated skeptically.

"Oh, yes. That man has racked up some frequent-flier miles. Comes out at least once a week to check on you."

"I don't believe you."

"No one ever does." She shook her head. "But that doesn't change the fact that he's always there, lurking in the shadows, watching over you. I'm surprised you haven't noticed." She bent forward just enough for her to see outside my front door. "Yo! Chuckie!" she screamed. "How's it hanging?"

A little click went off inside my head. Could he be the thing out there I'd been sensing? "Is he here right now?"

"Nope. I was just being polite."

Huh?

Cimil continued, "And so should you."

"Should what?"

"Be polite, child! Never ever get on an incubus's bad side. Hint: They love fruit baskets. With chocolate inside. And their egos are very fragile—I suggest you thank him for personally peeing on every inch of the yard around the house."

Dear God. "Why would he do that?"

She rolled her eyes. "To keep away any bad spirits, vampires, demons, and unwanted solicitors. Demon piss is a great repellent."

I crinkled up my face. "I'll take your word for it." *Now please leave. This is all too much crazy to take in one day.*

Cimil's jaw dropped. "You. Don't. Believe me."

"Well, I, uh—"

"Fine, but believe this: Your aunt Claire told your mother about Uncle Chuckie and put the fear of demons and monsters into her. From there, your sweet mama thought of nothing else, and there's a funny thing about thinkin' too much."

I felt an unwanted pearl of wisdom coming my way.

She continued, "When we think of something constantly, we attract it. I mean, look at me. I constantly think of my awesomeness and look how awesome I am!"

Yeah, you're oozy with it. "So you're trying to tell me that my mother chose to go mad?"

"No! You're totally missing the point! Why are humans so dense?" She took a breath and whooshed it out. "She kept thinking about monsters and ended up attracting them. Ask and the Universe shall deliver."

"So it's her fault I was attacked?" *What a load.*

"No! Gods! That was the Maaskab's fault, you silly squirrel. He made a choice to be an evil bastard, and as I just explained, he could've chosen to be something else. Just like dear old Uncle Chuckie. Have you not been listening?"

I nodded and then switched to shaking my head. "I'm not quite sure."

"No matter what the Universe plans for us, we all have free will. We are the captains of our own crunch! The dicks in our dictatorships. The French in our ticklers—"

"Okay. I get it."

"You ain't got *squat,* sister!" she said. "Uncle Chuckie needed someone to feed his good side, to help him see another possible future. And you were supposed to feed Tommaso the same way. But noooo…you had to go and feed his angry side, didn't cha?"

"Now I'm really lost."

"Why? It's perfectly clear to all of us!"

I looked around the room. "All of who?"

"Us. Me." Cimil pointed to herself and then to the corner of my living room, just through the doorway. "And all of them."

I didn't want to ask. So I didn't.

She shook her head, tsking at me. "Tommaso ran off to confront the Grand Poobah, the big evilness himself. The master of everything dark and unwholesome and cruel, including books that end in cliffhangers. Ick." She made a sour face.

"He's going to fight Satan?" I mean, if gods existed, then that meant he was real, too. Right?

"Satan?" Cimil cackled toward the sky. "That big pussy? Heck no! Satan sits around all day knitting little horned caps and coming up with ideas to get kids to vape e-cigs. He's a total loser. And spineless as a pickle. Get it? Spineless as pickles?"

"Yes?" I didn't get it at all.

"Awesome. Anywoo, I'm talking about the king of the Maaskab."

"There's a king." That sounded not-wonderful.

"Oh yeah. And he's so powerful that he got my brother Chaam, the God of Male Virility, to join Team Scab for a while. Of course, Chaam doesn't really remember much and thinks it was just some evil fluke; but trust me, Mr. Ass is always behind the scenes pulling the strings."

"Mr. Ass?" *Oh, God.* Her rant just kept getting weirder and weirder with no apparent point or end in sight.

"His real name is Ta'as, which I believe translates to 'banana' in Mayan, but don't quote me on that. Without paying me five dollars first— everything I say is copyrighted. But once Mr. Banana, there, recruits a few new head priests, he's going to start regrowing his army, and then we'll all be knee deep in Scabs again."

"Why don't you do anything about it? You're a...a..." I found it very difficult to say the words. "A god."

"(A) I'm Cimil. I can't help cheer for Team Evil. And Team Good. It's funner that way. (B) if the Universe is flip-flopping and I kill the most evil Scab of them all, then I'd really be killing the future nicest person on the planet, and then where would we be?"

"I really, *really* don't know," I groaned.

"Exactly. Of course, Ass Banana does have his eye on a special someone—one of my sisters, if you can believe that—and if he decides to give her his evil crusty heart, then he won't flip-flop, and he'll stay evil. So he probably should die."

"So what are you saying?" I asked.

"Haven't you been listening?"

At this point, I was so lost by her random story that I just wanted it to end. "Yes. Every word."

"Good. Now, I expect you to go and fix this mess you've created ASAP." She poked me again in the chest, and with my back to the wall, it really hurt.

"Ouch!" I rubbed the spot. "Please don't take this the wrong way, but putting this 'mess' on me is a huge stretch."

"Is it? Is it really? You were supposed to be mated to Andrus, and for whatever reason, his heart and soul weren't on the same page. The heart won, leaving you mateless. But then, the Universe in her infinite nincompoopery decided to give you another path to happiness. You didn't jump on it, and now look what happened? Chaos! You have twenty-four hours to fix it or that's that and I can't be held responsible."

Something told me that responsibility, along with sane behavior, was something she never held.

"Okaaay. What exactly do you want me to do again?" I was terrified to hear the answer, but I had to ask.

"You must go save Tommaso. And it must be

you and *only* you. Alone."

"I won't even ask why because I have a strong feeling you're not going to tell me. That said, I don't love him. He is one of those *things*."

"This is what I was afraid of." She tsked and shook her head at the floor.

"What?" I immediately regretted opening my mouth. I should've just kept it shut so she'd leave.

"I was afraid you'd turn out just like your old aunt Claire, who 'til this day is hiding in a cave in Peru."

"Aunt Claire is still alive?" No one had seen her for decades.

"If you call eating bugs for sustenance and not having access to the show *Outlander*—or *The Carbonaro Effect* or *John Oliver*—being 'alive,'" she made little air quotes with her fingers, "then you've got bigger problems than having Tommaso's death on your hands."

"Death?" I croaked.

"Yes. He's going to try to take Ass Banana down. Not a chance! Ass will squash him like a bug. Unless Tommy simply becomes Ass's second Mmm—Ass—Kab in command—get it? Maaskab? Ass? Oh, fuck you—that was funny. Anygiggles, I highly doubt, given that the Maaskab murdered Tommaso's family in cold blood, that he'd let that happen. He'd rather go down fighting than go back to Team Scabby."

The Maaskab murdered his family? All of them? And now he was becoming one of those beasts?

Ohmygod. My heart felt like it had sunk to the

bottom of the ocean. Everything finally made sense—his desperation to keep from flipping. The way he'd avoided telling me what was happening. The reason he'd felt so upset and run out after I'd told him what they'd done to me. He had a very deep emotional scar running through him. But here I'd been feeling disgusted by Tommaso and what he was becoming when the situation for him was unfathomably worse.

I ran my hands over the top of my head, pushing out a dread-filled breath. "God, this is so messed up."

Then the truth hit me like a bolt of lightning: Yes, my story was horrific, but I had been nineteen at the time, and here I was seven years later, letting that moment define and control me when what I should've been doing was taking back my life and putting the past where it belonged. Because, at the end of the day, the past no longer existed and never would again. Yet I'd single-handedly fueled the memory of that one night and kept it alive.

This was what ruined my mother: the not letting go. And it was ruining me. I kept seeing my entire world through the lens of one ugly, horrific night when really, there were so many beautiful moments, thousands perhaps, I could've focused on instead: The long hot summer days I spent at my best friend Mike's house when we were little. His mother watched us while mine worked. He didn't have a pool or air-conditioning, so we'd invent our own ways to escape the heat. My favorite had been filling up trash bags with the hose and trying to sit inside them without spilling the water. There was also the very special relationship I'd had with my mother and all the times we laughed together even when we got angry. But it was her laughter that always let me know she was still there for me. I loved the way she laughed. I could've even focused on the fact that for the past four years, I got up every morning and went to a job where I got to breathe fresh air and gaze out at the stunning desert mountains. People paid thousands for one day of what I got paid to do every day.

I'm such an idiot.

How could I have allowed myself to blame Tommaso when he was just as much a victim as anyone? He'd had his entire family wiped off the map, savagely murdered, and now he would be forced to essentially become the thing that killed the people he loved.

"You think he'll become this...this Ass's minion if he's not killed?" I asked Cimil.

"Tooootally. He'll then be the second most powerful A-hole in the world. And, despite being a sadistic A-hole myself, I am a god. Hardwired to protect you shitty creatures, so I *will* have to kill him." She grinned and held out her bony hands. "With my bare Minkies. Unless it's Wednesday, then it's actually Minky's turn to kill."

I seriously didn't understand what was happening. And I wasn't referring to Cimil's verbal trip around the wacky-go-round. I actually felt a horrific urge to protect Tommaso. I didn't want her or that Ass man to touch him.

That said, "What can I do?"

She shrugged. "Besides rescue him? Completely on your own because the Great and Powerful Cimi has prophesied this is the only way for a successful outcome?" Her mouth scrunched to one side. "How the hell should I know?"

Seriously? "Because you're a goddess."

"Wrong! I have zero powers. So you're totally solo on this mission."

Why did I get the distinct impression she was lying to me? "Can you at least tell me where to find him?"

"I could, but I won't. It's no fun that way."

"Wow," I said. "Suddenly, this fucked world is all making sense."

"Oh, boohoo." She fake fisted her eyes. "You try being alive for seventy thousand years with humans and their clusterfuckery, in this giant clusterfuckopolis, and try not to get clusterfuckafied!"

Dear God—sorry—dear gods, *please help me to not slap this deity.*

"Cimil, I know you can probably squash me like a ripe melon, but I swear to gods, or the Universe or whatever clusterfuckedupness you subscribe to, that if you don't tell me where to find Tommaso, I will turn to the dark side and eat your damned liver!"

She grinned. "That a promise?"

"Yes."

She made a little clap. "Yay! But I still won't tell you where he went. Because I don't really know if I know. You know? The master of the Maaskab is very skilled at hiding his presence. I recommend you drink heavily and replay every conversation you've had with Tommaso until you figure it out."

Nice. Wow. Great advice. "Please leave now."

She jerked back her head. "Well! I never!" She stomped out the front door. "Come, Minky."

"And give me back my putter," I griped.

I watched a twisted piece of metal drop from thin air to the floor. "Sick," I winced.

"Yup." Cimil reached into her pocket and handed me a card. "Call if you need anything. We're always here to help."

I slowly took the card. "Thanks." Of course, the card was blank.

"See you at the wedding. Or at Tommy's execution. Either way, I'll be wearing pink." Cimil sauntered away in her tight pink pants.

Someone needs to strangle her.

As for me, it was time to crawl out of the ugly hole I'd been living in and make a stand. Not just for Tommaso, but for myself.

Oh, crap. I have to do this alone.

CHAPTER TWENTY-ONE

I'd never been to Mexico, I did not speak Spanish, and I had no idea if I would live through the next few hours. Or this massive hangover. Turned out that having a few drinks and combing through my conversations with Tommaso, as Cimil suggested, had sparked one and only one idea as to where he might have gone.

Might.

The only thing I knew for sure, as I drove through the jungle in a thirty-year-old Jeep with bald tires, was that this insane trip to find him was just as much about me as it was about him. I needed him to triumph. And I certainly didn't want him dying. But also, I had to confront this darkness living inside my head. I'd wasted too much of my life feeling afraid.

Yes. This was a bit extreme, and I'd be the first to admit it. But my head was in a very jumbled place, searching for an end to my self-perpetuated nightmare.

So. If I did happen to find Tommaso and find him alive, what was my plan?

I didn't believe that loving him was a magical antivenin. Cimil said that all I had to do was help him imagine another future—a good one. Uncle Chuckie forged his own from there, and so could Tommaso. So while I couldn't promise him love, I could promise my friendship and understanding. Okay, and possibly some humping. But only if he asked nicely and apologized for lying to me. *Jerkface.* But I did like the man. I mean to say, I was attracted to him. I just wasn't happy about him deceiving me, even if I understood why and sympathized with his situation.

Still, I was here. Putting my ass on the line to help him because it seemed that I was the only one who could. Either that, or Cimil just wanted to watch me suffer and die terrified and alone.

I continued down the two-lane road, driving toward the only spot I could think of where Tommaso might be. He'd mentioned that he'd been taken to an underground cavern somewhere near a temple covered in "masks."

After a quick surf on the Internet, I had learned there was a place called "Kohunlich" that was thought to have been a stop on a Mayan trade route sometime around 200 B.C. then later built into a small city with some pretty dang impressive irrigation canals and temples, one of which was dedicated to the Sun God. *One of Cimil's siblings, perhaps?* Anyway, it just so happened that Kohunlich was home to the Temple of the Masks and that there was a cenote, or spring, that ran right underneath it. If the site looked anything like the pictures I'd found of other underground cenotes, there would be caverns there, too.

A cold shiver sliced right through me, despite the warm, muggy day—much too warm for October, in my book. Add to that, I'd only packed some cargo pants and a sweatshirt, I was sweating like crazy.

"Uncle Chuckie...please give me strength." So strange, right? Uncle Chuckie, my demonic, incubus relative had suddenly become a symbol of beating the odds. But as Cimil had said, he'd protected me. Okay, he'd peed all around my place—weird—but nevertheless, he'd been trying to help.

I kept going down the small highway, past the main road leading to the archeological site, about another kilometer, and then turned down a narrow dirt road that cut through the jungle. It was supposed to lead me to a spot about a quarter mile downhill from the ruins. From there, the guide at the Jeep rental slash self-guided adventure tour place told me I'd find a hiking trail leading to the only cenote he knew of in that area.

"But keep an eye out for jaguars," he'd said, scratching his long flaming red beard, sounding almost amused by the thought of me getting eaten. "And definitely bring a walking stick." Of course, he had a giant stack of them for sale for fifty bucks, right next to the bug spray, weird unicorn-themed baseball caps, and trail maps. *Self-guided jungle tours, my ass.* They really should've named their place "You're on Your Fucking Own, Buddy."

But girls in a hurry to rescue hot men from certain death didn't have the luxury of being choosy. There weren't many four-wheel-drive car rental options in this neck of the woods about forty miles from the border of Belize.

I stopped the Jeep at the end of the bumpy road, the lush green tree canopy so dense that only a smattering of sunlight filtered through to the damp, leaf-covered jungle floor. As I stepped out, there was an unexpected stillness all around me. Not even the wind was blowing.

The hairs on the back of my neck turned to quills. *Ohmygod. Why am I doing this?*

Clearly, because I had to, but that didn't make me question my sanity any less.

I pulled out my Maruman Majesty driver from my golf bag. It was a beauty. Heavy, gold plated, and could knock the block off anyone—human or otherwise. Yes, I'd brought my clubs along. I wasn't about to go in empty-handed, and I didn't think showing up at the airport with a gun was such a great idea—not that I owned one. I also couldn't bring just one club, because that would look weird. So I'd brought them all. Hey, maybe if I was lucky, I'd actually get in a few rounds. There were plenty of resorts up and down the Maya Riviera.

Wishful thinking, Char.

I slipped on my backpack containing bottled water, a map, and a few other essentials, and started down the trail. This was it. Somewhere around here had to be caverns, and if I was lucky, they'd be the ones Tommaso had told me about. Would Ass Banana—*what a name*—be here, too? I didn't know.

"It's time to face your monsters, Char," I muttered to myself just as a giant bug landed on my face. I screamed hysterically, swatting it, and it fell to the ground, hissing.

"Gah! Oh, hell no!" It was a cockroach the size of an iPhone. I could've sworn that the thing looked right at me and laughed. "Go away! Shoo!" Just as it skittered under a leaf, I felt something tickling the side of my neck. Staring at me from my shoulder was the world's biggest spider. Or scorpion. Or both?

"Holy shit!" I flung the thing off me and stumbled back over a rock, falling flat on my ass. Suddenly, the ground beneath me gave way, and I started falling.

ॐॐ

I used to be afraid of the dark. But as I fell toward what promised to be the center of the Earth, I decided that wet, slippery holes collapsing in on themselves as you clawed the muddy walls, hoping for anything to grab onto, were way, way shittier.

Yes, good old darkness now officially rocked.

This did not.

Neither did reaching the end of my downward journey. Because when my body fell through the ceiling of an underground cavern, landing in a cold, dark pond filled with muck and bubbles that smelled like rotten eggs, well...I just about died. Literally. The back of my head smacked on a rock a few feet below the surface, reopening my wound for a second time.

"Gah!" I yelled as my head popped up from the surface, the taste and smell of sewer-scented water sticking to my nostrils and mouth. I gagged and spit, trying to ignore the warm fluid running down my neck from the back of my head. Blood.

Shit. Shit. Fucking shit! Where am I? I spun around and noticed a crack in the ceiling on the other side of the giant, fifty-foot-high cavern. The light beamed in like a knife, slicing through the chill and blackness, but only giving off enough illumination to let me see that particular section. The rest of the place was completely obscured.

Okay. Fuck monsters. And scary mud holes. This place was way worse. Just the thought of what might be lurking beneath me in the black water made me want to wet myself.

Frantic, I swam toward the light, hoping and praying that there was a way out of this hellhole. At the very least, I'd accept a large rock to stand on or anything that would allow me to get out of the water.

Closing in on the patch of light glimmering on the water's surface, I began to make out a little beach about twenty yards beyond that, barely visible in the darkness.

I swam for it. *God, I promise never to whine again about being scared. Just help me get out of this. I'll donate all of my money, adopt some real children who need a home—not just the bald, ugly chickens or malevolent cats no one wants. And, most of all, I promise to strangle Cimil.* I sensed that I was not the first person on this planet to end up in a bad spot because of her.

Finally, I reached the sandy bank and crawled out of the water, panting and spitting and trying not to lose my fucking mind. My hand suddenly felt something warm and firm, round and...*toe!*

I looked up and saw what had haunted my every waking and sleeping hour for the last seven years: The monster from my dreams stood right in front of me.

"Oh fuck."

CHAPTER TWENTY-TWO

The thing dragged me through the gritty mud by the hair as I kicked and screamed, clawing at its hand. Somewhere between the madness, it dawned on me that I was going to die.

Who's going to take care of my babies? I'd only paid for a week's stay at Camp Critter. And stupidly, I hadn't let anyone know where I was going. Certainly not the people from work. Not my two best friends either. (Frankly, I would never risk them coming to look for me anyway.) Aside from that, there really weren't many other people in my life. I'd regrettably lived in an isolation bubble the last seven years.

Big mistake. "Let me go!" I yelled, despite knowing it would do absolutely no good.

Finally, we emerged from the darkness into the blinding afternoon sunlight, and I was shoved into a small holding cell made of a thatched roof and thick branches. Okay, it was a crappy hut. "Let me out of..."

I caught sight of the creature's face, and just like in my nightmares, I realized it was a man. He had ropes of long black dreads crusted with brown stuff. His entire body, including his face, was covered with inky soot, and his eyes were pits of garnet red and black. No. He wore no clothes, just a loincloth of sorts that looked like an animal hide. *Or...perhaps human skin?*

"Oh shit," I squeaked, thankful there was at least a set of branches between us, despite them being part of my cage.

The thing looked at me and smiled, baring its blackened teeth. "You. Stay. There." His voice sounded like Freddie Krueger's rusty razor-blade fingers shredding up a rusty bucket.

"Oh-oh-okay." I nodded my head.

It turned and walked across the small clearing we were in, disappearing into the dense foliage of the jungle.

Once it was out of sight, I let out a breath, but immediately went into hyperventilation mode. My head hurt like a sonofabitch and was still bleeding. *I have to get out of here.* I had to find Tommaso and plead my case. I jiggled the door, but it wouldn't open. The creepy part was how there wasn't anything latching the door to the structure itself.

What the hell? Was it some sort of mind control or evil magic? I didn't know.

Once again, I pushed with my entire body, but the seemingly flimsy thing felt like steel.

I studied it closely and blinked. Nothing about this cage was real. Not in my world. It was all sticks and branches with nothing binding them together. *I'm fucking losing my mind.* Or was I?

Gods. Fairies. Vampires. Incubuses—*Oops. I meant incubi*—and whateverelse-beings. *Let's not forget the unicorns.* Those all existed. And Cimil had mentioned something about her having powers that were taken away, which meant such things existed, too.

If you choose to believe Cimil. Okay and, yes, half of me did—the crazy half. So this meant that whatever was keeping me inside this structure wasn't exactly the sort of thing most rational people would believe in. But I believed in monsters. And now gods. And goddesses and unicorns and demons and...*and magical huts.*

I sighed at my newly embraced insanity and then looked up at the pristine blue sky, wondering if I could make another leap to save myself if I got the chance. Clearly, I was in the right place. No, not the stupid hut. This had to be where Tommaso had gone. So if I got the chance to see him, could I fix him? Could I get him to see another future? Possibly one with me?

My mind began to replay the brief moments we'd had together, and all of those subtle things that a girl might notice on a first date. The way he made me feel all fluttery when I looked into his eyes. The way he smelled so good that I found myself inhaling deeply, wanting to drink him in. And his lips, I could never have imagined feeling hot only touching a man's lips. But I had. There were so many small moments, even the way his eyes seemed to drift around my face as if he was taking me in when I spoke. The way he put me at ease and made me feel braver.

I collected those pieces to form a picture, and everything about them told me he was perfect. For me, that was.

"Hello, Charlotte," said a deep familiar voice.

My head whipped up. *Tommaso!* I rushed forward and gripped the wooden "bars" on the door of my hut. *Ohmygod or gods?* "Holy shit. Are you okay?"

Because, Christ Almighty, he sure as hell didn't look it. His hair, though still short, was matted with crusty red-brown muck. *Dried blood?* His beautiful body, stripped of any real clothing, was covered with that odiferous black soot, and his eyes were black. Completely black.

"Why have you come here?" he asked, his voice deeper than usual.

Screw the chitchat. Let's get down to business. "Tommaso, listen to me. You don't want to do this. You don't want to be here. You don't want to be one of them. And I know that I was supposed to be Andrus's mate—whatever the hell that means—but I don't want him. Yes, yes, I love his look—what woman can resist leather pants?—but that's not my heart speaking. My heart wants something that my brain can sign off on. It wants a best friend who's sexy and strong and who can kick ass when needed. So even though we don't know each other, I'm asking for the chance to find out if that's you." I drew a trembling breath. "Because I think it is. I mean to say—I want you." And I meant that. I really did, though it was difficult to imagine why at the moment. He really smelled.

His cold gaze narrowed on my face. "We will cut out your heart at sundown."

What? "What! How can that be your respon…" My voice trailed off as he simply disappeared. Like, as in, disappeared-disappeared. Gone. Poof. "What the…? Tommaso! Come back! You don't want to do this!"

The eerie silence of the surrounding jungle was the only response I got.

Crap. I dropped my head, resting my forehead on the door. This wasn't how I was going down. It couldn't be. And from the position of the sun, I had but a handful of hours left to save Tommaso. Because getting him to wake the hell up would be the only way to save myself.

Ohmygod. Why did I listen to Cimil?

Chapter Twenty-Three

As the sun dipped below the tree line, casting an orange hue over the sky, I felt my pulse rate rising steadily and the sweat trickling in a cold stream down my back.

I'd been sitting there for hours in my damp, horrible-smelling shirt and cargo pants, going through every inch of every conversation with Tommaso and Cimil and even Andrus and Sadie, but I didn't see the silver bullet I needed to get him to wake the hell up. There had to be something I could do to get through to him. There just had to be. But I realized I knew so little about Tommaso. His family had been murdered by the Maaskab. The Maaskab were a scary-as-hell cult of ancient Mayan priests who were really good at...okay, I wasn't clear on that part—they were good at being scary as hell. They were cruel and ruthless and I had the memories to back that up. They were recently all but exterminated in some end-of-the-world situation that didn't go their way—thankfully—but this end-of-the-world situation had caused some crazy reaction of sorts where single immortals were changing their moral polarity. The only known cure being having a mate, soul mate, or being in love.

Jesus, can this possibly get any more complicated?

"Hello, Charlotte. I understand I'll be dining on your heart this evening. While you watch."

My head snapped up to find the silhouette of a huge—and I mean *huge*—Maaskab. Eight or more feet of grime-covered horror film material with dreads that reached its waist, decorated with teeth. *Oh shit.* And thumbs. *And double oh-shit!* And a full-on severed finger running through the septum of his nose like some god-awful jewelry.

Taking the tribal look a little too far, dontcha think? Be that as it may, the malevolence oozing from his general direction could not be questioned. Even the animals and bugs wouldn't dare. The explosion of squawking, clicking, and roaring all around us was a testament to their fear of this man.

I gulped. "You must be…" What was his name again? All I remembered was Ass Banana. But calling him an ass probably wouldn't win me any points so I went with… "You must be Banana."

He growled in a tone so deep and horrifying that my knees started to give out, and I wasn't even standing. *Okay, I guess calling him "Banana" was a bad choice, too.*

"I am Ta'as, the king of the Maaskab. And you should watch your mouth, little human."

"Or what? You'll eat my heart and make me

watch?" I grumbled. Okay, perhaps my comment was mildly petulant, but in all seriousness, I was dehydrated, had lost some blood from my head injury (and probably had a concussion, too), and I didn't have very good prospects of living.

"I think I may eat that sharp tongue of yours as well, little girl."

"Super," I mumbled. "I don't suppose there's anything I could say to make you change your mind?" Purely a rhetorical question, of course.

"Nope." His dark eyes flickered with a glint of joy.

That was when it really sank in that this was going to happen. Tommaso wasn't going to rescue me. Nor were the gods—what a bunch of crazy A-holes. And I had no cavalry.

Thank you, Cimil! What a great idea coming alone.

I started to laugh hysterically, pushing my hands to my belly.

Ta'as looked at me curiously. "And *what* do you find *so* funny?"

I shook my head from side to side, chuckling. "You, actually. Okay, and me."

He crossed his crust-caked arms over his crust-caked chest that I realized was covered with scars, similar to what Tommaso had—speed bumps running straight across. They had to be some sort of Maaskab club membership ID.

"Do tell," he said.

I slowly got to my feet, unable to stop grinning. I'd lost my marbles. And noodle. I'd found my funny bunnies.

"Well, take your pick. I mean, there's the part about you being dressed like an evil baby in a shitty diaper. Then there's the fact that you want to kill me. Why? I can only guess, but the clock is ticking for you, just like it was ticking for Tommaso. It's fucking hysterical." It was ironic that he'd soon transform into something resembling Mother Teresa. Not that he'd ever be pure of heart and soul, but he'd sure the hell feel like...what had Cimil said? Oh yes. He'd become the nicest person on the planet. Anyway, that was what I wanted to say, but I couldn't stop laughing.

"Stop your cryptic insolence this moment!" he barked. "I will not have it."

Smiling, I jerked back my head. "Oh, but what are you going to do? Knit my cat a scarf in retaliation. Oh! Wait! I know! You'll recite a poem to my chickens!"

I suddenly wished that his switch would flip right now so I could witness him scrapbooking or rescuing worms from a rainy-day sidewalk. He'd probably be screaming on the inside while unable to resist the urge to do horribly nice things.

The large towering shadow of his body went perfectly still, and the life all around us fell deathly quiet. "Wha-wha-what do you speak of?"

"Wait." I pointed at him. "You don't even know what I'm talking about, do you?" Then it hit me hard. What would happen if I convinced this evil bastard that pursuing any paths leading to a soul mate would be impossible? Would his switch flip?

Really, I had nothing to lose.

I cleared my throat. "Hey, I just wanted to take a moment to acknowledge your smell. As a woman, I find it so incredibly repulsive that I do believe you've killed all of my future ovulations." I looked up at him, awaiting a response.

"What is this game that you're playing?" His black and crimson eyes flickered with rage.

"What game? I'm merely stating the facts. You're really disgusting. I mean, thumbs as jewelry? Wait! Don't tell me. You're trying to trick people into thinking you're a hitchhiker. Is that it?" I held out my thumb as if hitching for a ride.

He simply stared at me.

"No? Maybe you like using them for other things, then." I flashed a glance at his groin and motioned up with my thumb. "Oh, that's pretty nasty. I doubt you're going to find a lady who's into that, but who am I to—"

He reached out his hand in the direction of my neck and squeezed. Though he didn't touch me, I could feel his large sticky fingers closing my airway.

Dear gods, he has powers. I tried to stay focused and not panic, because one thing I knew for sure: I would die if this didn't work.

"Oh, wow," I croaked, my voice coming out slow and gritty. "I'm so-o-o impressed. You can do the Vader. I think he died single, too. If only he'd had a thumb necklace."

Ta'as's grip tightened, and I felt like my eyes were going to pop from their sockets. *Dammit,*

Char. Think of something! Cripple his ego! In a crazy flurry of horrific thoughts about these being my final breaths, my mind gravitated toward the one and only topic that plagued every male on the planet, even the damned hot ones who could probably do no wrong in us women's eyes.

"I know," I ground out my words, "that you're only like this…because…your penis is so small. But I'm sure there's someone out there, a nice evil girl, who enjoys a flaccid noodle. They say Hitler had the same problem, but even he managed to find a woman."

His magic hand of death squeezed harder, and then the world around me faded along with the oxygen supply to my brain. An obscure mist washed over me, and I felt myself blacking out.

Suddenly, I was falling down that dark, muddy hole again. I screamed with my eyes closed, bracing for the impact of the water that didn't come. When I opened my eyes again, I wasn't in that cold, dark, odiferous cenote, but lying in my bed. *Oh, God. Oh, God. Not this dream again.*

I was back in my room on that night seven years ago. It was a night I had relived a thousand times in my nightmares—the Maaskab touches me and cuts my skin. Its bloody-looking eyes glow in the dark, paralyzing me with fear. And when I scream, he curls those bloodstained lips into a horrifying smile. But then something happens, and I'm suddenly looking out the window as my mother beats the thing to death. I remembered those few moments like they were yesterday. But the one thing I never remembered was what drove the Maaskab away.

Why didn't he kill me? It was just as much of a blank to me then as it is now.

Fully aware that I was about to relive the nightmare once more, I gripped the sheets with my fists. Suddenly, I saw something move in the dark corner of my room, its massive form catching the light from my alarm clock.

Shit. I can't let him do this again. I can't. But before my brain could process or come up with a way out, his face hovered over mine.

"Save. Me," he mumbled in a deep gargle. "Please…save…me…"

What did he want me to do? I didn't have a clue, but I saw my chance and took it. I reached for my lamp and swung for his head, only to have it land straight in the palm of his hand.

Like all of the other times I'd relived this moment, his desperation turned to rage.

He grabbed me by the hair and flung me to the ground. I screamed as he pulled a large knife from his waistband and drove it down towards me as if he was going to slice me open. But he didn't. The knife stopped centimeters from my body, and he laughed into the air with delight, enjoying every ounce of fear he provoked.

"I am really going to enjoy this," he said in a low, gravelly voice while going to his knees at my side.

I then felt his ice-cold diseased hands on my skin as he cut my nightgown down the middle, nicking my skin in the process and making me bleed. His eyes lit up with sadistic joy, almost like he fed off my pain and drew strength from it.

Fight him, Char! Fight him. But there was an invisible tether holding me down.

He placed his hands on my bare breasts, and knowing what would happen next, I attempted once again to fight him off, only able to manage another scream.

Suddenly, the lights turned on, and I heard a female voice echo through the room. "Hey, there, Mr. Scabby. Now, Auntie Cimil is gonna give you exactly five point five, five, five seconds to take your icky paws off that human, or I'm gonna cut off your dick and make you eat it."

I looked over at the doorway, and there was a crazy-looking redhead wearing a pink scuba mask as a headband.

Cimil? Fucking Cimil was there? I thought to myself as I watched this memory replay, a spectator in my own hellish nightmare.

"One tiny little goddess doesn't frighten me," he said, rising to his feet.

Cimil cackled toward the ceiling. "First off," she held up her index finger, "I really should, because I'm the one you'll face when your time on this crazy planet is over. And I'll be makin' sure you go somewhere special—like the eternal ass-rape clown rodeo. Second off," she held up two fingers. "That moment is about to come a lot sooner than you think—but I know how people hate spoilers, so I'll just let that one stew in your nasty noggin. And third," she held up three fingers, "your five point five, five, five seconds are up."

Something—or someone—in white rushed at the Maaskab, and it flew across the room, hitting the wall with a loud *thump!*

"Oh! And fourth, I'm never alone." Cimil raised her arms to make the international symbol of the touchdown.

"You better run, motherfucker," said a tall, statuesque blonde wearing a white '60s-style minidress. "Because I maybe the Goddess of Forgetfulness, but I've got about twenty other awesome powers and one of them includes the ability to telepathically remove a man's privates."

The Maaskab picked himself up and bolted out the door.

"That's right!" Cimil belted. "Take your crusty nut sack with ya!" She then sighed contentedly and looked at the blonde. "Alrighty, let's get this one all fixed up." Cimil pointed to me.

"What about the Scab?" the blonde asked.

Still pointing in my direction, Cimil shrugged and then smiled gleefully. "Oh, this one's mother thought there was a burglar in the house and is presently beating the snot out of him with a golf club, realizing that—"

The sound of my mother's scream wailed outside.

"Ah!" Cimil said cheerily. "Annnd she just realized that ain't no burglar."

"Mom!" I got to my feet and ran to the window, holding the front of my gown closed with my hands.

Cimil blocked me. "Ewww…you really don't want to see that. But not to worry, Charlotte honey. I called good old Chuckie for backup. And of course, Minky is always on standby. Your mamma's gonna be just peachy!"

"Who are you?" I asked. Of course, now, looking back on this memory, I knew she was Cimil, the Goddess of the Underworld. But that night, I had thought she was just some crazy person who'd shown up with Go-go Boots Barbie to save me.

Cimil replied, "It doesn't matter who I am because my sister here is going to make you forget you ever saw us until the moment is right."

"Why? And what was that thing? Why did it attack me?"

Cimil then gave me a look so hard and cold that it made me shrink back. "Because the world is a messed-up place, Charlotte. And we all have our role to play—for the record, this moment wasn't your big touchdown."

What the heck did that mean?

She went on, "When the time is right, you will remember everything and do something very important. Ta'as is like El Chapo—great at evasion and rarely shows his face—but he'll show it to you. And then—" she slapped her hands together "—booya!"

"But I—"

"Just remember, everyone has a weakness. Even Ass Banana. Go Charlotte!" She pumped her little hand in the air.

"What the fuuu...?"

The woman in white stepped forward and grabbed my shoulders. "Okay, honey. Just relax. I'm only going to give you a light dose so it won't be permanent."

༚

I blinked and found myself waking up inside that nasty hut, lying on the muddy jungle floor, my throat burning and windpipe aching.

"Oh, good. You're back."

I looked up and saw Ta'as still standing there, holding out his clawed hand.

Oh gods. What was that? All these years, I'd been left to believe that the monster had done the unthinkable and that no one had been there to help me, when in reality I'd been made to forget. I couldn't fathom why, except that Cimil had wanted me to get to this place, to this exact moment. *To do this exact thing.*

I coughed and rolled over, trying to get the air to inflate my lungs again.

"I changed my mind about killing you," Ta'as said. "Just yet, anyway."

I continued coughing, trying to get to my feet, all the while thinking about what Cimil had said. Ta'as had a weakness. What was it? Of course, stupid Cimil could've simply told me, but nooo.

I am the captain of my own crunch. I am the captain of my own crunch. I can do this.

"Thank you," I said, gripping the branches of my rickety hut to hold me up.

"You're welcome. I realized that your fiery little heart will be put to better use as my appetizer. And not to worry, you will get to see it for yourself."

It just wasn't enough for him to kill me, was it? He wanted to make me watch. What a butthole.

"You know," I pushed out my words in a slow, raspy breath, "I met one of your minions once. My mother beat him to death with a five iron. And now, meeting you, a part of me wonders if that was what he wanted all along. To escape you."

"He was weak," Ta'as snapped.

The lack of cockiness in Ta'as's voice signaled that I'd hit a nerve. I wasn't sure why, but it made me think about what the monster in my room had said: He'd begged me to help him. I never understood what that meant, but now I wondered if what he really wanted was to be freed, through death or otherwise.

Oh, shit. Oh, shit. Tommaso told me that he'd been taken against his will, brainwashed, and forced to do things he wasn't proud of. Maybe they were all on the same boat, prisoners of some horrific evil.

"Cimil told me," I said, "that the gods killed off almost all of the Maaskab. But maybe they let themselves die. Maybe they're all trying to get away from their king."

Ta'as's eyes bubbled with rage. "They died because they were weak! Like you."

"I'm not weak. I'm observant. And right now, I'm wondering if on the inside you know you've turned into this horrible monster that no one will ever love, no woman will ever want, no army will follow willingly. It makes me wonder if deep down inside, you're just some guy who wants it all to end because there's no hope of stopping your agony and loneliness."

"Wha-wha-what are you trying to do, you witch?" His eyes began glowing bright red like a demonic Halloween decoration.

"You want to beg for my help, just like the Maaskab who died on my porch, don't you?"

He stumbled back, placing his dirt-caked hands over his chest. "What are you doing!" he yelled. "Cease this moment!"

I couldn't believe this was happening. "You know I'm saying the truth. You know that you can't ever be really important."

He held out his hand. "Stop. Stop, you witch. Stop!"

If I weren't so scared out of my freaking mind, I would've laughed at being called a witch.

All of a sudden, the wind began to gust and the black goo stuck to his skin began flaking off. His disgusting toothy dreads started falling to the ground like dead leaves on a chilly fall day.

He was changing right before my eyes, and while I wanted to claim it was due to my being a badass, I couldn't ignore the fact that it simply felt too easy. Like it was all meant to be somehow.

"All the killing," I dragged out my words, my breathing still labored, "and all the power in the world won't make you important. Won't make you loved." *And it certainly won't fix your tiny cock.*

He groaned and clawed at his face. "Stop!"

I could barely speak as he turned from a shadow to an olive-skinned man with blue, blue eyes and a short brown beard. He looked...he looked...he looked like a member of Mumford and Sons.

"You!" he bellowed. "You've ruined me!"

What came next was the part I wasn't sure I really saw, but I might almost swear I did: He began crying.

The man turned and ran, disappearing into the wilderness of the Mexican jungle.

I could do little more than stand there with my mouth hanging open. *I just took down the evilest being on the planet.*

CHAPTER TWENTY-FOUR

It wasn't long after Ta'as epic man-tantrum that the last ray of sunlight faded into oblivion and the jungle went still again. Somewhere off in the distance, an animal snorted or cackled or—I didn't know what to call the noise exactly. I imagined it was a wild boar or perhaps one of those jaguars I'd been warned about.

Of course, the animals weren't what frightened me. Tommaso did. And the fact that he hadn't come for me yet made every part of my body tense. *Dammit. I really need to pee.* But I wasn't about to drop trou only to have Mr. Evil T show up.

As I stood there, gripping the wooden bars, doing my little pee-pee dance, I heard screaming and grunting. Male screaming and grunting.

I froze and held my breath. *Holy hell, what is that?*

More battle cries roared through the night. *Oh, shit.* Someone was attacked by the Maaskab. That meant Tommaso was under attack!

"No! Goddammit! No! Let me the fuck out of here!" Not that I would know what to do—I mean, I was clubless and it wasn't like I would be jumping in to defend the Maaskab. Those suckers wanted to eat my innards. On the other hand, I still held out hope for Tommaso.

"Dammit!" I yelled.

After a short moment, the sounds stopped and a dark figure emerged from the jungle, heading right for me. I instinctively backed up until I could go no further.

"It is time, Charlotte."

The face of the shadowed being never came into focus—too dark out now for that—but his gravelly tone was familiar enough.

"Tommaso, what happened?"

He didn't reply, but the door flew open, and I felt myself propelled out. I landed at his feet with a thump. "Guess you're okay," I said, shaking my head from the impact.

Before I knew it, he had me to my feet and was dragging me along by the arm.

"You need to stop and think, Tommaso. I know that somewhere deep down you don't really want to do this."

"Oh, but I do."

"You don't," I grunted. "And Ta'as is gone. He turned good and ran off." I stupidly thought that pointing that out might give him the encouragement to push back on whatever thing had him by the balls.

"Ah, yes." He chuckled, leading me up a muddy embankment. "Thank you for that."

"Thank me? Why?"

"Because now that he's gone, I am the leader of the Maaskab and I have killed off his few remaining followers." But I'd thought there were only two Maaskab besides Tommaso. Ta'as already recruited new ones.

We suddenly came into a clearing surrounded by torches. Six or seven Maaskab bodies were piled in the center next to a stone altar. "And now that I've killed everyone," Tommaso said, "I will consume their power."

With a sour face, I imagined what that could possibly mean. "You're going to eat their hearts, aren't you?"

"Of course. Starting with yours, Charlotte. The chill inside yours will shut out the voice of the old Tommaso once and for all and free me to start the Maaskab again. Newer. Bigger. Stronger."

What were they? Glue strips?

"Tomma—" He yanked me forward so hard that I felt my arm dislodging from the socket. I screamed.

"Yes. Scream just like that," he said. "Your pain will make me stronger."

"Tommaso, don't do this. I know you care about me and, somewhere inside, you're fighting to do the right thing. Please," I whimpered, in so much pain that I thought I might pass out. "Please fight. I know you're a good man. With a really big penis." Okay, that last bit was lame, but if calling Ta'as's junk "tiny" made him change teams, it wasn't so ridiculous to think that complimenting Tommaso's manhood might cure him.

He threw me over the altar and bound my wrists with thick rope, causing me to scream again—my arm was throbbing and the back of my head wasn't feeling much better. That was when I caught sight of the huge machete tucked into the waistband of his man thong.

Oh, God. Oh, God. This was all too similar to my nightmares—the ones where I did not survive.

He began chanting, tilting his sooty face toward the starry night sky. The language sounded savage, just like him.

The tears now streaming down my face, all I could do was blubber at this point. "Please," I cried. "I'm sorry I didn't fall in love with you at first sight. I'm sorry that the Maaskab took everything from you. I'm sorry that the gods didn't try to help you. But they didn't help me either, which is why we have to help each oth—"

"I changed my mind," he said in a low, haunting tone. "The sound of your voice is really annoying." He pulled out a thick piece of knotted rope from somewhere and shoved it into my mouth, tying it tightly around the back of my head.

"Norrr! You basard! Doan. Doan!" I mumble-screamed.

He grabbed the knife from his waistband, placed it in his two hands, and raised it up over my heart.

Oh, fuck! "Norrr, Tommao!"

"Put that fucking knife down this instant!" yelled

a panting female voice just at the edge of the torchlit clearing.

Tommaso halted his stab in midair, the expression on his face perplexed.

My head whipped in the direction of the woman. It was a redheaded gal who looked to be in her early twenties. Though she was sweaty as hell, I could see she was beautiful with kind eyes.

"That's right," she said, "put the knife down."

"Why are you here, Emma?" he asked.

She approached cautiously. "Because I knew you were in trouble. And I bribed Cimil to tell me where you might be."

"What the fuck do you want, woman?" he asked. "To die on this altar like her? Because I bet your heart would make me even more powerful."

I looked back at her and noticed her eyes were full of tears. "No, Tommaso. I came to tell you the truth."

"Emma!" boomed another deep voice somewhere inside the jungle. Suddenly an enormous man with huge muscles and long black hair emerged. "Emma! Step away from him!"

Emma scowled. "No!" She pointed at the man. "You had no business coming here."

"Like hell," growled the large man. "I'm your husband. You're the mother of our son. Everything you do is my business."

She blinked at him and then a sad, sad look washed over her face. "I didn't want you to have to hear this, but I guess you're going to." She looked back at Tommaso, who still held the knife above me, like he was in suspended animation, trying to work something out. "Tommaso, do you remember that day you captured me and handed me over to be sacrificed? Do you remember how guilty you felt after everything was over and I had you cured of the Maaskab's poison? Well, think of what's going to happen if you kill her. Because there will be no second chances for you. The gods will kill you, Tommaso. And I love you. I don't want to see you die."

"You-you-you love me?" he stuttered.

She nodded. "You're a friend and a brother and an ex-crush all rolled into one."

"What the fuck, woman?" the large man snarled.

"I love you, too, Guy," Emma said. "And I chose you. I married you. But that doesn't mean I didn't have feelings for him." She pointed at Tommaso.

"You-you lied to me?" Guy looked like he'd been shot in the stomach.

"Yes. Because I knew you wouldn't understand and that you couldn't handle the truth. But I can't keep it a secret anymore. I don't want to see him destroy his life when he still has a chance at happiness." She turned her attention back to Tommaso. "I'm sorry, Tommaso. I'm sorry for loving Guy more. I'm sorry for lying or hurting you by hiding the truth. But more than anything, I'm sorry for not settling this sooner. I think if I had, you would've seen your life differently somehow. That you would've seen you're worth loving and risking everything for. Just like I am doing now."

He dropped the knife to the ground and buckled

at the knees. I watched as he covered his face and the air filled with the sound of his groans. Emma ran to him and wrapped her arms around him.

"I'm so sorry, Tommaso," she said, crying and petting the back of his head. "I'm sorry this happened to you."

He wrapped his arms around her and buried his face in her neck.

"That's right," she muttered softly. "I'm here. I'm here for you and always will be."

I felt my heart sink into the abyss. He loved this woman. He loved her so much that she'd been able to break whatever evil spell had wrapped around his heart.

My eyes teared with sadness, knowing that I was not her. I couldn't save him. He didn't want a future with me. It was always her.

I looked over at the towering man, Guy, who just stood there watching his wife hold another man. The look on his face was devastation, as if he'd just watched his entire life die.

I felt the same way, frankly. I'd somehow become emotionally attached to Tommaso in a way I couldn't understand. And that was what hurt the most. Realizing that I wanted him so much, but didn't have a chance.

CHAPTER TWENTY-FIVE

Three weeks later.

"Charlotte, I am not asking. I'm telling you."

I swiveled in Uncle Chuck's direction. Now that I'd been spending time with him, I'd begun to notice how handsome he was for an older gentleman. He had a full head of dark gray hair and a hypnotic laugh. Both made me wonder if they were part of his bag of tricks to lure in the ladies.

"Sorry. You're not my dad, and if you were, I'd still say no." I went back to loading the dishwasher while everyone finished digesting the enchilada meal I'd made. Turned out, incubi ate people food. Along with people. It was all still pretty weird.

"Don't be a brat. You're going!" Sadie said, who sat beside her father, petting Bitch Pants. She happened to be my cat's one and only favorite "person."

Leave it to my satanic cat to love a demon.

"I happen to agree." Andrus, who was helping bring the dishes from the table, set down a pile of plates in the sink and then crossed his meaty arms over his chest. As if showing me his giant biceps would intimidate me and get me to do what he said. "And if you don't go, I will personally spank you."

"How was it that the Universe thought to mate us?" I scoffed. I mean, yeah, he was really good looking, but his serrated edges and lack of understanding of how to treat a woman—or people in general—left something to be desired. Sadie, with her flowing auburn hair and intense dark eyes, was definitely the right woman for him. She didn't take crap from anyone. Case in point…

"You'll touch my cousin over my dead body!" Sadie barked, her eyes glowing succubus orange.

"It was just a threat, honey," Andrus said sheepishly. "You know I would never spank anyone but you."

I covered my face and groaned. It was great having family back in my life again. Truly. But I still had a long way to go to understand them and their nonhuman ways, including their humor.

"Now, see what you did?" Sadie scolded Andrus. "Poor Charlotte is going to run and hide in the closet again."

I dropped my hands and looked over at her. "That happened one time." I held up my finger. "One! And it was because you were getting that weird look on your face and I've never seen anyone turn into a sex-slurping demon."

"Sex-slurping." She snorted. "You're so funny."

"Shut up. All of you," said my uncle and then looked right at me. "Charlotte, you can't not go to the party. You are the guest of honor, and the gods will see it as an insult of the gravest sort."

I shrugged.

He shook his head. "Do you truly want to get on Cimil's bad side? Because I've been there and let me tell you, she has a special kind of torture she inflicts upon people she doesn't like. Ask the clowns." He scratched his chin. "Of course, the same can be said for those she likes. Just ask the cast of *The Love Boat*."

"Huh?" I frowned.

"Never mind," said my uncle. "The point is that it's a few hours of your time. You go, you sip a few drinks, accept your award, and then you leave."

"Yeah, but I didn't do anything," I said.

"You took down the most powerful, dangerous Maaskab ever to walk the earth, and while I know you don't want to share what happened that day, I for one am proud to call you my niece. I would call you daughter, too, if you'd let me." His golden eyes filled with sentiment.

My own father had left my mother before I was born. I never knew him, never learned his name, and I never cared to.

"Since I am…" Uncle Chuckie added.

I blinked at him. "What?"

"What?" Sadie gasped.

"What?" Andrus barked.

Uncle Chuckie raised his chin. "Yes. It's true. I met your mother first, Charlotte. She was very special to me, enough so that I was able to resist the urge to kill her. But then," he turned to Sadie, "I met *your* mother, and I knew that she was my intended mate.

"I couldn't help but want to try to make a life with Claire, but in the end, when I told her what I was, that Charlotte was my first daughter, she couldn't handle it. She called me a monster and left. Luckily, I met your stepmother, who is truly my partner and best friend."

Sadie's eyes began trickling. "You mean...you mean...Charlotte is really my half sister?"

"Yes." He nodded his head. "And Nell, too, but she doesn't know either."

Sadie covered her mouth, and I did the same. People always said that we looked like twins, but I equated it to the fact that our mothers were identical. In truth, however, it was that plus the fact we had the same father.

Oh wow. Now it all made so much sense. My mother moving to Palm Springs by herself, away from her sister. Her distance from my aunt. Her hate for Uncle Chuck and fear of him. It was all one giant traumatic mess for her and the likely reason she never told me the truth about my father.

Had she also feared that I would end up like my dad? She had been obsessed, especially as I got older, with all that crazy supernatural stuff.

"Ohmygod," I whispered. "It's like all of the missing pieces of my life just fell out of the sky."

Sadie got up from the table and rushed toward me, throwing her arms around my neck. "You're my sister!"

I was speechless. Absolutely speechless.

I pushed her back gently and then looked at my uncle—I mean father. "Does this mean that I'm a…" I couldn't say the word. I just couldn't.

He shook his head no. "While you have my blood, you're not like us."

"How is that possible?" I asked.

He shrugged. "Like Nell, your human side is too strong perhaps. I don't really know. But if you haven't shown any signs of being a succubus by now, then you never will—although, I'm sure your recessive traits do add to your sex appeal."

Was this why men continually hit on me? *Dear gods.* "Wow. I'm…I'm…I'm speechless."

My father rose from the table and came over to wrap his arms around me. "And I'm an evil demonic bastard for not coming to you sooner. But I thought it would be best to leave you alone until I knew if you had my traits. You never showed any, but I still couldn't let you go. And yet, I didn't know how to approach you, knowing how your mother was." He began to tear up, and it instantly reminded me of Tommaso. How he was so strong and indestructible, but had that little piece of him hidden inside that was plagued with regret and sorrow. "I'm so sorry, honey, that I wasn't there when you needed me."

I immediately understood what he meant. The day I was attacked by the Maaskab.

"But you were there. You fought them off," I realized. He'd been the creature with the orange eyes and defended my mother. And I already knew that he'd watched over me these past years, too. He'd been the "monster" I sensed lurking in the shadows.

"I didn't do enough," he said. "They hurt you."

I didn't know what to say. I felt bad that he felt bad, but I'd moved on. He needed to as well.

I shrugged. "As Cimil once said, it was the Maaskab's fault. Not yours or mine. The one who attacked me decided his own path."

"Right you are," my dad said, wiping his tears with his sleeve. "And now it's time for you to decide what comes next in your life. You should go to the party."

Back to this again? I really didn't want to go because Tommaso might be there—or worse, be there with Emma—and I just couldn't handle confronting the whole thing just yet. Which was also why I hadn't answered any of Tommaso's calls. What could he possibly say that I wanted to hear? Besides, he stopped calling after the first week, so clearly he'd moved on.

"I've been through a lot," I said. "And now I have one more huge piece of my life to try to digest."

My father continued, "There'll be plenty of time for digesting later. You should meet the immortal community—get to know them and what it means to be immortal."

I looked at him and didn't quite follow. "Sorry?"

"All right, you got me there," he said. "You're not immortal, but you do have my blood. You will live a very, very long time."

What the hell? "How long?"

He shrugged. "A thousand years, perhaps?"

"Oh, crap." I couldn't begin to comprehend the full meaning of that. "How old are you?"

"I lost count. Ten. Fifteen thousand. I don't recall."

Wow.

"So will you go to the party?" he asked. "You will need friends in your life who understand you and what you will go through as you age differently from humans. And perhaps you'll meet a nice immortal man to share all of those years with."

Ah. Now I understood why he felt so strongly about my going. He was hoping I might meet someone to help me get over Tommaso. But I wasn't ready to face what happened, and... "I'm not ready to face Tommaso yet. The memories are too fresh. And I'm definitely not ready to think about dating."

My father—gods, it was so surreal to say or think that—my father squeezed my hand. "The sooner you confront your demons, the sooner you can move on, Charlotte. Don't waste another day of your life hiding from the things you fear."

I blinked at him and smiled, pushing back a little tear. He was so, so right. I'd wasted enough time avoiding life, keeping the world at arm's length—or a putter's length—because I was afraid. I didn't need to be afraid anymore.

I bobbed my head. "Yeah, I'll go. But one condition."

My father smiled. "I'd be delighted to go with you."

"Not that. I mean—yes, I'd love for you to come with me, but I was going to say: Andrus has to spank me. A promise is a promise."

I looked over at Sadie, waiting for her reaction. Big mistake.

As her eyes turned a glowing orange, I stuck out my hands. "Just kidding! Ohmygod! Kidding!"

She smiled. "Me too!" And then began cracking up.

For the first time in my life, I finally felt like I belonged. And most importantly, I was no longer frightened of anything. Because I was part monster.

CHAPTER TWENTY-SIX

Just after eight o'clock, I pulled up to the Shangri La Hotel in Santa Monica in my red Jeep, feeling a bit out of place among the expensive-looking sports cars, limos, and other very pricy vehicles. The valets, however, were quick to attend to me just the same.

Wearing a long, spaghetti-strap red satin dress—compliments of Cimil, who'd sent it to my house, along with a note that said "Booya!"and nothing more—I felt like I was going to my immortal coming-out party.

As I rode the elevator up to the rooftop bar where the party was being held, I couldn't help feeling all fluttery and nervous. I prayed Tommaso was not there. I prayed I wouldn't have to see him or Emma. Luckily, Andrus and Sadie said they'd be here later, so I'd at least know a few friendly faces, and my dad said he'd make an appearance after he took care of some business downtown. Sadly, he'd be flying back to Cleveland to be with his wife—who I supposed was now my stepmother—and his other daughter—who was now my other half sister. He explained that he needed to talk to them both and come clean before introducing me.

I tried to imagine how that conversation might go, him telling his wife slash best friend that he had another daughter but never told her or anyone. If it were me, I'd be upset about the lie, not about the daughter. Why did people go to such lengths to hide things that no one really cared about? If anything, life's little dramas only made us more interesting.

The elevator chimed and the doors slid open. Loud music and laughter immediately flooded my ears.

I stepped out, taking a moment to let my eyes adjust to the dark space that was lit with red lighting, giving the room a velvety lounge-type feel. *Oh wow.* The bar was crowded with people in tuxes and gowns. There were so many faces, so many beautiful people, and everyone was so godsdamned tall.

Okay, I straightened my spine, pasted on a smile, and headed for the bar. Champagne was a great place to start.

A waiter passed by with a tray full of shots, the crowd plucking them off quickly as he went by.

Okay, tequila works, too. I grabbed a small glass and threw it back.

"Charlotte, you've arrived," I heard a female voice say.

I turned and saw a medium height woman with

dark creamy skin, dark curly hair, and the most loving smile I'd ever seen. She held out her hand. "I'm Ashli. And I'm so sorry I couldn't make it to you earlier."

I shook her hand and instantly felt...well...super good. "Sorry?"

"I'm Ashli, the Goddess of Love? Zac said you needed my help? I would've come sooner, but I was taking some time off to be with my baby and husband. I just got in this afternoon, and then, of course, I heard you were the guest of honor, so here I am."

What in the world was she talking about? "I'm sorry, uh...Goddess—do I call you 'Goddess'?"

"Ashli. Just Ashli."

I nodded. "Okay, *Ashli*. I don't mean to be rude, especially because you seem like the nicest person I've ever met and I suddenly have the urge to go around hugging everyone, but I think you've mistaken me for someone else."

She crinkled her brow. "No. I don't think so. You're the Charlotte who was supposed to be mated to Andrus, right?"

"Errr...yeah, but—"

"Well, don't you worry," she said, giving my arm a little squeeze. "I know Tommaso was anxious to speed up your falling in love with him, for obvious reasons, but that doesn't mean you two aren't meant to be."

Tommaso asked this woman to make me fall in love with him? I was at a loss for words.

Ashli must've picked up on my confusion. "You

have no idea what I'm talking about, do you?"

"Ashli, you finally made it," said a deep silky voice.

Standing there was an impressively tall man, probably around seven feet, with a shaggy mane of black hair, startling blue eyes—or turquoise or green or something like that—too dark to tell—and a surreally sculpted face hiding beneath a thick growth of stubble.

"Zac, there you are," said Ashli. "I was looking for you, but bumped into our guest of honor here. Can you explain why she has no clue who I am?"

The gorgeous man suddenly looked guilty. "Well, I, uh…you know…I thought you should be here as a backup. Just in case."

"Dammit, Zac!" Ashli griped. "What did I say about using my gifts on people? They have to agree to my help. They have to want it. I'm not going to run around using my powers on unsuspecting victims."

"That's how the rest of the gods do it," he argued.

She rolled her eyes. "Falling in love is a serious matter! And I'm not like the rest of the gods, and I will certainly never be a giant asshole like you and Cimil." She looked at me. "I was a plain old human up until about a year ago when I met Máax, the God of Time Travel."

I just stood there listening with my mouth hanging open. "Oh…uh…I-I wasn't aware humans could become gods." Or that there was a god of time travel. *Holy crap, I have so much to learn.*

Ashli smiled. "Apparently, no one else was aware either. Well, except for Cimil. But we all know how that is." She shrugged sweetly and then turned back to Zac to dish out another warning. "That's the last time I'll tell you, Zac. Got it? Or you and Cimil can forget my help and you'll be on your own to help the masses find mates."

"I got it." He held up his hands in surrender. "But since you're here, I'm wondering if you can help me seduce a woman—"

"Zac!" Ashli scorned and then turned away.

"Wait!" he yelled over the loud dance music. "I really like her, and you're…" His voice faded as he followed her into the crowd.

As for me, my mind was spinning a little. Okay, a lot. Not from the bizarre exchange I'd just witnessed—one of just many more to come, I suspected—but because Ashli had said Tommaso asked for some love spell to be put on me? At least, that was what I think she said.

What a complete jerk. Not only was he in love with someone else, but he'd wanted me to fall in love with him? Why would he do that?

As I stood there fuming in the center of the crowded room of formally dressed mingling guests, pretending to check out the DJ—a tall blond wearing a mini skirt and white go-go boots—I felt a wave of nervous flutters wash over me.

I turned and spotted Tommaso exiting the elevator. There was a moment where the light behind him illuminated his tall, lean, masculine silhouette, making him seem like an ancient warrior from another time. Not because of his clothes, which I couldn't really see, but because there was something about the way he carried himself—chin lifted, shoulders and back straight, a slight swagger to his step—it was the kind of way a confident man, a powerful man, a fearless man moved.

I couldn't peel my eyes away as the elevator doors behind him closed and the red light of the room enveloped him. His gaze zeroed right in on me, and as hard as it was to admit, I couldn't lie to myself. I was afraid. Afraid of looking at him. Afraid of wanting him and afraid of knowing his desire was elsewhere. Ego, pride, fear, weakness. It was an ugly soup of insecurity stewing around inside my head, and it shamed me. *Oh, goodie! Add shame.* One more carrot for the pot.

Still, I would never get over him if I didn't have closure.

I squared my shoulders and reminded myself who I really was—the woman who'd hopped on a plane and flew to Mexico all by herself to confront the Maaskab. *Yeah, and you're genetically half succubus. How badass is that?*

Tommaso, who I now realized wore a tux—*gods, so, so handsome*—slowly made his way toward me and me to him. We stopped with a few feet of distance between us.

"Charlotte, you look," his eyes crawled down my dress, all the way to my red-painted toenails and red strappy shoes, and then up again, "stunning."

"Thank you." I patted the side of my pinned-up hair. I honestly felt a little awkward in such a nice outfit. Most days I dressed like a tomboy to avoid being hit on so much by my clients. Now I knew that had been completely useless.

"You look, very, very well yourself," I said.

He grinned and two little divots puckered in each smoothly shaved cheek. "Compared to the last time you saw me, I'm sure it's quite a shock."

"It's a relief, actually."

We both stared in awkward silence, me trying not to fight how I felt—or how my pulse was out of control or how he smelled so good, all clean and citrusy, or how standing near his tall frame made me feel so safe. It was silly to deny the attraction or how much it hurt to lose what could've been between us had things been different.

The best way to deal with this was to face it head-on.

"Charlotte, I—"

"Tommaso, I—"

We spoke over each other and then both said, "You first."

He lifted his hand to stop me. "No, I insist. You're entitled to speak first. But might I suggest we step out onto the terrace?"

It was a bit loud inside. "Sure."

He dipped his head and gestured for me to proceed. We walked outside where we had a view of Santa Monica beach and a long dock with beautiful twinkling lights.

Once outside, I found a small table for us to sit at on the crowded patio.

Tommaso sat across from me and leaned his

large frame back into the wrought-iron seat, running his hand over his black bow tie. He was so beautiful—that fierce, dangerously sexy expression in his eyes, the way his angular jaw flexed, the way he commanded a presence that made everyone want to look but not mess with him.

"I believe you have the floor, Charlotte." He flashed a cool smile.

"Oh. Sorry." I had been gawking. "I just wanted to say—"

"Can I get you two something to drink?" said a googly-eyed redheaded waitress who practically popped out of nowhere.

"Oh, uh. Nothing for me," I said.

"I'll have a scotch. Neat. Make it a double."

"Well, in that case," I said, "I'll have the same. But make mine tequila. And a triple. With a wedge of lime."

Tommaso gave me a look.

Yeah, so it wasn't the same drink. And I'd just ordered a triple tequila shot. So what? I was going to need a little numbing after I got done saying what I had to say.

"Comin' right up, honey," said the waitress, smacking her gum. "But it will be a few. Our bartender is MIA and we got Bees behind the counter."

"Sorry, but did you say there are bees inside?" I asked.

"Yeah." She blew a bubble and let it pop. "But they don't hurt no one unless you provoke them."

She strutted away, and I was left scratching my head.

Tommaso must've noticed. "She meant Bees, as in the Goddess of Bees. Her sacred hive goes everywhere she goes."

Okaaaay. "Glad you explained; I never would've figured that one out."

"But you would've had one hell of a shock when you went to the bar. She wears the hive on her head."

"Interesting." I nodded.

"Quite. So, what was it you wanted to say?"

Ugh. This was so uncomfortable. I really wished that waitress would hurry up with my drink.

"I, uh, wanted to say that...that..." Crap. I wanted to say that he'd hurt me. I wanted to say that I wished he'd told me the truth from the beginning about who he was and what he'd wanted from me, even if I might not have been ready to accept it. I wanted to say that I was pissed as hell that he'd led me on and made me like him so much when we never had a chance. I wanted to say that I missed him. So, so much that it hurt to breathe.

Instead, I pasted on a smile and gazed into his eyes. *Holy crap.* They were turquoise, I realized. Yes, now that I could see him with a bit of regular light from the gas lamps outside, I could see his beautiful light eyes.

Great. Now he's even hotter. Jerk!

"Yes?" he prodded.

"I'm happy things worked out for you. I mean, with the whole not turning evil and not going to prison thing. And that you and Emma were able to finally," I swallowed hard, "connect."

Tommaso laughed. "Connect?"

"Well, yeah. Or get back together or finally admit your feelings—whatever you want to call it."

He crossed his arms over his chest. "So you think Emma and I are together."

"I saw the way you two looked at each other. She wanted you, and you clearly have feelings for her."

"Do you actually think her husband would let me live if I had romantic feelings for her? He's the God of Death and War. In that order. I think. Okay, I forget. But I'm fairly certain. The point is, he wouldn't think twice about removing my head if I touched his mate."

I figured that much. I had flown back with the man and watched him stab his own hand repeatedly while reciting Tommaso's name. The hand kept closing up, but it was still very disturbing.

"It's none of my business how you two—or three—settle your business," I said, my tone level.

He shook his head. "There is no two. And there sure as hell is no three." I lifted my brows, and he slid his hand across the table to grab mine. "Yes, I had strong feelings for Emma when we first met, and as you heard, she once had feelings for me, too."

"She said she *loves* you, not 'loved.'"

"And she does—but not the way you think. We have a history and will always be there for one another. But she didn't choose me. She didn't marry me. She didn't have children with me. She had them with Guy because what she has with him is meant to be. I'm not the man for her. I never could be. And now I know she is not the woman for me either—I love her, but like a sister, a best friend, but nothing more."

"But I heard her say—"

"You weren't listening, then. She and I don't want to be together. But that doesn't negate that we care about each other. And I think somewhere in the back of her mind it made her feel guilty not to say how important I am to her simply because her husband is a jealous idiot."

"I understand," I said. "I do, but—"

"I don't think you do."

His condescending tone whipped me right over the fence—you know, the one I was trying to mend. Well, now I wanted to stomp on it. "Don't tell me what I think, Tommaso." I jerked back my hand.

"Charlotte, I didn't come here to fight. I came here because I wanted to ask—"

"You don't even know me," I snarled.

He tipped his head to the side. "Oh, but I do. I know everything about you, Charlotte Marie Meyer. I know that you love to rescue very unlikeable creatures you feel the world has forgotten. I know that you are as kind as you are brave because you spend your days making horny elderly men smile and feel young again. I know that you were once afraid to sleep and close your eyes because monsters are real. And," he leaned in, "I know that your nipples are pink and that you don't like to shave your legs every day."

"What! Ohmygod. So I skipped a day. Or five. So what?" I was a real woman, not some fantasy Barbie doll.

"I'm not complaining." He lifted a brow. "Other than the fact we were interrupted and I haven't been able to stop thinking about finishing what we started.   Which brings me to the point I wanted to—"

"I can't believe you." I stood up, wanting to spit in his gorgeous face. "Is that all I am to you, some woman to fuck? Is that why you called in Ashli, because you wanted to get into my pants?" I'd risked my life to save him. I'd confronted my worst fears. I deserved to be a little more than some sexual conquest.

He looked up at me with the most horrifically pissed-off expression I'd ever seen on a man. I instinctively wanted to step back, but didn't. Those days of being afraid were over.

He slowly rose from the table, fuming. "I won't lie, Charlotte. When we first met, the only thing I wanted was for you to accept me as your new mate so I wouldn't turn. And for that, I'm sorry. But can you really blame me? What would you do to prevent becoming a Maaskab, the thing that violently killed your family?"

"I would do just about anything. But I wouldn't wreck another person's life just to unwreck my own."

"You think I wrecked your life?" he growled.

"*You* almost ended it! And you definitely wrecked it." And he'd looked damned fucking hot while he'd done it. Except for that Maaskab episode. Not hot.

"You think I used you and never had any feelings whatsoever." It wasn't a question; it was an accusation.

"Yes. Again, asshole."

He stared at me for a long moment. "I see." He turned and walked away. Just like that.

"Where are you going?" I yelled.

"Char? What the hell is going on?" said a woman.

I turned my head and found Sadie and Andrus glaring at me.

"He's a giant asshole, that's what!" I said.

"Charlotte, as your once intended mate, I feel obligated to point out to you that you are, in fact, the giant asshole."

"Fuck you!" I snapped. "And stop bringing up the fact that the stupid Universe thought we'd be awesome together."

"Hear, hear." Sadie held out her fist for a sisterly bump.

I obliged, but Sadie quickly started digging into me. "But he's right, Char. You are a giant asshole."

"What?" I scoffed, pointing accusatorially in the direction Tommaso had disappeared. "He's the one who lied and tried to use me. He's the one who pretended to want me when we never had a chance."

Andrus stepped forward and grabbed me by the shoulders. "Your head, woman, is stuck up your ass. I suggest you pull it out immediately because

Tommaso is like a brother to me, and I will not see you hurt him."

Sadie stepped in and pried Andrus off. Thank goodness, because I was about ready to go to my car and grab my clubs.

"Honey," Sadie said, "what my barbaric husband here is trying to say is that Tommaso hasn't stopped obsessing over you since the first moment he saw you. And he fought like hell to find you after he had a vision that he'd hurt you—he did everything to make sure you were okay. And later, when he found out what the Maaskab did, he went down there to kill them all off once and for all. Single-handedly. Yes, a silly idea because Ta'as was too strong, but Tommaso didn't care. He just wanted you to feel safe again. He wanted to be able to tell you that he'd slayed your dragon and that you never had to be afraid again."

My mind bounced around from emotionally charged thought to emotionally charged thought. "But…but…what about Emma?"

"Emma is in New York with Guy, right where she will always be: by her mate's side," said Andrus.

"Oh." So Tommaso had been telling the truth about Emma and him not being more than just two people with a past. "So why didn't he come and tell me this himself?"

"(A) he said he tried to call you," Sadie said, "but you wouldn't answer. (B) he's a man and was probably ashamed that he almost ripped out your heart." She scratched the side of her mouth.

My eyes teared up. "How do you know all of this?"

"Because I've spent the last few weeks helping him plan this engagement party and listening to him gush about how much he loves you."

Engagement party? I looked around at the crowd of elegantly dressed people, none of whom I knew.

"These are Tommaso's friends," Sadie said, guessing my thoughts. "And every person in this room is prepared to tell you how Tommaso once helped them, was there when they needed a friend, or how he made a sacrifice for them."

I took another look. There were so many people here. Hundreds.

Andrus added, "I'm sorry we didn't invite your *two* friends, you giant hermit, but they would probably crap themselves given the immortal guest list."

"Oh, stop." Sadie smacked his arm.

*Engagement part*y. This was an engagement party. Tommaso had arranged all of this to ask me to marry him.

"I-I don't understand. He doesn't even love me," I said, more thinking aloud than anything else.

Sadie shook her head slowly. "Trust me, he loves you. Which is why he insisted on going the grand gesture route. He said it was the only thing," she made little air quotes with her fingers, "'befitting of the courage you showed to go and save him.'"

"Oh." I looked down at my hands, which I was subconsciously wringing together.

Sadie grabbed them both and squeezed. "Char,

he's a good man. And he does love you. But you need to meet him halfway if you want it to be the kind of lasting love you really want. A man is as only as strong as his woman—it's the one thing I've learned through all of this."

"Heeey..." Andrus protested. "I'm...strong..." His deep voice cracked as he absorbed the warning she shot him with her eyes. "I'm only as strong as you, my love."

She gave him a nod of approval.

Meanwhile, I stood there doing some absorption of my own.

Tommaso loved me? I honestly couldn't believe it. Did I love him back? I thought I did. I had risked my life to save him. And I had felt devastated, profoundly so, when I'd thought I'd lost him to Emma.

Wow. I blew out a breath. *When did this happen?* I always envisioned falling in love would feel like a bolt of lightning or getting thumped over the head. But this had just sort of snuck up on me. I guessed not everyone got the fairy tale and fell hard. They simply fell. And then, if they were lucky, they kept on falling. Deeper and deeper in love as time went on.

I suddenly hoped that would be us. A long life together of falling in love. A little more each day.

"Where did he go?" I asked.

Sadie smiled. "He either went to the Randy Unicorn to drink it off, or he went home."

"What's the Randy Unicorn?" I asked.

"A very disturbing nightclub," Andrus said. "I suggest you wait for him at home. I'll text you the address."

CHAPTER TWENTY-SEVEN

Zac's attempt to tempt Ashli, the Goddess of Love, into helping him snag Tula's heart had failed miserably. He'd offered to buy Ashli a year's worth of Belgian chocolates—so tempting, right?—he'd offered a lifetime subscription to that cleaning service where the maids were men in kilts—she'd said, "Thanks, but I'm pretty sure my husband would object." He'd even offered to never call her again for help, to which she laughed and said, "Yeah, right. You're a god—you live from crisis to crisis. You'd keep that promise for a week at best."

True. But that was their gig. Saving the world, rescuing everyone from evil. Zac yawned. *Damn, this is getting old.* Seventy thousand years into his eternity, and he was already wondering what the point was to all of this. There was no end in sight of the monotony—people made problems, tried to destroy themselves, the gods stepped in to save the day, and repeat.

Who knew being so awesome would be so boring.

"Enjoying the party?"

Zac looked down almost two entire feet to find Tula's sweet pink lips curving into a sweet little smile and her big blue eyes gazing up. There was something about the way she looked at him. She was always so cheerful and lively. So at peace with herself. Frankly, just standing next to her gave him a certain tranquility he'd never known—all right, it gave him that and the urge to fuck her senseless because she was so hard to get. But that was his temptation talking.

He sighed. *I'm such a dick. A hot dick, yes, but nevertheless a dick.*

He looked out across the dance floor at an ocean of people dancing. "Considering the couple of honor ran out and my brother Belch is nowhere to be found, so the drinks taste like piss punch, I suppose the party is adequate."

Tula giggled. "Mr. Zac, you do have a way with words."

He shrugged, feeling a bit beaten down.

"Hey." She grabbed his arm, sending little surges of tingles through half his body. The lower half. "You okay, Mr. Zac?"

He continued looking away. "Sure. Why?"

"Uhhh...because I wore this disgusting dress for you, and you haven't said a word."

He looked her over quickly finding that Tulu, for once, had ditched the schoolmarm gear—muumuus, turtlenecks, culottes, overalls, or *Little House on the*

Prairie dresses. Yes, he used to watch the show. So what? Cimil watched *The Love Boat* incessantly. Why couldn't he have a TV obsession? Anyway, tonight she wore a sleek black dress that hugged her curves all the way down to her calves, with a neckline that went so low, her voluptuous bosom was practically pouring out.

He sighed again and looked away.

"What?" she chirped defensively. "It's not slutty enough for you?"

"It's fine," he said.

"Then what's the problem? You asked me to dress provocatively, so I did. This is my peace offering to you."

While Tula's heart was in the right place, trying to accommodate him by looking like a woman who didn't require any temptation—therefore, hypothetically subduing his urge to tempt—it hadn't worked.

"Mr. Zac?" This time, she dug her nails into his arm. "Talk to me."

He looked at her fingernails attempting to break his very resilient skin. *She* was angry? Didn't she understand how she was wrecking his life?

"Just go, Tula. Leave me be."

She stepped in front of him and stared up at his face. "What's going on with you, Mr. Zac? I'm trying here. I'm really trying."

"Trying what?"

"To be your friend. To make you happy."

She was making him miserable. Fucking miserable. Just a few months ago, he'd been banished to L.A., his powers stripped, and he'd been forced to run this ridiculous matchmaking agency as a penance. All of this intended to teach him a lesson about the meaning of true love and how it couldn't be bought or stolen. It had to be given freely or it wasn't love. Well, he got that. He did. But that would never change who he was: the God of Fucking Temptation. And knowing who he was, who he'd always be, had given him confidence. Only now, he was beginning to doubt everything. Except his awesomeness, of course.

"You can't make me happy, Tula."

"I didn't mean it like that. I was just trying to make things easier for you." Her voice, as usual, was filled with sincerity and warmth. "I know you've been through a lot, and it makes me feel bad that being near me always upsets you."

Ugh! Why does she have to be so nice and so...pure of heart? It's so annoying! "Leave, Tula. You know nothing." He didn't bother to look her way when he spoke. Probably because he didn't want to see the wounded look in her eyes.

"O-okay..." she said sadly.

The moment she began walking away, he immediately felt it—that annoying fucking guilt in his gut. She came near him—good. It felt good. She left; he felt like shit.

"Wait." He followed after her and caught up quickly, grabbing her by the arm. "I'm sorry, Tula." He spun her around to face him. "I don't mean to be so...*mean.*"

"Then why are you doing it? Why do you insult

me and treat me like my feelings don't matter? You're no different than *he* is."

Tula was referring to her now ex-fiancé, who'd dumped her because she'd insisted on leaving her virtue intact until marriage.

"You're wrong, Tula. I am far, far worse. At least he dumped you, whereas I cannot seem to let you go."

The look in her beautiful wide blue eyes toggled between longing and conflict.

Before he knew what he was doing, Zac wrapped his arm around her, pulled her into his body, and bent down to kiss her. Not because he wanted to conquer her or tempt her, but simply because he needed to feel the warmth of her mouth on his.

With their mouths touching, their breath mixing, and their bodies pressing tightly together, Zac fully expected her to push him away. And then knee him. But Tula unexpectedly threw her arms around him and lifted herself onto her tiptoes to deepen the kiss.

Zac could hardly believe it when Tula's soft, sweet mouth opened to him like a blooming flower, waiting to be entered and explored.

Startled, he jerked back. "Dear gods, woman. Did you just kiss me back?"

Tula's eyes were filled with soft affection, so delicate and fragile, that he wondered if the wind would blow and take it all away.

"Wait," he said, hoping she wouldn't start overthinking this and ruin the moment. "Don't answer that. Just…come and dance with me."

She blinked at him and smiled. "I'd like that, Mr.

Zac." He could see the relief on her face. With her, things had to happen in their own time. On her terms. Because she wasn't looking to open her pure heart to just anyone.

Dammit. I'm not the right man for her. I'll only hurt her and ruin her and...

He stopped and was about to make up some lame excuse to leave, but then she stepped up to him and dropped her head on his broad chest.

His breath whooshed out. *Dear gods.* He'd never felt so much want.

"Put your arms around me," she asked so sweetly.

Gods, please forgive me. He slid his arms around her, pulled her into his body, and the two of them began swaying to the music.

"Zac! Get your dang hands off that human, this lickety splitness!"

Zac and Tula turned their heads to find Cimil in a dress entirely made out of flattened Dr. Pepper cans. And she had on a long red beard.

Yikes. "Cimil, never a pleasure to see you," said Zac. "My compliments on the redneck facial hair. Very edgy."

"Wha—" Cimil reached up and felt her chin. "Whoops!" She yanked the thing off. "No wonder Roberto kept calling me Buford." She threw the thing to the floor. "Okay, now where were we?"

"You were leaving." He pulled Tula back into his arms.

"Gah!" Cimil wedged herself right in there, separating the two. "Zac, brother," she growled, "I meant what I said when we hired her. Tula is not for you. She is not a toy. And she will never love you."

Zac suddenly felt enraged.

"I'm so sorry, Ms. Cimil," said Tula. "We were just dancing. And, yes, he did kiss me, but it was all perfectly innocent."

"Innocent?" Zac snapped at Tula. "That kiss was *not* innocent."

Cimil grabbed his arm.

"Ow!" Zac yelped. "Let go, you she-demon of refreshment."

"You listen to me, brother. Tula is important. I can't explain why or how, because that is not the way of the Cimi. You must trust in the process."

"You mean your insanity," he said.

"That too," Cimil agreed, "but for once in your life, please listen to me. You will ruin Tula's life because you could never truly love anyone and you cannot make her happy. You're not like her. You're not good."

"What?" he said defensively. "I'm good. I'm a god, which makes me involuntarily good. Most of the time. And who's talking about love, here? We were just dancing." Of course, that wasn't quite the truth, and he knew it. But Cimil's declaration stung a little; what else could he say?

"Gilbert wants me back," Tula blurted out.

Both Cimil and Zac looked at the little woman, who wasn't much taller than Cimil, actually.

"He called me this morning and begged me to forgive him," Tula elaborated. "And he said he was sorry and would wait for me as long as it took me to be ready."

"There! You see!" Cimil shoved her finger in Zac's face. "All is right in the Universe again. Tula is reconciling with the man she's intended to be with and who will make her happy."

"Do you think he'll make me happy, Zac?" Tula asked Zac.

Fuck. She wasn't really asking his opinion about Gilbert; she was asking about her and him. She was giving him a chance to make his move.

Zac felt a sharp pain in his chest. Cimil was right. He would never be able to give someone like Tula what she needed. He had to stop pursuing her and let her be. That was what was best for the woman. But dammit all to hell, he so wanted to ruin her. Every inch, from her head of blonde locks down to her pretty pink toes.

Zac looked over at Tula and was taken aback by her expression. She looked conflicted. *Join the club.*

He cleared his throat. "My apologies for interfering with your destiny, Tula. As you are aware, my predisposition to tempt those around me is involuntary." He dipped his head. "It's been a pleasure toying with you this evening." He watched as her expression turned the deepest shade of hurt. "Good luck with Gilbert." He turned around to a group of three hot women dancing—a blonde in a skimpy gold dress, a brunette in a potato-sack-looking thing to hide her extra pounds, and a redhead who wore a leather bustier. "Well, hello there," he said to the DUFF. "Don't you look lovely this evening." The woman's mouth sort of just fell open, as did her friends'. "I'd like to shove my tongue down your throat and then take you back to my place and pound you with my giant cock all night long." He said it nice and loud so Tula would hear. "How does that sound?"

Seducing this woman was too easy, of course. But at least he'd give this cute, plump little lady a night that would change her life and make her friends jealous. And Tula would see he was a bastard.

The brunette nodded, but still didn't speak. He then grabbed her and kissed her hard, throwing her back into an almost horizontal dip. The crowd on the dance floor cheered wildly as he mouth fucked the living hell out of this woman.

That ought to do the trick. When he put her upright again and released her from the kiss, Tula was nowhere to be seen. Cimil, of course, was grinning with satisfaction. She'd gotten her way.

But there was this moment, a split second, where he could've sworn he saw a devilish gleam in Cimil's eyes. She was up to something, wasn't she?

Need you really ask? This was Cimil he was talking about. But what was her game?

Perhaps Tula is meant to be mine. But if he was wrong and Cimil was telling the truth, then he would ruin the woman's life.

He looked down at his date for the night. "Let's get out of here." He took her hand and headed for the elevator. Tonight he would not think of Tula. He would only think of himself. As it was meant to be.

CHAPTER TWENTY-EIGHT

Tommaso couldn't believe what a giant ass he'd been. He'd understood perfectly well what that moment a few weeks ago, back in the jungle, must've looked like to Charlotte. But that was the reason he'd insisted on going this route. The big epic apology. The grand public declaration of love. He hadn't wanted there to be any doubt in Charlotte's mind about his desire to spend his life with her.

He supposed a big part of him knew it from the first moment he laid eyes on her, but there wasn't an ounce of uncertainty left in his body after she'd so bravely come to find him at the Maaskab encampment. It was *her* grand gesture that had opened his heart to the knowledge that perhaps he'd been waiting for this moment—for a woman who was as loyal, who loved her family as deeply as he did, and who wasn't afraid to fight.

And while Char was busy feeling wounded that Emma had pulled him from the fiery pits of mental hell, he had been relieved. There was no amount of gratitude on the planet that could express the importance of what Emma had done. Emma had reached deep inside his heart and tugged on the part of him that loved her still. It was enough to yank him from the dark place he'd been forced to go and prevent him from killing Charlotte—the woman he now knew was meant to be his. Char had risked everything to help him. She'd confronted the crippling fears for him. She was his equal in every way, if not superior in many.

Emma, while strong and beautiful, had never connected with him in such a way. Was it because Emma's heart had been spoken for from the moment she met Guy? Or was it because he had been waiting for Charlotte all along?

Perhaps both.

But "not meant to be" was "not meant to be" regardless of how one got there. He and Emma were not meant to be.

Neither are you and Charlotte, apparently. He'd been a fool to think he could be the hammer that would break through that brick wall surrounding her heart.

Idiot.

He reached for another piece of empty luggage on the top shelf of his walk-in closet and pulled it down.

"Tommaso!" Charlotte appeared in the doorway, panting hard, startling him.

The luggage slipped from his hands and crashed to the floor. "What are you doing here?"

"I came—" Pant. Pant. "To talk to you." Pant. Pant.

"Did you run? Because they have things called cars. Much easier way to travel."

She gave him a look. "I drove. But damn, this house is huge. I need to exercise more."

He shook his head. "Why are you here, Charlotte?"

She stood upright. "Is this your closet? It's the size of my entire house!"

No. It was bigger. But how was a man of means supposed to organize such an extensive collection of Italian suits and shoes, silk ties, and custom-made shirts? And still leave room for his woman's things?

"Technically," he said, "it is your closet. Or was to be your closet. Now it is just a closet that will soon belong to whomever buys this place."

Still panting, she looked at him with confusion. "What do you mean 'my closet'?"

"I bought this house for you. For us."

"What?"

"That is what men do, Charlotte. They take care of their family. They give them a home and make them feel safe."

"I'm going to pass on having a discussion about modern gender roles and the feminist revolution, and instead focus on the fact that you bought us a mansion. In the Hollywood Hills. Seriously?"

"Yes. And clearly that was an error on my part, so now it will be sold."

She gripped him by the arm as he turned to get

more clothing from the automatic shirt rack. "Tommaso, why would you do this?"

"I think you already know the answer to that question."

"Hearing it from Andrus isn't the same as hearing it from you."

He turned and gazed into her eyes. She truly looked stunning this evening in her silky red dress. He could hardly breathe earlier at the party when he'd seen her as he'd stepped off the elevator. So unforgettably beautiful.

"What is your point, Charlotte? You made your opinion clear about me." She'd practically called him a monster, saying that he had wrecked her life and wrecked her.

"Well, it's your own damned fault," she spouted. "Did it ever occur to you that maybe being honest with me might've avoided all this? I mean, come on. Why not tell me about Emma and how you felt? Why not tell me that you wanted to propose? But no, you opened up to everyone but me. Instead, I get bits and pieces and half-truths. So that's why I'm here, Tommaso. This is your chance. Tell me everything. Tell *me*. Not your friends. Not your ex-heartthrob. Not my sister. Tell me."

He wanted to, but it wasn't easy. Not after he'd gone to such lengths to put together that party— ridiculous idea. Why hadn't he listened to Sadie? She'd warned him that Charlotte was a bit of a recluse.

"The truth is that a few months ago, Cimil prophesied I would meet my mate at that mixer party you went to. And the moment I learned you were going to enter my life, I began telling myself lies. I told myself I would buy my mate a nice house to keep her comfortable. I would care for her and make sure she was safe. And I would do so by staying away because I am the opposite of safe. Everyone I've cared for ends up dead. Except for Andrus—he's impossible to kill. In any case, after I realized you and I weren't going to happen and I'd be hauled off to prison, I decided to make the most of my life by going to kill off the Maaskab once and for all."

"So basically a suicide mission."

He nodded. "Perhaps, but I wanted to make this world a quieter place for you."

"But aren't they all going to turn good?"

"For how long, Char? For a year? For a decade? The Universe is in turmoil, but it has a way of working itself out, and then what? How will you sleep soundly forty years from now when you have children and a husband you love?"

She looked down at her feet, working out the scenario he'd just laid out. "So you really wanted to help me."

"Yes. And, unfortunately, I came to the same realization as you had once I got down there."

She looked at him, confused.

"Ta'as had already been recruiting," he explained. "And he was too strong to take on directly. But I also knew he would flip sides eventually. So I would wait patiently for that to happen and then kill him. Once he was out of the

way, I could take out the other Maaskab. Especially
if I turned. Then it would be only a matter of time
before the Uchben caught up to me. Problem
solved. One Maaskab to take out. Just one. And
you'd be free."

She gasped and covered her mouth. "You
changed on purpose. You let them make you a
Maaskab again." Her eyes began to tear.

He nodded. "It was the only way to be powerful
enough to kill them. Unfortunately, I never
expected you to show up."

Her mouth opened and then closed and then
opened again. "You became the one thing you hated
most in this world simply to give me a chance at a
peaceful life? It's-it's beyond heroic. I don't know
wha-what t-to say."

He shrugged. "Goodbye will do sufficiently for
me." He turned and started grabbing his shirts. He'd
never gone so far out on a limb, done something so
morally difficult for anyone, but he'd done it for
her. And the result was her telling him how he
wasn't worthy. Well, screw that.

"I want to see the house," she said hurriedly.

He looked over his shoulder. "Why?"

"Because I want to see my new home."

CHAPTER TWENTY-NINE

Crap. I'd screwed up. So, so badly. Now hearing the truth, I finally understood why I wanted Tommaso so much. He hadn't just gone down to Mexico to fight my demons, he'd gone down to confront his own, too.

"Please?" I asked, my voice filled with vulnerability, knowing that he could stomp on my heart right then and there and I would deserve it. That said, I'd had no way of knowing any of this. He should've just told me, and I was banking on the fact that he knew it. We were both responsible.

"You really want to see the house?" His surreal, turquoise eyes were bursting with volatile emotions.

"The whole damned thing. Even the garage." Strangely, though, this closet seemed familiar somehow. Like I'd seen it in a magazine or had been here once.

He held back a little smile. "You sure? Because it's a big fucking house—it needs a lot of attention. You can't just move into it and then leave next week because you decide it's too big and too beautiful to handle."

I almost cracked up. He was too much. Too hot, too adorable, too tough.

"You'll have to pry me out. My cold dead body."

"That's a bit morbid," he said.

"I was trying to make a point."

He looked at me and then sighed. It was the kind of sigh a person made when they couldn't express their state of contentment with words. How'd I know? Because I made the same one at the same time.

"I also made a coop for your chickens," he added. "It has central heat since you said they're always cold."

"You did?"

He nodded.

"God, I so want you." I rushed toward him and threw my arms around his neck, our mouths colliding. We fell back, and he must've unintentionally grabbed onto too many shirts—a reaction to being love-tackled—because the rail of the auto shirt rack came down but was still moving.

The shirts began piling on top of us, but I wasn't about to let go. I kissed him hard—full tongue, hands plowing through his soft messy dark hair, my breath unable to find a comfortable spot inside my body. My heart was in no better shape; it was exploding with happiness.

I ground myself against him, and he laughed. "Charlotte, what are you doing? I feel like I'm being love-mauled."

I jerked back my head, laughing. "Next I plan to tie that shit up and bang it hard."

"Dear gods, woman!" He was no longer smiling.

"Too much?" I smiled blushingly. "Sorry. I was just joking around."

"No. No, it was hot. I mean...what man could resist such passion?" He laughed. I laughed. And while we stared into each other's eyes, I think we both realized we were...happy. Stupid happy. Imperfect happy. In love happy. Happy.

His smile faded away into an intense gaze, and the air spiked with tension. "I love you, Charlotte."

This time I smiled from deep inside my soul. "My chickens love you back."

"What?" He pulled me down and rolled on top of me, pinning my hands above my head. "Tell me you love me back or I'll eat them."

"You wouldn't dare eat my ugly children."

"Try me. Tell me you love me or they're nuggets, woman."

"I love you," I said, more serious than I'd ever been.

He lowered his mouth to mine and kissed me hard. This kiss felt so good. So free. So sensual and right.

He released his grip, and I felt his hand roam down to cup my breast. Feeling his weight on top of me, pressing every inch of his hard lean frame into my body, made me melt. It made me feel like his. Wanted, loved, protected.

I kissed him back, running my tongue against his, enjoying the feel of his fresh five o'clock stubble. Hard and soft. Rough and tender. That was Tommaso. That was this kiss.

His hot breath growing faster and mine becoming frantic, I began tugging on the back of his shirt. He lifted his body to help out the process. Once the shirt was chucked to the side, somewhere among the pile of clothes we were in, I was able to see his chest.

"Oh, God, Tommaso," I gasped. His chest was covered with fresh pink scars that ran horizontally. The raised pink flesh of each one had to be about a quarter of an inch thick. "What did they do to you?" I whispered.

His arms pillared to the sides of my shoulders, he stared into my eyes. "I did what I had to. For you, Charlotte. The only thing I regret was that I almost hurt you. I don't know what I would've done."

"I know I was crazy to go down there. But I couldn't let you give up everything for me."

"I'm not sorry you went. Because you saved me." At first, I didn't know what he meant, because Emma had been the one to save him. But then I realized he wasn't talking about that one moment. He was talking about his life, his future, his existence. I knew because I felt the same way.

I lifted my head and pushed my mouth to his, wrapping my arms around his neck to hold him tightly to me.

We kissed. And then we kissed some more. I just wanted to feel his skin and savor this moment.

Finally, he broke away. "I'm sorry. I can't take it anymore." He began pulling up the hem of my dress and working my panties down to my knees. He unbuttoned his pants and laid himself between my thighs, somehow working my underwear down around my ankles.

His hot mouth was quickly back to mine, and I felt his hand working between us to position his hard cock at my heated entrance.

He stopped kissing me and simply stared into my eyes. "You're so damned brave, Charlotte. I'm a very lucky man."

I opened my mouth to say something, but instantly forgot as he thrust forward, burying his cock deep inside me.

I gasped from the unexpected sting.

"Did I hurt you?" he asked, his voice low and deep.

"Don't stop," I panted. "Don't stop."

He returned to kissing me, and his taste only kept getting sweeter and sweeter. I couldn't get enough.

He pulled out and thrust again, stealing my breath. I tilted my hips to angle him more comfortably toward that sweet spot deep inside.

"More," I begged, beginning to get my rhythm and feeling my walls accommodating his thickness.

He placed his hands beside my head, lifting up his muscled frame. He began pumping hard. I was so close already, but didn't want the moment to end. Him inside me was ecstasy, sensual sinful euphoria, where nothing else existed besides our sweaty bodies.

After several minutes—five, ten, twenty, I didn't know—he picked up the pace, hammering hard, me meeting him thrust for thrust, knowing I had but seconds before…

I sucked in a deep breath and my body exploded into stardust—magical, weightless powder just floating around in the atmosphere.

He leaned in hard, and I heard the deep, masculine groan rumbling from his chest. His hot cock twitched deep inside me, bursting with cum. The sensation made me climax all over again. There was nothing more sexually raw than a hot man you loved pouring himself into you.

We held each other tight for several long moments, coming down off of our sinful cloud.

Panting hard, savoring the feeling of him still deep inside, I had to ask, "How do you feel about kids?"

He jerked back his head and looked at me with an unreadable but surprised expression.

"Oops. Too soon?"

A slow, charming smile crept over his sensual mouth. "Did I mention the house has ten bedrooms?"

"Ten?" *Oh crap.* That was a lot of children. "You won't mind if we adopt a few, do you?"

"As long as they're human."

I gave him a look.

"I'm not going to win this one, am I?" he said.

I shook my head no.

He grinned. "Anything for you, Charlotte."

I sighed contentedly. "Let's get on with seeing the rest of the house." I pulled him back to my mouth and started moving my hips for him.

He groaned. "Have you seen the walk-in closet? It's very big. You should see it."

I laughed. "I'd love to."

CHAPTER THIRTY

"Parties, parties, fucking parties," the God of Wine and Intoxication groused, riding the elevator up to the rooftop bar at the Shangri La Hotel in Santa Monica, two hours late for the party. Like usual, he was supposed to be bartending—his special gift right along with being the life of the party. He could simply look at a person and know the perfect beverage. Lychee martini, a randy monk (Frangelico on the rocks with whipped cream), slippery nipple (Irish cream with peppermint Schnapps), boogers in the grass (a shot glass of peach Schnapps, Midori, and Baileys) or anything else. There wasn't a drink on this planet he didn't know how to prepare, and there wasn't a party— shitty high school reunion, a wake, a Thanksgiving dinner with in-laws—*or your mother's Sunday meatloaf leftover guilt-trip extravaganza*—that he couldn't turn into a mind-blowingly fun event.

He let out a long, deep belch—thus his nickname "Belch"—the result of having just consumed a keg of beer. Yes. All by himself. Yes, while he was driving over here. Yes, at the stoplight in sixty seconds.

What can I say? It's a gift.

He poked the button of the elevator, realizing it hadn't moved. He was still sitting on the first floor.

Gods, I'm so drunk. Poke. Poke. *Hurry the fuck up.*

The elevator doors opened and in stepped a beautiful blonde wearing running shoes, teeny tiny black shorts, and a purple tank top. Her legs were pure muscle, her ass was rock hard and shapely, her tits looked like two perfect halves of a coconut like the ones he'd made mai tais in just last night at a luau.

Hot.

She was in her late forties or possibly early fifties by his estimation, but she had the body of a fucking goddess on sexy steroids.

"Well, hiya," he slurred, "wuz yur name?"

Frowning, she stepped inside, pushed the button for the tenth floor, and gave him her back.

"I'm Acan," he offered. "There's a party upstairs if you're free."

She didn't respond.

What? She dares ignore me?

"Hey now. You're being kind of ruuude," he slurred. "I hate ruuude people. Especially when they have really tight asses and nice tits."

"Ugh." She flashed a glance over her shoulder as the doors slid closed and they began ascending. "You're disgusting."

"Disgusting?" He looked down at his giant belly and began making circles over the thing. He certainly didn't see anything wrong with it. "This belly is the result of thousands of years of dedicated alcohol consumption." Did she not understand the intense training and stamina it required to help so many people let loose? Humans needed fun. They needed to party every now and again, and he was their champion. Their messiah to lead the way to party Mecca. "I'm a god. A fucking good one, too! You'd be so lucky to have me. Even for just one night."

She turned and looked at him. "You. Are. Disgusting."

"Well, you dunno what yur missin', sweethurt. One night with Belch is like a night in heaven."

She scowled. "Sure. I'll spend the night with you just as soon as you lose the eighty-pound gut, brush your beer breath, comb your hair, and," her eyes flashed down to his groin, "wear some damned pants."

The elevator doors opened, and she headed out.

"You're kind of picky for such an old broad," he barked.

She swiveled on her heel, shooting death darts with her eyes. "Old? Did you, pantless drunk man, call *me* old?"

Compared to him, she was a spring chicken. But where did she get off? "Yep. Old like dirt."

She narrowed her beautiful green eyes. "Club Crossfit down the street. Five a.m. Be there and I'll show you old, you degenerate, disgusting slob."

The doors slid closed as he stood there in awe. So much fire in her eyes. And so much hate.

Well, you did call her "old." Yeah, but I'm drunk.

"I'll be busy puking!" he yelled at the already closed doors.

As the elevator traveled the rest of the way up, his anger only grew. *How dare she insult me. I am a deity. I represent a time-honored tradition of excess and bad judgement. I am...I am...going to kick her ass.* "Game on, sweetheart. Game fucking on..."

TO BE CONTINUED...
ON THE NEXT PAGE...
YES, KEEP GOING. I'M TALKING TO YOU!

ॐ∽ॐ

CIMIL

There you are! Welcome to the end of the book!

Okay, my scrumptious little people pets! Dishes have gone unwashed. Dinners have gone cold. Homework has gone unchecked. My work here is done! Yes! I am talking to you, human! The one holding this delightful book in your hands!

Wait. What is that you say, Minky?

Ah, Minky is very unhappy. The horny little minx—get it? Horny? She's a unicorn... Oh, piss off! That was funny! Anynoodle, Minky is complaining because she says there weren't enough nasty bits in the book. Yep, she means sexy-time. She urges you to email the author—that silly mortal who believes erroneously that she is in control of this story. (Fool! She is but a puppet in my divine scheme to become Goddess of Garage Sales. And to destroy the world.) Annnyway, Minky urges you to write Mimi and demand she tell the truth and the whole truth about Belch, aka God of Wine. His story is full of naughty, dirty sex, and it must be told properly! So it is up to you, dear reader, to influence this Mimi person and appease my Minky! So email, Tweet, Facebook, skywrite, smoke signal, postcard, meme—do what you must to get the message to this Mimi mortal. #Godofwine #MakeitdirtyMimi!

All righty, now that we have that out of the way,

Minky and I have noticed that Mimi has not yet completed the story. I mean, seriously, Mimi. Can you say "hole"? Oh, yes. I for one know every gritty detail of Tommaso's story. I was there! But the world still has questions about the story!

#1: Why did Tommaso believe he'd tied Charlotte up and put her in his closet?

#2: What exactly did Tommaso do during his blackouts?

#3: Why didn't Charlotte remember meeting Tommaso at my awesome immortal singles mixer?

#4: Why didn't Tommaso realize that Charlotte looked like her cousin Sadie?

#5: How did Char learn to golf?

#6: In what two parts of the story do I appear in disguise?

Now you see, don't you, human? So many unanswered questions! But fret nyet, my little pets. Auntie Cimi has you covered.

I giveth you another quizeth!

Go to this lovely page on Mimi's website:

www.mimijean.net/tommasotrivia.html

And take the multiple choice quiz! Minky will select several winners for a glorious bounty of books and other useless crap you cannot possibly want. Yes, there might be unicorn poop involved, but I cannot say for certain.

Winners will be chosen on JULY 4th, 2016. Answers to the quizeth and the winners' names will be posted on the same page AND in Mimi's newsletter.

All righty, my tiny Ciminions, it is time for me to get to work. Zac awaits me at the office and there are many immortals to fuck with—whoops, I mean help.

Hasta La We Go!

Cimil

P.S. This list of items in my basement, found in the back of this book, is so incomplete. They forgot to mention my Funyun collection!

TO BE CONTINUED...
GOD of WINE Coming FALL, 2016!

www.mimijean.net/godofwine.html

AUTHOR'S NOTE

Hi All!

I hope you enjoyed TOMMASO. I have no idea why I envisioned him being with a preppy-looking golfer gal who doesn't shave her legs every day, but I'll just blame it on Cimil! She's the matchmaker, after all!

If you're looking for a signed bookmark, don't forget to email me with your shipping address (mimi@mimijean.net). As always, I have super yummy magnets, too, as a thank you to my awesome readers who take the time to show some book-love and post reviews! (First come basis, but I did buy extra this time!)

Just a quick note on GOD OF WINE, book #3: I plan to have it out late fall.

(Along with IT'S A FUGLY LIFE!)

GOTO: www.mimijean.net/godofwine.html for updates and news!

OR SIGN UP FOR MY NEWSLETTER (link also at the back of the book) if you'd like an alert. I send out welcome swag for new subscribers upon request. ☺

A BIG THANK YOU to my fans who shared with me what they think might be in Cimil's basement. So funny! You can check out the posts here in the back of the book!

FINALLY, for those who enjoy the story breakdown, I hope you like the true meaning of this one. Because, for me, it was really interesting to put some serious mental elbow grease into this topic: perception. How we see the world, others, and ourselves isn't necessarily shared by those around us.

Okay, keep reading on the next page if you're interested! And "see" you in AUGUST for the release of HAPPY PANTS #2, TAILORED FOR TROUBLE. It's fun, it's sexy, and as usual, it's an adventure.

HAPPY READING,
MIMI
mimi@mimijean.net
www.mimijean.net

P.S. FOR YOU PLAYLIST FANS:

"Brown Eyed Girl" by Van Morrison
"Pity Party" by Melanie Martinez
"Firestone" by Kygo
"Paris" by Magic Man
"All I Want" by Kodaline
"One Day" by Kodaline
"All Comes Down" by Kodaline
"Cold Cold Man" by Saint Motel
"My Type" by Saint Motel
"Out Of My League" by Fitz and the Tantrums
"Waste My Time" by Tilian
"Someday" by Tilian
"You'll Forget Me Soon" (feat. Sofia Sweet) by Tilian
"Lost In My Bedroom" by Sky Ferreira
"You And Me" by Vega 4
"Memory" by Violent Femmes
"All Through the Night" by Sleeping At Last

WHAT'S TOMMASO REALLY ALL ABOUT?

Some people love a movie or TV show, while you hate it. Popcorn with butter makes you gag, and others will stand in line for an extra few minutes just to have their crispy kernels drenched beyond all popcorny recognition. (I like light butter myself. Kettle corn is even better!) But, there's no surprise in the fact that we're all different. That said, have you ever thought about it at the intimate level? Sure, there's a public out there who vote differently, eat differently, and dress differently, but what about the people closest to you? I think many of us assume that our closest friends and family see us for who we really are.

But do they really?

Maybe. Maybe not.

And when it comes to our men—how they see us and how we see them—I often wonder how far apart our self-perceptions are from theirs. And vice versa.

So the first half of the book, we get to see the world through Tommaso's eyes. We feel a bit more distant from him—after all, he's a man. Hehe. He's thinking about survival, fucking, and his place in this world. He's lost everything and afraid of "owning" or caring for anything ever again. But the one thing he does know? He's not going to let anyone diminish his dignity. He is looking for freedom. Not because he cherishes it, but because feeling captive to another makes him feel ashamed—not a man. He feels the same way about Charlotte not having her freedom. She is, after all, an extension of himself, even if he doesn't know it yet.

The other thing we learn about Tommaso is how he sees Charlotte. He thinks she's emotionally unavailable and uninterested in him. But really, his perceptions around what's really going on are completely off.

Then, in the second half of the story, we switch perspectives. Now we see Tommaso through Charlotte's eyes. She's intimidated by his beauty and afraid of letting him into her life simply because she thinks it will ultimately end badly for him—having to watch her go insane, like her mother. Yet, she can't help but be inspired by his strength and confidence. She realizes that she doesn't need him to survive, but things could be a lot better with him around. Of course, we all need people, if not to help us, then to inspire us and teach us. Sometimes we just need them to be there and hold our hands for comfort. Charlotte realizes there is no shame in that. From there, she gets a taste of life with Tommaso and wants way more.

And finally, when Charlotte learns the truth about Tommaso, she begins to see that he is a reflection of her own life. He's been robbed of his happiness due to circumstances beyond his control. It's then she decides that he's worth fighting for because she's worth fighting for. It's time to stop living in the past with memories that haunt her. Nothing good can come of it.

In the end, they both confront their ghosts and open their lives to new possibilities together.

And that's what this story is really about. The truth about people or situations is rarely handed to us on a silver platter. Sometimes it requires effort to get to it. But I think the cool thing about being a woman is that most of us are born with internal BS sensors (my kids hate that), and we have this ability to read people and empathize and to look beyond the surface. Damn, we rock! Don't we, ladies?

Hope you enjoyed this mental detour...

HAPPY READING!

Mimi

ACKNOWLEDGEMENTS

I never get tired of saying it, because it's true! I can't thank my readers enough for their continued enthusiasm for this series and all of my books. Without you, I'd still be writing commodity reports. Blah!

And, as always, a HUUUUUGE thank you to my demigods: Kylie, Ally, Dalitza, and Nana for providing the much-needed sanity check on my insanity.

Another big fist bump and grovel to the folks who help make the book happen: Dali (again), Latoya, Pauline, Su, and Stef!

And, of course, I can't forget the awesome ladies on my street team, some of whom have been cheering me on since the very first book. I love you guys.

Okay…and now back to writing!

Mimi

WHAT'S IN CIMIL'S BASEMENT?

I asked my readers on Facebook what they thought would be inside Cimil's basement. The answers were too funny not to share. So a big thank you to my readers who joined in!

Rebecca Hammer: The set from the show Wipeout complete with swinging blades, flame throwers and land mines. Cuz the kids need a play gym.

Nikki Manzella: What wouldn't Cimil have in her basement?

Heather Foley Francis: Tag sale signs from around the world lol

Hannah Roberson: Giant wedding cake with a stripper midget inside

Kristin Felts: What wouldn't she have?

Isabel Campos: Just about anything!! Unicorn, fluffy dragon, purple elephant!!

Sian Anderson: Rainbow unicorns, bouncy castles with spray cream

Chez Rodgers: Fluffy fire breathing puppies

Tammy Jungmann: Rainbow farts…Bahaaha sorry smile emoticon

Michelle Norberg: A hot boy toy?!

Emily Hartzell Wheeler: Uh, a ball pit. Duh.

Kristin Felts: Extinct species as pets. An empty room with no apparent use. A sweat shop of some kind. Maybe a laundry service. (Hey as long as they do my laundry. It's none of my concern what they do with their free time. Plus Minky likes having fresh meat nearby for occasional chewing needs. But only when they're on break. No blood on the merchandise.)

Sandra Pride: Endless supply of pumpkin puree, because one can never have enough pies. 1000's of gnomes, because she can't help but steal them from people's lawns. Loveboat memorabilia.

Susan Hoger Guerreiro: Obscure neon signs, torture implements from throughout history—probably with cows attached or locked to a wall and forced some horribly cute and mind-numbing video on repeat, a pepper – shaker collection (but not salt), other obscure things always left over at garage sales that people end up tossing or donating

Lindsey Drake: A wizard, every Love Boat piece of memorabilia in existence, a pink Cadillac with leopard print seats (limited edition), 4 flame throwers for the kids to play with and a broken juke box which only ever plays cotton eyed joe on loop smile emoticon

Carolyn Maciejko: But with a live person, trapped, answering her ridiculous questions, like "should I make pasta for dinner tonight, or tacos?"

Jennifer Bryson: well we know she loves yard sales so she is bound to have a bean bag chair or 2 floating around oh wait this is Cimil probably a sex swing lol

Michelle Amato: As soon as i saw this all i thought about was the stuff she had in the cave..

Lori Bock: I know she's holding the Teletubbies hostage !! lol

Christine Hubbard Robertson: The guys from Tallywackers!!

April Allen: Leisure Lollipops…shaped like unicorns and sexy man parts!

Trenna Harris: Life size cut out of Isac from the Love boat!

Terri Casolaro Seminuk: Did anyone mention a sex swing cause I could totally imagine one hanging from a beam…

Annette N Ryan Reyes: Leprechauns and Menehunes!

Krystina Beck: Lol license plates from every state.

Dina Reyna: The monsters from the tremors movies? Or 50 pound penis.

Tobias Chintz: Teapots from around the world and one shaped like a flamingo

Linsey Rollo: Zak's mate? So he can't get his mitts on her until the opportune moment?

Deby Henneman: A pin all machine and a disco ball....

Miranda Nemeth: A giant goose named SEXY Rexy that lays magical jewels.

Cynthia Cua: Ball Plastic ball pit. wink emoticon

Katherine Ann: Puff the magic dragon!

Bethany Klein: Tightrope?

GLOSSARY

Black Jade: Found only in a particular mine located in southern Mexico, this jade has very special supernatural properties, including the ability to absorb supernatural energy—in particular, god energy. When worn by humans, it is possible for them to have physical contact with a god. If injected, it can make a person addicted to doing bad things. If the jade is fueled with dark energy and then released, it can be used as a weapon. Chaam personally likes using it to polish his teeth.

Demilords: Once upon a time, they were a group of immortal badass vampires who'd been infused with the light of the gods. Now free from their jobs (killing Obscuros), and their vampire bloodline dead, they have all turned into plain old demigods, but are still just as deadly and lethal as ever.

Maaskab: Originally a cult of bloodthirsty Mayan priests who believed in the dark arts. It is rumored they are responsible for bringing down their entire civilization with their obsession for human sacrifices (mainly young female virgins). Once Chaam started making half-human children, he decided all firstborn males would make excellent Maaskab due to their proclivity for evil.

Obscuros: Evil vampires who do not live by the Pact and who like to dine on innocent humans since they really do taste the best.

The Pact: An agreement between the gods and good vampires that dictates the dos and don'ts. There are many parts to it, but the most important rules are vampires are not allowed to snack on good people (called Forbiddens), they must keep their existence a secret, and they are responsible for keeping any rogue vampires in check.

Payal: Although the gods can take humans to their realm and make them immortal, Payals are the true genetic offspring of the gods but are born mortal, just like humans. Most do not have any powers.

Uchben: An ancient society of scholars and warriors who serve as the gods' eyes and ears in the human world. They also do the books and manage the gods' earthly assets.

Character Definitions

The Gods

Although every culture around the world has their own names and beliefs related to beings of worship, there are actually only fourteen gods. And since the gods are able to access the human world only through the portals called cenotes, located in the Yucatán, the Mayans were big fans.

Another fun fact: The gods often refer to each other as brother and sister, but the truth is they are just another species of the Creator and completely unrelated.

Acan—God of Wine and Intoxication: Also known as Belch, Acan has been drunk for a few thousand years. He generally wears only tightie whities, but since he's the life of the party, he's been known to mix it up and go naked, too. Whatever works.

Ah-Ciliz—God of Solar Eclipses: Called A.C. by his brethren, Ah-Ciliz is generally thought of as a giant buzz kill because of his dark attitude.

Akna—Goddess of Fertility: She is so powerful, it is said she can make inanimate objects fornicate and that anyone who gets in the same room as her ends up pregnant. She is often seen hanging out with her brother Acan at parties.

Backlum Chaam—God of Male Virility: He's responsible for discovering black jade and figuring out how to procreate with humans.

Camaxtli—Goddess of the Hunt: Also once known as Fate until she was discovered to be a fake and had her powers stripped away by the Universe. She's now referred to as "Fake."

Colel Cab—Mistress of Bees: Though she has many, many powers, "Bees" is most known for the live beehive hat on her head. She has never had a boyfriend or lover because her bees get too jealous.

Goddess of Forgetfulness: She has no official name that is known of and has the power to make anyone forget anything. She spends her evenings DJing because she finds the anonymity of dance clubs to be comforting.

Ixtab—Goddess of Happiness (ex-Goddess of Suicide): Ixtab's once morbid frock used to make children scream. But since finding her soul mate, she's now the epitome of all things happy.

K'ak (Pronounced "cock"): The history books remember him as K'ak Tiliw Chan Yopaat, ruler of Copán in the 700s AD. King K'ak is one of Cimil's favorite brothers. We're not really sure what he does, but he can throw bolts of lightning, wears a giant silver and jade headdress with intertwining serpents, and has long black and silver hair.

Kinich Ahau—ex-God of the Sun: Known by many other names, depending on the culture, Kinich likes to go by Nick these days. He's also now a vampire—something he's actually not so bummed about. He is mated to the love of his life, Penelope, the Ruler of the House of Gods.

Máax—Once known as the God of Truth, Máax was banished for repeatedly violating the ban on time travel. However, since helping to save the world from the big "over," he is now known as the God of Time Travel. Also turns out he was the God of Love, but no one figured that out until his mate, Ashli, inherited his power. Ashli is now the fourteenth deity, taking the place of Camaxtli, the Fake.

Votan—God of Death and War: Also known as Odin, Wotan, Wodan, God of Drums (he has no idea how the hell he got that title; he hates drums), and Lord of Multiplication (okay, he is pretty darn good at math so that one makes sense). These days, Votan goes by Guy Santiago (it's a long story— read ACCIDENTALLY IN LOVE WITH…A GOD?), but despite his deadly tendencies, he's all heart.

Yum Cimil—Goddess of the Underworld: Also known as Ah-Puch by the Mayans, Mictlantecuhtli (try saying that one ten times) by the Aztec, Grim Reaper by the Europeans, Hades by the Greeks…you get the picture! Despite what people say, Cimil is actually a female, adores a good bargain (especially garage sales) and the color pink, and she hates clowns. She's also bat-shit crazy, has an invisible pet unicorn named Minky, and is married to Roberto, the king of all vampires.

Zac Cimi—Bacab of the North: What the heck is a Bacab? According to the gods' folklore, the Bacabs are the four eldest and most powerful of the gods. Once thought to be the God of Love, we now know differently. Zac is the God of Temptation, and his tempting ways have landed him in very hot water. Because no matter how tempting your brother's mate might be, trying to steal her is wrong. He is currently serving time in Los Angeles with Cimil, running the Immortal Matchmakers agency.

Not the Gods

Andrus: Ex-Demilord (vampire who's been given the gods' light), now just a demigod after his maker, the vampire queen, died. According to Cimil, his son (who hasn't been born yet) is destined to marry Helena and Niccolo's daughter, Matty.

Ashli: Ashli actually belongs over in the GODS section, but since she was born human, we'll keep her here. Ashli is mate to Máax, God of Time Travel. Unbeknownst to him, he was also the God of Love. Ashli inherited his power after they started falling in love. Maybe the Universe thought a woman should have this power?

Brutus: One of the gods' elite Uchben warriors. He doesn't speak much, but that's because he and his team are telepathic. They are also immortal (a gift from the gods) and next in line to be Uchben chiefs.

Charlotte: Sadie's cousin and the intended mate to Andrus Grey. Only, Andrus, being the rebel that he is, decided he could pick his own damned woman! Sadie and he are now happily mated.

Helena Strauss: Once human, Helena is now a vampire and married to Niccolo DiConti. She has a half-vampire daughter, Matty, who is destined to marry Andrus's son, according to Cimil.

Matty: The infant daughter of Helena and Niccolo, destined to marry Andrus's son.

Niccolo DiConti: General of the Vampire Army. Now that the vampire queen is dead, the army remains loyal to him. He shares power with his wife, Helena Strauss, and has a half-vampire daughter, Matty.

Reyna: The dead vampire queen.

Roberto (Narmer): Originally an Egyptian pharaoh, Narmer was one of the six Ancient Ones—the very first vampires. He eventually changed his name to Roberto and moved to Spain—something to do with one of Cimil's little schemes. He now spends his days lovingly undoing Cimil's treachery, being a stay-at-home dad, and taking her unicorn Minky for a ride.

Sadie: Charlotte's cousin and mated to Andrus Grey, Sadie is an aspiring actress who discovered she's also half incubus.

Tommaso: Once an Uchben, Tommaso's mind was poisoned with black jade. He tried to kill Emma, Votan's mate, but redeemed himself by turning into a spy for the gods.

Tula: The incorruptible administrative assistant at Immortal Matchmakers, Inc.

IT'S A FUGLY LIFE

Don't miss the continuation of Max and Lily.
Sign up for Mimi's newsletter!
Coming October, 2016!

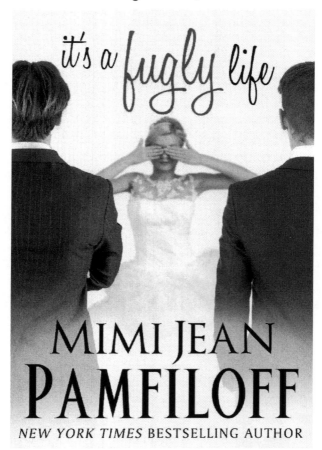

FOR BUY LINKS, BOOK EXTRAS, AND NEWS:
www.mimijean.net/fugly2.html

GOD OF WINE

Immortal Matchmakers, Inc.
Book #3
Coming 2016

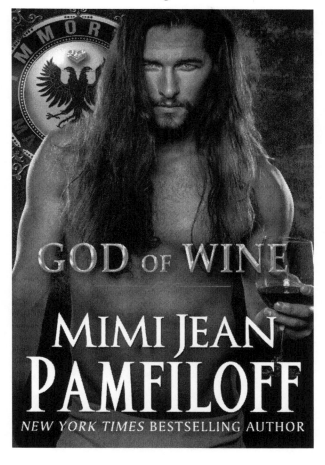

FOR BUY LINKS, BOOK EXTRAS, AND NEWS:
www.mimijean.net/godofwine.html

THE HAPPY PANTS SERIES IS BACK!

TAILORED FOR TROUBLE
Coming August 2016

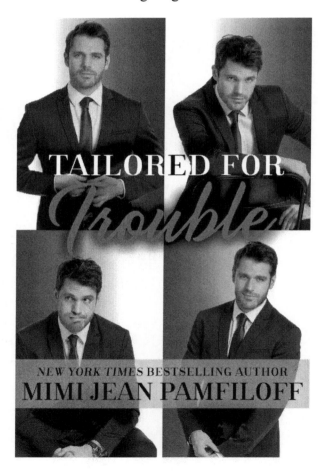

TAILORED FOR *Trouble*

NEW YORK TIMES BESTSELLING AUTHOR
MIMI JEAN PAMFILOFF

SHE WANTS TO CHANGE THE WORLD.

Taylor Reed is no stranger to selfish, uncaring CEOs. She was fired by one, which is why she has created her own executive training program—helping heartless bosses become more human. So Taylor shocks even herself when she agrees to coach Bennett Wade, the cutthroat exec who got her unceremoniously canned. She'd love to slam the door in his annoying but very handsome face, but the customers aren't exactly lining up at her door. Plus, this extreme makeover will give Taylor the golden opportunity to prove her program works like a charm.

HE WANTS TO BUY IT.

Bennett Wade is many things—arrogant, smug, brusque—but trusting isn't one of them. Women just seem to be after his billions. So when he hires Taylor, he has no desire to change. Bennett is trying to win over the feminist owner of a company he desperately wants to buy. But something about the fiery Taylor thaws the ice around his heart, making Bennett feel things he never quite planned on. And if there's one thing Bennett can't stand, it's when things don't go according to plan.

They are a match tailor-made…for trouble.

FOR BUY LINKS, EXCERPTS, and MORE:
www.mimijean.net/tailored.html

ABOUT THE AUTHOR

 MIMI JEAN PAMFILOFF is a *USA Today* and *New York Times* bestselling romance author. Although she obtained her MBA and worked for more than fifteen years in the corporate world, she believes that it's never too late to come out of the romance closet and follow your dream. Mimi lives with her Latin lover hubby, two pirates-in-training (their boys), and the rat terrier duo, Snowflake and Mini Me, in Arizona. She hopes to make you laugh when you need it most and continues to pray daily that leather pants will make a big comeback for men.

Sign up for Mimi's mailing list for giveaways and new release news!

LEARN MORE:

mailto: mimi@mimijean.net

www.mimijean.net

https://twitter.com/MimiJeanRomance

www.radioslot.com/show/mancandyshow/

www.facebook.com/MimiJeanPamfiloff